The Great Court Scandal

The Great Court Scandal

William Le Queux

MINT EDITIONS

The Great Court Scandal was first published in 1907.

This edition published by Mint Editions 2021.

ISBN 9781513280882 | E-ISBN 9781513285900

Published by Mint Editions®

minteditionbooks.com

Publishing Director: Jennifer Newens
Design & Production: Rachel Lopez Metzger
Project Manager: Micaela Clark
Typesetting: Westchester Publishing Services

Contents

Prologue

"The Ladybird will refuse to have anything to do with the affair, my dear fellow. It touches a woman's honour, and I know her too well."

"Bah! We'll compel her to help us. She must."

"She wouldn't risk it," declared Harry Kinder, shaking his head.

"Risk it! Well, we'll have to risk something! We're in a nice hole just now! Our traps at the Grand, with a bill of two thousand seven hundred francs to pay, and 'the Ladybird' coolly sends us from London a postal order for twenty-seven shillings and sixpence—all she has!"

"She might have kept it and bought a new sunshade or a box of chocolates with it."

"The little fool! Fancy sending twenty-seven bob to three men stranded in Paris! I can't see why old Roddy thinks so much of her," remarked Guy Bourne to his companion.

"Because she's his daughter, and because after all you must admit that she's jolly clever with her fingers."

"Of course we know that. She's the smartest woman in London. But what makes you think that when the suggestion is made to her she will refuse?"

"Well, just this. She's uncommonly good-looking, dresses with exquisite taste, and when occasion demands can assume the manner of a high-born lady, which is, of course, just what we want; but of late I've noticed a very great change in her. She used to act heedless of risk, and entirely without pity or compunction. Nowadays, however, she seems becoming chicken-hearted."

"Perhaps she's in love," remarked the other with a sarcastic grin.

"That's just it. I honestly think that she really is in love," said the short, hard-faced, clean-shaven man of fifty, whose fair, rather scanty hair, reddish face, tightly-cut trousers, and check-tweed suit gave him a distinctly horsey appearance, as he seated himself upon the edge of the table in the shabby sitting-room *au troisieme* above the noisy Rue Lafayette, in Paris.

"'The Ladybird' in love! Whatever next!" exclaimed Guy Bourne, a man some ten years his junior, and extremely well, even rather foppishly, dressed. His features were handsome, his hair dark, and outwardly he had all the appearance of a well-set-up Englishman. His gold sleeve-links bore a crest and cipher in blue enamel, and his dark moustache was carefully trained, for he was essentially a man of taste and refinement. "Well," he added, "I've got my own opinion, old chap, and you're quite welcome to yours. 'The Ladybird' may be in love, as you suspect, but she'll have to help us in this. It's a big thing, I know; but look what it means to us! If she's in love, who's the jay?" he asked, lighting a cigarette carelessly.

"Ah! now you ask me a question."

"Well," declared Bourne rather anxiously, "whoever he may be, the acquaintanceship must be broken off—and that very quickly, too. For us the very worst catastrophe would be for our little 'Ladybird' to fall in love. She might, in one of her moments of sentimentality, be indiscreet, as all women are apt to be; and if so—well, it would be all up with us. You quite recognise the danger?"

"I do, most certainly," the other replied, with a serious look, as he glanced around the poorly-furnished room, with its painted wood floor in lieu of carpet. "As soon as we're back we must keep our eyes upon her, and ascertain the identity of this secret lover."

"But she's never shown any spark of affection before," Bourne said, although he knew that the secret lover was actually himself. "We must ask Roddy all about it. Being her father, he may know something."

"I only wish we were back in London again, sonny," declared Kinder. "Paris has never been safe for us since that wretched affair in the Boulevard Magenta. Why Roddy brought us over I can't think."

"He had his eye on something big that unfortunately hasn't come off. Therefore we're now landed at the Grand with a big hotel bill and no money to pay it with. The Johnnie in the bureau presented it to me this morning, and asked for payment. I bluffed him that I was going down to the bank and would settle it this evening."

"With twenty-seven and sixpence!" remarked the clean-shaven man with sarcasm.

"Yes," responded his companion grimly. "I only wish we could get our traps away. I've got all my new rig-out in my trunk, and can't afford to lose it."

"We must get back to London somehow," Harry said decisively. "Every moment we remain here increases our peril. They have our photographs at the Prefecture, remember, and here the police are pretty quick at making an arrest. We're wanted, even now, for the Boulevard Magenta affair. A pity the Doctor hit the poor old chap so hard, wasn't it?"

"A thousand pities. But the Doctor was always erratic—always in fear of too much noise being made. He knocked the old fellow down when there was really no necessity: a towel twisted around his mouth would have been quite as effectual, and the affair would not have assumed so ugly a phase as it afterwards did. No; you're quite right, Harry, old chap; Paris is no place for us nowadays."

"Ah!" Kinder sighed regretfully. "And yet we've had jolly good times here, haven't we? And we've brought off some big things once or twice, until Latour and his cadaverous crowd became jealous of us, and gave us away that morning at the St. Lazare station, just when Roddy was working the confidence of those two American women. By Jove! we all had a narrow escape, and had to fly."

"I remember. Two agents pounced upon me, but I managed to give them the slip and get away that night to Amiens. A good job for us," the younger man added, "that Latour won't have a chance to betray his friends for another fifteen years."

"What! has he been lagged?" asked the horsey man as he bit the end off a cigar.

"Yes, for a nasty affair down at Marseilles. He was opening a banker's safe—that was his speciality, you know—and he blundered."

"Then I'm not sorry for him," Kinder declared, crossing the room and looking out of the window into the busy thoroughfare below.

It was noon, on a bright May day, and the traffic over the granite setts in the Rue Lafayette was deafening, the huge steam trams snorting and clanging as they ascended the hill to the Gare du Nord.

Guy Bourne was endeavouring to solve a very serious financial difficulty. The three shabbily-furnished rooms in which they were was a small apartment which Roddy Redmayne, alias "The Mute," alias Ward, alias Scott-Martin, and alias a dozen other names beside, had taken for a month, and were, truth to tell, the temporary headquarters of "The Mute's" clever and daring gang of international thieves, who moved from city to city plying their profession.

They had been unlucky—as they were sometimes. Harry Kinder had succeeded in getting some jewellery two days before, only to discover to his chagrin that the diamonds were paste. He had seen them in a bad light, otherwise, expert that he was, he would never have touched them. He always left pearls religiously alone. There were far too many imitations, he declared. For three weeks the men had done themselves well in Paris, and spent a considerable amount in ingratiating themselves with certain English and American visitors who were there for the season. Kinder and Bourne worked the big hotels—the Grand, the Continental, and the Chatham, generally frequenting the American bar at the latter place each afternoon about four o'clock, on the keen lookout for English pigeons to pluck. This season, however, ill-luck seemed to constantly follow them, with the result that they had spent their money all to no purpose, and now found themselves with a large hotel bill, and without the wherewithal to discharge it.

Guy Bourne's life had been a veritable romance. The son of a wealthy country squire, he had been at Eton and at Balliol, and his father had intended him to enter the Church, for he had an uncle a bishop, and was sure of a decent preferment. A clerical career had, however, no attractions for Guy, who loved all kinds of sport, especially racing, a pastime which eventually proved his downfall. Like many other young men, he became mixed up with a very undesirable set—that unscrupulous company that frequents racecourses—and finding his father's door shut to him, gradually sank lower until he became the friend of Kinder and one of the associates and accomplices of the notorious Roddy Redmayne—known as "The Mute"—a king among Continental thieves.

Like the elder man who stood beside him, he was an audacious, quick-witted, and ingenious thief, very merry and easy-going. He was a man who lived an adventurous life, and generally lived well, too; unscrupulous about annexing other people's property, and therefore retaining nowadays few of the traits of the gentleman. At first he had not been altogether bad; at heart he hated and despised himself; yet he was a fatalist, and had long ago declared that the life of a thief was his destiny, and that it was no use kicking against the pricks.

An excellent linguist, a well-set-up figure, a handsome countenance, his hair slightly turning grey, he was always witty, debonair and cosmopolitan, and a great favourite with women. They voted him a charming fellow, never for one moment suspecting that his polished exterior and gentlemanly bearing concealed the fact that he had designs upon their jewellery.

His companion, Harry Kinder, was a man of entirely different stamp; rather coarse, muscular, well versed in all the trickery and subterfuge of the international criminal; a clever pickpocket, and perhaps one of the most ingenious sharpers in all Europe. He had followed the profession ever since a lad; had seen the interior of a dozen different prisons in as many countries; and invariably showed fight if detected. Indeed, Harry Kinder was a "tough customer," as many agents of police had discovered to their cost.

"Then you really don't think 'the Ladybird' will have anything to do with the affair?" Guy remarked at last, standing beside him and gazing aimlessly out of the window.

"I fear she won't. If you can persuade her, then it'll all be plain sailing. They'll help us, and the risk won't be very much. Yet after all it's a dirty trick to play, isn't it?"

His companion shrugged his shoulders, saying, "Roddy sees no harm in it, and we must live the same as other people. We simply give our services for a stated sum."

"Well," declared Kinder, "I've never drawn back from any open and straightforward bit of business where it was our wits against another's, or where the victim is a fool or inexperienced; but I tell you that I draw a line at entrapping an innocent woman, and especially an English lady."

"What!" cried Bourne. "You've become conscientious all at once! Do you intend to back out of it altogether?"

"I've not yet decided what I shall do. The only thing is that I shall not persuade 'the Ladybird' either way. I shall leave her entirely in Roddy's hands."

"Then you'd better tell Roddy plainly when he comes back. Perhaps you're in love, just as you say 'the Ladybird' is!"

"Love! Why, my dear Guy—love at my age! I was only in love once—when I was seventeen. She sat in a kind of fowl-pen and sold stamps in a grocer's shop at Hackney. Since then I can safely say that I've never made a fool of myself over a woman. They are charming all, from seventeen to seventy, but there is not one I've singled out as better than the rest."

"Ah, Harry!" declared Guy with a smile, "you're a queer fellow. You are essentially a lady's man, and yet you never fall in love. We all thought once that you were fond of 'the Ladybird.'"

"'The Ladybird!'" laughed the elder man. "Well, what next? No. 'The Ladybird' has got a lover in secret somewhere, depend upon it. Perhaps it is yourself. We shall get at the truth when we return to town."

"When? Do you contemplate leaving your things at the Grand, my dear fellow? We can't. We must get money from somewhere—money, and to-day. Why not try some of the omnibuses, or the crowd at one of the railway stations? We might work together this afternoon and try our luck," Guy suggested.

"Better the Cafe Americain, or Maxim's to-night," declared Kinder, who knew his Paris well. "There's more money there, and we're bound to pick up a jay or two."

At that moment the sharp click of a key in the lock of the outer door caused them to pause, and a moment later they were joined by an elderly, grey-haired, gentlemanly-looking man in travelling-ulster and grey felt hat, who carried a small brown kit-bag which, by its hotel labels, showed sign of long travel.

"Hulloa, Roddy!" Kinder cried excitedly in his Cockney dialect. "Luck, I see! What have you got?"

"Don't know yet," was the newcomer's reply, his intonation also that of a born Londoner. "I got it from a young woman who arrived by the *rapide* at the Gare de l'Est." And throwing off his travelling get-up he placed the kit-bag upon the table. Then touching a spring in the lock he lifted it again, and there remained upon the table a lady's dressing-bag with a black waterproof cover.

"Looks like something good," declared Guy, watching eagerly.

The innocent-looking kit-bag was one of those specially constructed for the use of thieves. The bottom was hinged, with double flaps opening inward. The interior contained sharp iron grips, so that the bag, when placed upon any object smaller than it, would cover it entirely, the flaps forming the bottom opening inward, while the grips, descending, held the bag or other object tight. So the kit-bag, when removed, would also remove the object concealed within it.

Roddy, a grey-faced, cool, crafty old fellow of sixty, bore such a serious expression that one might readily have taken him for a dissenting minister or a respectable surgeon. He carefully took off the outer cover of the crocodile-skin dressing-case, examined its gilt lock, and then, taking from his pocket a piece of steel about six inches long, with a pointed end, almost a miniature of a burglar's jemmy, he quickly prised it open.

The trio eagerly looked within, and saw that it was an elegantly-fitted bag, with gold-topped bottles, and below some miscellaneous articles and letters lay a small, cheap leather bag.

In a moment the wily old thief had it open, and next instant there was displayed a magnificent bodice ornament in diamonds, a pair of exquisite pearl earrings, several fine bracelets, a long rope of splendid pearls, a fine ruby brooch, and a quantity of other ornaments.

"Excellent!" exclaimed Guy. "We're on our feet once more! Well done, Roddy, old man! We were just thinking that we'd have to pick the pockets of some poor wretches if things didn't change, and I never like doing that."

"No," remarked the leader of the gang, critically examining one after another of the articles he had stolen. "I wonder to whom these belong?" he added. "They're uncommonly good stuff, at any rate. Ascertain what those letters say."

Guy took up the letters and glanced at the superscriptions upon the envelopes.

"By Heaven!" he gasped next instant, and crushing the letters in his hand stood staring at the open bag. "What infernal irony of Fate is this? What curse is there upon us now? Look! They are hers—hers! And we have taken them!"

The three men exchanged glances, but no word was uttered.

The startling truth held Guy Bourne speechless, staggered, stupefied.

I

Concerns a Court Intrigue

The bright moon shed a white light over the great, silent courtyards of the Imperial palace at Vienna.

A bugle had just sounded, the guards had changed with a sudden clang of arms that rang out in the clear night, followed by the sound of men marching back to the guardhouse. A sharp word of command, a second bugle note, and then all was quiet again, save for the slow, measured tread of the sentries at each angle of the ponderous palace.

From without all looked grim and gloomy, in keeping with that strange fate that follows the hapless Hapsbourgs; yet beyond those black walls, in the farther wing of the Imperial palace were life and gaiety and music; indeed there was presented perhaps the most magnificent scene in all Europe.

The first Court ball of the season was at its height, and the aged Emperor Francis-Joseph was himself present—a striking figure in his uniform and orders.

Filled with the most brilliant patrician crowd in all the world—the women in tiaras and blazing with jewels, and the men in Court dress or in gorgeous uniforms—the huge ballroom, with its enormous crystal electroliers and its gold—and—white Renaissance decorations, had never been the scene of a more dazzling display. Archdukes and archduchesses, princes and princesses, nobles and diplomatists, ministers of the empire and high functionaries of State danced or gossiped, intrigued or talked scandal; or those whose first ball it was worried themselves over points of etiquette that are always so puzzling to one not born in the Court atmosphere.

The music, the scent of the flowers, the glare and glitter, the beauty of the high-born women, the easy swagger of the bestarred and beribboned men, combined to produce a scene almost fairy-like.

Laughter rang from pretty lips, and men bent to whisper into the ears of their partners as they waltzed over the perfect floor, after having paid homage to their Emperor—that lonely, broken man whose good wife, alas! had fallen beneath the assassin's knife.

A sovereign's heart may be broken, but he must nevertheless keep up a brave show before his subjects.

So he stood at the end of the room with the Imperial circle about him, smiling upon them and receiving their homage, although he longed to be back in his own quiet room at the farther end of the palace, where their laughter and the strains of music could not reach his ears.

One pale, sweet-faced woman in that gay, irresponsible crowd glanced at him and read his heart.

Her fair beauty was extremely striking, and her neat-waisted figure perfect. Indeed, she had long ago been acknowledged to be the most lovely figure at the Austrian Court—the most brilliant Court of Europe—a countenance which even her wide circle of enemies could not criticise without showing their ill nature; a perfect countenance, which, though it bore the hallmark of her imperial birth as an Archduchess, yet was sweet, dimpled, and innocent as a child's.

The Princess Claire—Cecille-Marie-Alexandrine was twenty-four. Born and bred at that Court, she had three years before been married to the Crown Prince of a German house, the royal house of Marburg, and had left it for the Court at Treysa, over which her husband would, by reason of his father's great age, very soon be sovereign.

At that moment she was back in Vienna on a brief visit to her father, the Archduke Charles, and had taken a turn around the room with a smart, well-set-up man in cavalry uniform—her cousin Prince George of Anhalt. She was dressed in ivory white, wearing in her fair hair a wonderful tiara; while in the edge of her low-cut bodice there showed the crosses and ribbons of the Orders of St. Elizabeth and Teresa—decorations bestowed only upon Imperial princesses.

Many eyes were turned upon her, and many of the friends of her girlhood days she saluted with that charming frankness of manner which was so characteristic of her open nature. Suddenly, while walking around the room, a clean-shaven, dark-haired, quick-eyed man of thirty in Court dress bowed low before her, and in an instant, recognising him, she left her cousin's side, and crossing spoke to him.

"I must see your Imperial Highness before she leaves Vienna," he whispered quickly to her in English, after she had greeted him in German and inquired after his wife. "I have something private and important to tell you."

The Crown Princess looked at him quickly, and recognised that the man was in earnest. Her curiosity became aroused; but she could ask no questions, for a hundred eyes were now upon her.

“Make an appointment—quickly, your Highness. I am here expressly to see you,” he said, noticing that Prince George was approaching to carry her off to the upper end of the room, where the members of the Imperial family were assembled.

“Very well. In the Stadtpark, against the Caroline Bridge, at eight to-morrow night. It will be dark then.”

“Be careful that you are not followed,” he whispered; and then he bowed deeply as she left him.

When her cousin came up he said,—

“You are very foolish, Claire! You know how greatly such a breach of etiquette annoys the Emperor. Why do you speak with such people?”

“Because I like to,” she answered defiantly. “If I have the misfortune to be born an Imperial Archduchess and am now Crown Princess, it need surely not preclude me from speaking to people who are my friends?”

“Oh, he is a friend, is he? Who is the fellow?” inquired the Prince, raising his eyebrows.

“Steinbach. He is in our Ministry of Foreign Affairs.”

“You really possess some queer friends, Claire,” the young man said, smiling. “They will suspect you of being a Socialist if you go on in this way. You always shock them each time you come back to Vienna because of your extraordinary unconventionality.”

“Do I?” she laughed. “Well, I’m sure I don’t care. When I lived here before I married they were for ever being scandalised by my conduct in speaking to people. But why shouldn’t I? I learn so much them. We are all too narrow-minded; we very little of the world beyond the palace walls.”

“I heard yesterday that you’d been seen walking in the Kamthnerstrasse with two women who were not of the nobility. You really oughtn’t to do that. It isn’t fair to us, you know,” he said, twisting his moustache. “We all know how wilful you are, and how you love to scandalise us; but you should draw the line at displaying such socialistic tendencies openly and publicly.”

“My dear old George,” she laughed, turning her bright eyes to him, “you’re only my cousin and not my husband. I shall do exactly what I like. If it amuses and interests me to see the life of the people, I shall do so; therefore it’s no use talking. I have had lots of lectures from the Emperor long ago, and also from my stiff old father-in-law the King. But when they lecture me I only do it all the more,” she declared, with a mischievous laugh upon her sweet face. “So they’ve given me up.”

"You're incorrigible, Claire—absolutely incorrigible," her cousin declared as he swung along at her side. "I only *do* hope that your unconventionality will not be taken advantage of by your jealous enemies. Remember, you are the prettiest woman at our Court as well as at your own. Before long, too, you will be a reigning queen; therefore reflect well whether this disregard of the first rule of Court etiquette, which forbids a member of the Imperial family to converse with a commoner, is wise. For my own part, I don't think it is."

"Oh, don't lecture me any more for goodness' sake," exclaimed the Crown Princess with a little musical laugh. "Have this waltz with me."

And next moment the handsome pair were on their way down the great room with all eyes turned upon them.

When, ten minutes later, they returned to join the Imperial circle about the Emperor, the latter motioned his niece towards him.

"Come to me when this is ended," he said in a serious voice. "I wish to talk to you. You will find me in the white room at two o'clock."

The Crown Princess bowed, and returned to the side of her father, the Archduke Charles, a tall, thin, grey-haired man in a brilliant uniform glittering with orders.

She knew that his Majesty's quick eye had detected that she had spoken with the commoner Steinbach, and anticipated that she was to receive another lecture. Why, she wondered, was Steinbach there? Truth to tell, Court life bored her. She was tired to death of all that intrigue and struggle for place, power, and precedence, and of that unhealthy atmosphere of recklessness wherein she had been born and bred. She longed for the free open life in the country around Wartenstein, the great old castle in the Tyrol that was her home, where she could tramp for miles in the mountains and be friendly with the honest country folk. After her marriage—a marriage of convenience to unite two royal houses—she had found that she had exchanged one stiff and brilliant Court for another, more dull, more stiff, and where the etiquette was even more rigid.

Those three years of married life had wrought a very great change in her.

She had left Vienna a bright, athletic girl, fond of all sports, a great walker, a splendid horsewoman, sweet, natural, and quite unaffected; yet now, after those three years of a Court, smaller yet far more severe than that of Austria, she had become rebellious, with one desire—to forsake it all and live the private life of an ordinary citizen.

Her own world, the little patrician but narrow world behind the throne, whispered and shrugged its shoulders. It was believed that her marriage was an unhappy one, but so clever was she that she never betrayed her bitterness of heart. Like all her Imperial family, she was a born diplomatist, and to those who sought to read her secret her face was always sphinx-like. Her own Court saw her as a merry, laughter-loving woman, witty, clever, a splendid dancer, and with a polished and charming manner that had already endeared her to the people over whom she was very shortly to reign. But at Court her enemies looked upon her with distrust. She exhibited no sign of displeasure on any occasion, however provoking. She was equally pleasant with enemies as with friends. For that reason they suspected her.

Her charming ingenuousness and her entire disregard of the traditional distinction between the Imperial house and the people had aroused the anger of her husband's father, the aged King, a sovereign of the old school, who declared that she was fast breaking up all the traditions of the royal house, and that her actions were a direct incentive to Socialism and Anarchism within the kingdom.

But she only laughed. She had trained herself to laugh gleefully even when her young heart was filled with blackest sorrow; even though her husband neglected and despised her; even though she was estranged for ever from her own home and her own beloved family circle at the great mountain stronghold.

Next to the Emperor Francis-Joseph, her father, the Archduke Charles, was the greatest and wealthiest man in Austria. He had a Court of his own with all its appendages and functionaries, a great palace in the Parkring in Vienna, another in Buda-Pesth, the magnificent castle of Wartenstein, near Innsbruck, besides four other castles in various parts of Austria, and a beautiful villa at Tivoli, near Rome. From her birth the Princess Claire had always breathed the vitiated air of the courts of Europe; and yet ever since a girl, walking with her English governess at Wartenstein, she had longed and dreamed of freedom. Her marriage, however, was arranged for her, and she awakened from the glamour of it all to find herself the wife of a peevish prince who had not finished the sowing of his wild oats, and who, moreover, seemed to have no place for her in his heart.

Too late she realised the tragedy of it all. When alone she would sit for hours in tears. Yet to no living soul, not even to her father or to the dark-haired, middle-aged Countess de Trauttenberg, her lady-in-waiting and confidante, did she utter one single syllable. She kept her secret.

The world envied her her marvellous beauty, her exquisite figure, her wealth, her position, her grace and ineffable charm. Yet what would it have said had it known the ugly truth? Surely it would have pitied her; for even an Imperial archduchess, forbidden to speak with the common world, has a human heart, and is entitled to human sympathy.

The Crown Prince was not present. He was, alas I seldom with the Princess. As she stood there in the Imperial circle with folded hands, laughing merrily and chatting vivaciously with the small crowd of Imperial Highnesses, no one would have guessed that she was a woman whose young heart was already broken.

Ah yes! she made a brave show to conceal her bitterness and sorrow from the world, because she knew it was her duty to do so—her duty to her princely family and to the kingdom over which she was soon to be queen.

The Emperor at last made his exit through the great white-and-gold doors, the Imperial chamberlains bowing low as he passed out. Then at two o'clock the Crown Princess managed to slip away from the Imperial circle, and with her rich train sweeping behind her, made her way rapidly through the long, tortuous corridors to his Majesty's private workroom, known as the White Chamber, on the other side of the great palace.

She tapped upon the door with her fan, and obtained entrance at once, finding the Emperor alone, standing near the great wood fire, for it was a chilly evening, close to his big, littered writing-table. His heavy expression told her that he was both thoughtful and displeased. The chamber, in contrast to the luxury of the splendid palace, was plainly furnished, essentially the workroom of the ruler of a great empire—the room in which he gave audiences and transacted the affairs of the Austria-Hungarian nation.

"Claire," he said, in a low, hard voice, "be seated; I wish to speak to you."

"Ah, I know," exclaimed the brilliant woman, whose magnificent diamonds glittered beneath the electric light, "I know! I admit, sire, that I committed an unpardonable breach of etiquette in speaking with Steinbach. You are going to reprove me—I know you are," she pouted. "But do forgive me. I did not reflect. It was an indiscretion."

"You never reflect, Claire; you are too irresponsible," the Emperor said in a tone of distinct displeasure. "But it is not that. I have called you here to learn why the Crown Prince is not in Vienna with you."

He fixed his grey, deep-sunken eyes upon hers, and awaited her answer.

"Well—" she faltered. "There are some Court dinners, and—and I believe he has some military engagements—anniversaries or something."

The Emperor smiled dubiously.

"You are shielding him, Claire," he said slowly; "I see you are. I know that Ferdinand is estranged from you. Of late I have learnt things concerning you—more than you imagine. You are unloved by your husband, and unhappy, and yet you are bearing your burden in silence, though you are a young and beautiful woman. Now, Claire," he said in a changed voice, placing his hand tenderly upon his niece's shoulder, "tell me the truth. I wish to hear the truth from your own lips. Do you know what they say of you? They say," he added, lowering his voice—"they say that you have a lover!"

"A lover!" she gasped hoarsely, starting from her chair, her beautiful face as white as the dress she wore; "a lover! Who—who told you so?"

II

Her Imperial Highness

Whatever passed between the Emperor and his niece, whether she confessed the truth or defied him, one fact was plain—she had been moved to bitter tears.

When, half an hour later, she went back through those long corridors, her rich train sweeping over the red carpets, her white-gloved hands were clenched, her teeth set hard, her eyes red, her countenance changed. Her face was changed; it was that of a woman heart-broken and desperate.

She did not return to the ballroom, but descended to the courtyard, where one of the Imperial servants called her carriage, and she returned alone to her father's splendid palace in the Parkring.

Ascending straight to her room, she dismissed the Countess de Trauttenberg, her lady-in-waiting, and Henriette, her French maid; and then locking the door, she tore off her tiara and her jewels and sank upon her knees upon the old carved prie-dieu before the ivory crucifix placed opposite her bed.

Her hands were clasped, her fair head bent, her sweet lips moved in fervent prayer, her eyes the while streaming with tears. Plunged in grief and unhappiness, she besought the Almighty to aid and counsel her in the difficult situation in which she now found herself.

"Help me, my Father!" she sobbed aloud. "Have mercy upon me—mercy upon a humble woman who craves Thy protection and direction." And her clasped hands trembled in the fervency of her appeal.

Those who had seen her an hour ago, the gay, laughing figure, blazing with jewels, the centre of the most brilliant Court of Europe, would have been astounded to see her at that moment prostrated before her Maker. In Austria, as in Germany, she was believed to be a rather giddy woman, perhaps by reason of her uncommon beauty, and perhaps because of her easy-going light-heartedness and disregard for all Court etiquette. Yet the truth was that the strong religious principles instilled into her by her mother, the deceased Archduchess Charles, had always remained, and that no day passed without one hour set apart for her devotions, in secret even from the Countess, from Henriette, and from the Crown Prince, her husband.

She was a Catholic, of course, like all her Imperial house, but upon one point she disagreed—that of confession.

Her husband, though he professed Catholicism, at heart scoffed at religion; and more than once when he had found her in the private chapel of the palace at Treysa had jeered at her. But she bore it all in patience. She was his wife, and she had a duty to perform towards his nation—to become its queen.

For nearly an hour she remained upon her knees before the crucifix, with the tiny oil-light flickering in its cup of crimson glass, kneeling in mute appeal, strong in her faith, yet humble as the humblest commoner in the land.

"My God!" she cried aloud at last. "Hear me! Answer my prayer! Give me strength and courage, and direct my footsteps in the right path. I am a weak woman, after all; a humble sinner who has repented. Help me, O God! I place all my trust in Thee! Amen."

And, crossing herself, she rose slowly with a deep-drawn breath that sounded weirdly through the fine room, and walking unsteadily towards the big cheval glass, gazed at her own reflection.

She saw how pale and haggard was her face, and looked at her trembling hands.

The ribbons and stars at the edge of her bodice caught her eye, and with a sudden movement she tore them off and cast them heedlessly upon the table as though the sight of them annoyed her. They had been conferred upon her on her marriage. She sighed as she looked back at them.

Ah, the hollow mockery of it all!

She glanced out of the window, and saw in the bright moonlight the sentry pacing up and down before the palace. Across the wide boulevard were the dark trees of the park. It recalled to her the appointment she had made there for the next evening.

"I wonder why Steinbach has followed me here?" she exclaimed to herself. "How did he obtain entrance to the Court ball? Probably he has some friend here. But surely his mission is urgent, or he would never have run this risk. I was, however, foolish to speak to him before them all—very foolish. Yet," she added slowly to herself, "I wonder what he has to tell me? I wonder—" And, without concluding her sentence, she stood gazing out upon the dark park, deep in thought, her mind full of grave apprehensions of the future.

She was a Hapsbourg—and evil fate follows a Hapsbourg always. She had prayed to God; for God alone could save her.

She, the most brilliant and the most envied woman in the Empire, was perhaps the most heart-broken, the most unhappy. Casting herself into an armchair before the log fire, she covered her drawn, white face with her hands and sobbed bitterly, until at last she sat immovable, staring straight into the embers watching the spark die out, until she fell asleep where she sat.

Next day her sweet, fresh face bore no traces of her desperation of the night. She was as gay and merry as ever, and only Henriette noticed in her eyes a slight redness, but discreetly said nothing.

The Countess, a rather pleasant-faced but stiff-mannered person, brought her her engagement-book, from which it appeared that she was due at a review by the Emperor at eleven o'clock; therefore, accompanied by her lady-in-waiting, she drove there, and was everywhere admired by the great crowds assembled. The Austrian people called her "our Claire," and the warm-hearted Viennese cheered when they recognised that she was back again among them.

It was a brilliant scene in the bright spring sunlight, for many of the Imperial Court were present, and the troops made a brave show as they marched past his Majesty and the assembled members of the Imperial house.

Then she had a luncheon engagement with the Archduchess Gisela, the wife of Prince Leopold of Bavaria, afterwards drove in the Ringstrasse and the Prater, dined early at her father's palace, after giving Henriette leave of absence for the evening, and also allowing the Countess de Trauttenberg her freedom, saying that she intended to remain at home. Then, shortly before eight o'clock, she ascended to her room, exchanged her turquoise-blue dinner-gown for a plain, stiff, tailor-made dress, put on a hat with a lace veil that concealed her features, and managed to slip across the courtyard of the domestic offices and out of the palace unseen.

The night was cloudy and dark, with threatening rain, as she crossed the broad Parkring, entering the park near the Kursalon, and traversing the deserted walks towards the River Wien. The chill wind whistled in the budding trees above, sweeping up the dust in her path, and the statuesque guard whom she passed in the shadow glanced inquisitively at her, of course not recognising her.

There was no one in the Stadtpark at that hour, and all was silent, gloomy, and dismal, well in keeping with her own sad thoughts. Behind her, the street lamps of the Parkring showed in a long, straight line, and before her were the lights on the Caroline Bridge, the spot appointed for the meeting.

Her heart beat quickly. It was always difficult for her to escape without the knowledge of De Trauttenberg or Henriette. The former was, as a good lady-in-waiting should be, ever at her side, made her engagements for her, and saw that she kept them. That night, however, the Countess desired to visit her sister who was in Vienna with her husband, therefore it had happened opportunely; and, freed of Henriette, she had now little to fear.

The dress she wore was one she used when in the country. She had thrown a short cape of Henriette's about her shoulders, and was thus sufficiently disguised to avoid recognition by people in the streets.

As she came around a sudden bend in the pathway to the foot of the bridge the dark figure of a man in a black overcoat emerged from the shadow, and was next instant at her side, holding his hat in his hand and bowing before her.

"I began to fear that your Imperial Highness would not come," he said breathlessly in German. "Or that you had been prevented."

"Is it so very late, then?" she inquired in her sweet, musical voice, as the man walked slowly at her side. "I had difficulty in getting away in secret."

"No one has followed you, Princess?" he said, glancing anxiously behind him. "Are you quite sure?"

"No one. I was very careful. But why have you asked me to come here? Why were you at the ball last night? How did you manage to get a card?"

"I came expressly to see you, Princess," answered the young man in a deep earnest voice. "It was difficult to get a command to the ball, but I managed it, as I could approach you by no other way. At your Highness's own Court you, as Crown Princess, are unapproachable for a commoner like myself, and I feared to write to you, as De Trauttenberg often attends to your correspondence."

"But you are my friend, Steinbach," she said. "I am always to be seen by my friends."

"At your own risk, your Highness," he said quickly. "I know quite well that last night when you stopped and spoke to me it was a great breach of etiquette. Only it was imperative that I should see you to-night. To you, Princess, I owe everything. I do not forget your great kindness to me; how that I was a poor clerk out of work, with my dear wife ill and starving, and how, by your letter of recommendation, I was appointed in the Ministry of Foreign Affairs, first as French translator, and now as a secretary. Were it not for you, Princess, I and my family would have starved. You saved me from ruin, and I hope you are confident that in me, poor and humble though I am, you at least have a friend."

"I am sure of that, Steinbach," was her Highness's kindly reply. "We need not cross the bridge," she said. "It is quiet along here, by the river. We shall meet no one."

For a few moments a silence fell between them, and the Princess began to wonder why he had asked her there to meet him.

At last, when they were in a dark and narrower pathway, he turned suddenly to her and said,—

"Princess, I—I hardly know how to speak, for I fear that you may take what I have to say in a wrong sense. I mean," he faltered, "I mean that I fear you may think it impertinent of me to speak to you, considering the great difference in our stations."

"Why?" she asked calmly, turning to him with some surprise. "Have you not just told me that you are my friend?"

She noticed at that moment that he still held his hat in his hand, and motioned to him to reassume it.

"Yes. I am your Highness's friend," he declared quickly. "If I were not, I would not dare to approach you, or to warn you of what at this moment is in progress."

"What is in progress?" she exclaimed in surprise. "Tell me."

She realised that this man had something serious to say, or surely he would never have followed her to Vienna, and obtained entrance to the Imperial Court by subterfuge.

"Your Highness is in peril," he declared in a low voice, halting and standing before her. "You have enemies, fierce, bitter enemies, on every side; enemies who are doing their utmost to estrange you from your husband; relentless enemies who are conspiring might and main against you and the little Princess Ignatia. They—"

"Against my child?" cried the Princess, amazed. "Do you really mean that there is actually a conspiracy against me?"

"Alas! that is so, Highness," said the man, seriously and distinctly. "By mere chance I have learnt of it, and being unable to approach you at your own Court, I am here to give you timely warning of what is intended." She was silent, gazing straight into her companion's face, which was, however, hardly distinguishable in the darkness. She could scarcely believe the truth of what this commoner told her. Could this man, whom she had benefited by her all-powerful influence, have any ulterior motive in lying to her?

"And what is intended?" she inquired in a strange, hard voice, still half dubious and half convinced.

"There is a plot, a dastardly, widespread conspiracy to cause your Highness's downfall and part you from the Crown Prince before he comes to the throne," was his answer.

"But why? For what motive?" she inquired, starting at the amazing revelation.

"Cannot your Highness discern that your jealous enemies are in fear of you?" he said. "They know that one day ere long our invalid King must die, and your husband will then ascend the throne. You will be Queen, and they feel convinced that the day of your accession will be their last day at Court—frankly, that having seen through their shams and intrigues, you will dismiss them all and change the entire entourage."

"Ah! I see," replied the Crown Princess Claire in a hoarse, bitter voice. "They fear me because they have realised their own shortcomings. So they are conspiring against me to part me from my husband, and drive me from Court! Yes," she sighed heavily, "I know that I have enemies on every side. I am a Hapsbourg, and that in itself is sufficient to prejudice them against me. I have never been a favourite with their Majesties the King and Queen because of my Liberal tendencies. They look upon me as a Socialist; indeed, almost as a revolutionist. Their sycophants would be glad enough to see me banished from Court. And yet the Court bow to me with all that hateful obsequiousness."

"Your Highness is, unfortunately, quite right," declared the man Steinbach. "The Crown Prince is being enticed farther and farther from you, as part of the ingenious plot now afoot. The first I knew of it was by accident six months ago, when some letters from abroad fell into my hands at the Ministry. The conspiracy is one that permeates the whole Court. The daily talk of your enemies is the anticipation of your downfall."

"My downfall! But how is that to be accomplished?" she demanded, her fine eyes flashing with indignation. "I surely have nothing to fear—have I? I beg of you to be quite candid with me, Steinbach. In this affair your information may be of greatest service, and I am deeply indebted to you. It staggers me. What have I done that these people should seek my ruin?" she cried in blank dismay.

"Will your Highness pardon me if I tell the truth?" asked the man at her side, speaking very seriously. "You have been too free, too frank, and too open-minded. Every well-meant action of yours is turned to account by those who seek to do you evil. Those whom you believe to be your friends are your worst antagonists. I have longed to approach you and tell you this for months, but I always feared. How could I reach you? They are aware that the secret correspondence passed through my hands, and therefore they suspect me of an intention of betraying them."

"Then you are here at imminent risk to yourself, Steinbach," she remarked very slowly, looking again straight into his dark face.

"I am here as your Highness's friend," replied the young man simply. "It is surely worth the risk to save my gracious benefactress from falling victim to their foul, dastardly conspiracy?"

"And who, pray, are my worst antagonists?" she asked hoarsely.

He gave her rapidly half a dozen names of Court officials and persons in the immediate entourage of their Majesties.

"And," he added, "do not trust the Countess de Trauttenberg. She is playing you false. She acts as spy upon you and notes your every action."

"The Countess—their spy!" she gasped, utterly taken aback, for if there was one person at Court in whom she had the utmost confidence it was the woman who had been in her personal service ever since her marriage.

"I have documentary proof of it," the man said quietly. "I would beg of your Highness to make no sign whatever that the existence of the plot is known to you, but at the same time exercise the greatest caution, both for your own sake and that of the little Princess."

"Surely they do not mean to kill me, Steinbach?" she exclaimed in alarm.

"No—worse. They intend to banish your Highness from Court in disgrace, as a woman unworthy to reign over us as Queen. They fear you because you have discovered their own intrigues, corruptions, and scandals, and they intend that, at all costs, you shall never ascend the throne."

"But my husband! He should surely know this!"

"Princess," exclaimed the clean-shaven young man, speaking very slowly and seriously, "I regret that it is I who am compelled to reveal this to you, but the Crown Prince already believes ill of you. He suspects; and therefore whatever lies they, now invent concerning you he accepts as truth. Princess," he added in a low, hard voice, "you are in deadly peril.

There, the truth is out, for I cannot keep it from you longer. I am poor, unknown, without influence. All I can do is to give you this warning in secret, because I hope that I may call myself your friend."

The unhappy daughter of the Imperial house was silent. The revelation was startling and amazing. She had never realised that a plot was afoot against her in her husband's kingdom. Words entirely failed her. She and her little daughter Ignatia were marked down as victims. She now for the first time realised her peril, yet she was powerless to stem the tide of misfortune that, sooner or later, must overwhelm her and crush her. She stood there a defenceless woman.

III

The Revelations of a Commoner

Princess and commoner walked in silence, side by side. The rough night wind blew the dust in their faces, but they bent to it heedlessly, both too full of their own thoughts for words; the man half confused in the presence of the brilliant woman who ere long would be his sovereign; the woman stupefied at the dastardly intrigue that had not only estranged her husband from her, but had for its object the expulsion from the kingdom of herself and her child.

Open-hearted as she was, liberal-minded, pleasant, easy-going, and a delightful companion, she had never sufficiently realised that at that stiff, narrow-minded Court there were men and women who hated her. All of us are so very loth to believe that we have enemies, and more especially those who believe in the honesty and integrity of mankind.

She reflected upon her interview with the Emperor. She remembered his Majesty's hard words. Had those conspiring against her obtained his ear?

Even De Trauttenberg, the tall, patient, middle-aged woman in whom she had reposed such confidence, was their spy! Steinbach's story staggered belief. And yet—and yet was not the Emperor's anger plain proof that he knew something—that a foul plot was really in progress?

Along those dark winding paths they strolled slowly, meeting no one, for the place was utterly deserted. It was an exciting escapade, and dangerous withal.

The man at last broke the silence, saying,—

"I need not impress upon your Imperial Highness the necessity for discretion in this matter. To betray your knowledge of the affair would be to betray me."

"Trust me," was her answer. "I know how to keep a secret, and I am not likely to forget this important service you have rendered me."

"My only regret is that I was unable to approach you months ago, when I first made the discovery. Your Highness would have then been able to avoid the pitfalls constantly set for you," the man said meaningly.

The Princess Claire bit her lip. She knew to what he referred. She had been foolish, ah yes; very foolish. And he dare not be more explicit.

"Yes," she sighed. "I know—I know to what you refer. But surely we need not discuss it. Even though I am Crown Princess, I am a woman, after all."

"I beg your Highness's pardon," he exclaimed quickly, fearing that she was annoyed.

"There is nothing to pardon," was her reply. "You are my friend, and speak to me in my own interests. For that I thank you. Only—only—" she added, "all that you've just told me is such a startling revelation. My eyes are opened now. I see the dastardly ingenuity of it all. I know why my husband—"

But she checked herself instantly. No. However ill-treated she had been she would preserve her secret. She would not complain to a commoner at risk of her domestic infelicity going forth to her people.

It was true that within a year of marriage he had thrown her down in her room and kicked her in one of his paroxysms of temper. He had struck her blows innumerable; but she had borne all in patience, and De Trauttenberg had discovered dark marks upon her white shoulders which she had attributed to a fall upon the ice. She saw now the reason of his estrangement; how his sycophants had poisoned his mind against her because they feared her.

"Steinbach," she said at last, "tell me the truth. What do the people think of me? You are a commoner and live among them. I, imprisoned at Court, unfortunately, know nothing. The opinions of the people never reach us."

"The people, your Highness, love you. They call you 'their Claire.' You surely know how, when you drive out, they raise their hats and shout in acclamation."

"Yes," she said in a low, mechanical voice, "but is it real enthusiasm? Would they really love me if I were Queen?"

"Your Highness is at this moment the most popular woman in the whole kingdom of Marburg. If it were known that this plot was in progress there would in all probability be a revolution. Stuhlmann and his friends are hated everywhere, and their overthrow would cause universal satisfaction."

"And the people do not really think ill of me?"

"Think ill of you, Princess?" he echoed. "Why, they literally worship you and the little Princess Ignatia."

She was silent again, walking very slowly, and reflecting deeply. It was so seldom she had opportunity of speaking with one of the people unless he were a deputy or a diplomatist, who then put on all his Court manners, was unnatural, and feared to speak. From the man beside her, however, she saw she might learn the truth of a matter which was ever uppermost in her mind. And yet she hesitated to approach what was, after all, a very delicate subject.

Suddenly, with her mind made up, she halted, and turning to him, said,—

"Steinbach, I want you to answer me truthfully. Do not evade the question for fear of annoying me. Speak openly, as the friend you are to me. I wish to know one thing," and she lowered her voice until it almost faltered. "Have you heard a—well, a scandal concerning myself?"

He made no answer.

She repeated her question; her veiled face turned to his.

"Your Highness only a few moments ago expressed a desire not to discuss the matter," he replied in a low, distinct voice.

"But I want to know," she urged. "I must know. Tell me the truth. If you are my friend you will at least be frank with me when I command."

"If you command, Princess, then I must obey, even with reluctance," was his response. "Yes. I have heard some gossip. It is spoken openly in Court by the *dames du palais*, and is now being whispered among the people."

She held her breath. Fortunately, it was dark, for she knew that her countenance had gone crimson.

"Well?" she asked. "And what do they say of me?"

"They, unfortunately, couple your Highness's name with that of Count Leitolf, the chief of the private cabinet of his Majesty," was his low answer.

"Yes," she said in a toneless voice. "And what more?"

"They say that Major Scheel, attache at the Embassy in Paris, recognised you driving with the Count in the Avenue de l'Opera, when you were supposed to be at Aix-les-Bains with the little Princess Ignatia."

"Yes. Go on."

"They say, too, that he follows you everywhere—and that your maid Henriette helps you to leave the palace in secret to meet him."

She heard his words, and her white lips trembled.

"They also declare," he went on in a low voice, "that your love of the country is only because you are able to meet him without any one knowing, that your journey here to Vienna is on account of him—that he has followed you here."

She nodded, without uttering a word.

"The Count has, no doubt, followed your Highness, indiscreetly if I may say so, for I recognised him last night dining alone at Breying's."

"He did not see you?" she exclaimed anxiously.

"No. I took good care not to be seen. I had no desire that my journey here should be known, or I should be suspected. I return to-night at midnight."

"And to be frank, Steinbach, you believe that all this has reached my husband's ears?" she whispered in a hard, strained voice.

"All that is detrimental to your Highness reaches the Crown Prince," was his reply to the breathless woman, "and certainly not without embellishments. That is why I implore of you to be circumspect—why I am here to tell you of the plot to disgrace you in the people's eyes."

"But the people themselves are now speaking of—of the Count?" she said in a low, uncertain voice, quite changed from her previous musical tones when first they met.

"A scandal—and especially a Court one—very soon spreads among the people. The royal servants gossip outside the palace, and moreover your Highness's many enemies are only too delighted to assist in spreading such reports. It gives motive for the Crown Prince's estrangement."

Her head was bent, her hands were trembling. The iron had entered her soul.

The people—the people whom she so dearly loved, and who had waved their hands and shouted those glad welcomes to her as she drove out—were now whispering of Leitolf.

She bit her lip, and her countenance went pale as death as the truth arose before her in all its hideous ghastliness.

Even the man at her side, the humble man who had stood by her as her friend, knew that Leitolf was there—in Vienna—to be near her. Even Steinbach could have no further respect for her as a woman—only respect because she was one day to be his sovereign.

Her hands were clenched; she held her breath, and shivered as the chill wind cut through her. She longed to be back in her father's palace; to be alone in her room to think.

"And nothing more?" she asked in that same blank voice which now caused her companion to wonder.

"Only that they say evil of you that is not worth repeating," was his brief answer.

She sighed again, and then when she had sufficiently recovered from the effect of his words, she whispered in a low voice,—

"I—I can only thank you, Steinbach, for giving me this warning. Forgive me if—if I am somewhat upset by it—but I am a woman—and perhaps it is only natural. Trust me to say nothing. Leave Vienna to-night and return home. If you ever wish to communicate with me write guardedly, making an appointment, and address your letter to Madame Emond at the Poste Restante in Brussels. You will recollect the name?"

"Most certainly I shall, your Highness. I can only ask pardon for speaking so openly. But it was at your request."

"Do not let us mention it further," she urged, her white lips again compressed. "Leave me now. It is best that I should walk down yonder to the Parkring alone."

He halted, and bowing low, his hat in his hand, said,—

"I would ask your Imperial Highness to still consider me your humble servant to command in any way whatsoever, and to believe that I am ever ready to serve you and to repay the great debt of gratitude I owe to you."

And, bending, he took her gloved hand and raised it to his lips in obeisance to the princess who was to be his queen.

"Adieu, Steinbach," she said in a broken voice. "And for the service you have rendered me to-night I can only return you the thanks of an unhappy woman."

Then she turned from him quickly, and hurried down the path to the park entrance, where shone a single gas lamp, leaving him standing alone, bowing in silence.

He watched her graceful figure out of sight, then sighed, and turned away in the opposite direction.

A few seconds later the tall, dark figure of a man emerged noiselessly from the deep shadow of the tree where, unobserved, he had crept up and stood concealed. The stranger glanced quickly up and down at the two receding figures, and then at a leisurely pace strode in the direction the Princess had taken.

When at last she had turned and was out of sight he halted, took a cigarette from a silver case, lit it after some difficulty in the tearing wind, and muttered some words which, though inaudible, were sufficiently triumphant in tone to show that he was well pleased at his ingenious piece of espionage.

IV

His Majesty Cupid

As the twilight fell on the following afternoon a fiacre drew up before the Hotel Imperial, one of the best and most select hotels in the Kartner Ring, in Vienna, and from it descended a lady attired in the deep mourning of a widow.

Of the gold-laced concierge she inquired for Count Carl Leitolf, and was at once shown into the lift and conducted to a private sitting-room on the second floor, where a young, fair-moustached, good-looking man, with well-cut, regular features and dark brown eyes, rose quickly as the door opened and the waiter announced her.

The moment the door had closed and they were alone he took his visitor's hand and raised it reverently to his lips, bowing low, with the exquisite grace of the born courtier.

In an instant she drew it from him and threw back her veil, revealing her pale, beautiful face—the face of her Imperial Highness the Crown Princess Claire.

"Highness!" the man exclaimed, glancing anxiously at the door to reassure himself that it was closed, "I had your note this morning, but—but are you not running too great a risk by coming here? I could not reply, fearing that my letter might fall into other hands; otherwise I would on no account have allowed you to come. You may have been followed. There are, as you know, spies everywhere."

"I have come, Carl, because I wish to speak to you," she said, looking unflinchingly into his handsome face. "I wish to know by what right you have followed me here—to Vienna?"

He drew back in surprise, for her attitude was entirely unexpected.

"I came here upon my own private affairs," he answered.

"That is not the truth," she declared in quick resentment. "You are here because you believed that you might meet me at the reception after the State dinner to-night. You applied for a card for it in order that you could see me—and this, after what passed between us the other day! Do you consider that you are treating me fairly? Cannot you see that your constant attentions are compromising me and causing people to talk?"

"And what, pray, does your Imperial Highness care for this idle Court gossip?" asked the well-dressed, athletic-looking man, at the same time placing a chair for her and bowing her to it. "There has been enough of it already, and you have always expressed the utmost disregard of anything that might be said, or any stories that might be invented."

"I know," she answered. "But this injudicious action of yours in following me here is utter madness. It places me in peril. You are known in Vienna, remember."

"Then if that is your view, your Highness, I can only apologise," he said most humbly. "I will admit that I came here in order to be able to get a few minutes' conversation with you to-night. At our Court at home you know how very difficult it is for me to speak with you, for the sharp eye of the Trauttenberg is ever upon you."

The Princess's arched brows contracted slightly. She recollected what Steinbach had revealed to her regarding her lady-in-waiting.

"And it is surely best that you should have difficulty in approaching me," she said. "I have not forgotten your foolish journey to Paris, where I had gone incognito to see my old nurse, and how you compelled me to go out and see the sights in your company. We were recognised. Do you know that?" she exclaimed in a hard voice. "A man who knew us both sent word to Court that we were in Paris together."

"Recognised!" he gasped, the colour fading instantly from his face. "Who saw us?"

"Of his identity I'm not aware," she answered, for she was a clever diplomatist, and could keep a secret well. She did not reveal Scheel's name. "I only know that our meeting in Paris is no secret. They suspect me, and I have you to thank for whatever scandal may now be invented concerning us."

The lithe, clean-limbed man was silent, his head bent before her. What could he reply? He knew, alas! too well, that in following her from Germany to Paris he had acted very injudiciously. She was believed to be taking the baths at Aix, but a sudden caprice had seized her to run up to Paris and see her old French nurse, to whom she was much attached. He had learnt her intention in confidence, and had met her in Paris and shown her the city. It had been an indiscretion, he admitted.

Yet the recollection of those few delightful days of freedom remained like a pleasant dream. He recollected her childish delight of it all. It was out of the season, and they believed that they could go hither and thither, like the crowds of tourists do, without fear of recognition. Yet

Fate, it seemed, had been against them, and their secret meeting was actually known!

"Cannot you see the foolishness of it all?" she asked in a low, serious voice. "Cannot you see, Carl, that your presence here lends colour to their suspicions? I have enemies—fierce, bitter enemies—as you must know too well, and yet you imperil me like this!" she cried reproachfully.

"I can make no defence, Princess," he said lamely. "I can only regret deeply having caused you any annoyance."

"Annoyance!" she echoed in anger. "Your injudicious actions have placed me in the greatest peril. The people have coupled our names, and you are known to have followed me on here."

Her companion was silent, his eyes downcast, as though not daring to meet her reproachful gaze.

"I have been foolish—very foolish, I know," she cried. "In the old days, when we knew each other at Wartenstein, a boy-and-girl affection sprang up between us; and then, when you left the University, they sent you as attache to the Embassy in London, and we gradually forgot each other. You grew tired of diplomacy, and returned to find me the wife of the Crown Prince; and in a thoughtless moment I promised, at your request, to recommend you to a post in the private cabinet of the King. Since that day I have always regretted. I ought never to have allowed you to return. I am as much to blame as you are, for it was an entirely false step. Yet how was I to know?"

"True, my Princess!" said the man in a low, choking voice. "How were you to know that I still loved you in silence, that I was aware of the secret of your domestic unhappiness, that I—"

"Enough!" she cried, drawing herself up. "The word love surely need not be spoken between us. I know it all, alas! Yet I beg of you to remember that I am the wife of another, and a woman of honour."

"Ah yes," he exclaimed, his trembling hand resting on the back of the chair upon which she sat. "Honour—yes. I love you, Claire—you surely know that well. But we do not speak of it; it is a subject not to be discussed by us. Day after day, unable to speak to you, I watch you in silence. I know your bitterness in that gilded prison they call the Court, and long always to help you and rescue you from that—that man to whom you are, alas! wedded. It is all so horrible, so loathsome, that I recoil when I see him smiling upon you while at heart he hates you. For weeks, since last we spoke together, how I have lived I scarcely know—utter despair, insane hopes alternately possess me—but at last the day came, and I followed you here to speak with you, my Princess."

She remained silent, somewhat embarrassed, as he took her gloved hand and again kissed it.

She was nervous, but next instant determined.

"Alas! I have not failed to notice your strong affection for me, Carl," she said with a heavy sigh, her beautiful face slightly flushed. "You must therefore control this passion that seems to have been rekindled within your heart. For my sake go, and forget me," she implored. "Resign your appointment, and re-enter the diplomatic service of the Emperor. I will speak to Lindenau, who will give you an appointment, say, in Rome or Paris. But you must not remain at Treysa. I—I will not allow it."

"But, Princess," he cried in dismay, "I cannot go and leave you there alone among your enemies. You—"

"You must; for, unintentionally, because you have my interests at heart, you are my worst enemy. You are indiscreet, just as every man is who loves a woman truly."

"Then you really believe I love you still, Claire," he cried, bending towards her. "You remember those delightfully happy days at Wartenstein long ago, when—"

She held up her hand to stop the flow of his words.

He looked at her. For an instant her glance wavered and shrank.

She was his idol, the beautiful idol with eyes like heaven.

Yes, she was very beautiful—beautiful with all the beauty of woman now, not with the beauty of the girl.

And she, with her sad gaze fixed upon him, remembered all the past—the great old castle in the far-off Tyrol, her laughter at his awkwardness; their chats in English when both were learning that language; the quarrel over the lilac blossom. At Arcachon—the shore and the pine forest; the boyish kiss stolen under the mistletoe; the declaration of their young love on that lonely mountain-side with the world lying at their feet; the long, sweet, silent kisses exchanged on their homeward walk; the roses she had given him as farewell pledge when he had left for London.

All had gone—gone for ever.

Nevertheless, though everything was past, she could not resist an impulse to recall it—oh, very briefly—in a few feeling words, as one may recall some sweet and rapturous dream.

"We were very foolish," she said.

He was silent. His heart was too full for words. He knew that a woman who can look back on the past—on rapture, delight, the first thrilling kiss, the first fervent vow—and say, "We were very foolish," is a woman changed beyond recall.

In other days, had he heard such sacrilegious words a cry of horror would have sprung from his lips. But now, though he shuddered with anguish, he simply said,—

"I shall always remember it, Princess;" adding, with a glance at her, "and you."

Her wonderful eyes shrank once more and her lips quivered, as though for one second touched again by the light wing of love—as if, indeed, she felt she had done something unworthy of her, something which might bring her regret hereafter.

In the midst of his confusion, the man remained victorious. She would never be his, and yet she would be his for ever. No matter how she might strive, she would never entirely forget.

She sighed, and rising, walked unsteadily to the window, where, below, the street lamps were just being lit. Daylight had faded, and in the room it was almost dark.

"To-night, Carl, we meet for the last time," she said with an effort, in a hard, strained voice. "Both for you and for me it is best that we should part and forget. I did wrong to recommend you to the post at Court, and I ought to have foreseen the grave peril of the situation. Fortunately, I have realised it in time, even though our enemies already believe ill and invent lies concerning us. You must not return to Court. Remember, I forbid you. To-night, at the State dinner, I will speak to Lindenau and ask him to send you as attache to Rome or to Petersburg. It is the wisest course."

"Then your Highness really intends to banish me?" he said hoarsely, in a low, broken voice of reproach.

"Yes," she faltered. "I—I must—Carl—to—to save myself."

"But you are cruel—very cruel—Princess," he cried, his voice trembling with emotion.

"You must realise my peril," she said seriously. "Your presence at Court increases my danger hourly, because"—and she hesitated—"because, Carl, I confess to you that I do not forget—I never shall forget," she added as the tears sprang to her blue eyes. "Therefore, go! Let me bear my own burden as best I can alone, and let me remember you as what you have always been—chivalrous to an unhappy woman; a man of honour."

Slowly she moved across the room towards the door, but he arrested her progress, and took her small hand quickly in his grasp.

For some moments, in the falling gloom, he looked into her sweet, tearful face without speaking; then crushing down the lump that arose in his throat, he raised to his hot, passionate lips the hand of the woman he loved, and, imprinting upon it a tender, lingering kiss, murmured,—

"Adieu, Claire—my Princess—my first, my only love!" She drew her hand away as his passionate words fell upon her ear, sighed heavily, and in silence opened the door and passed out from his presence.

And thus were two brave hearts torn asunder.

V

Some Suspicions

State dinners, those long, tedious affairs at which the conversation is always stilted and the bearing of everybody is stiff and unnatural, always bored the Crown Princess Claire to death.

Whenever she could she escaped them; but as a Crown Princess she was compelled by Court etiquette to undergo ordeals which, to a woman not educated as an Imperial Archduchess, would have been impossible. She had trained herself to sit for hours smiling and good-humoured, although at heart she hated all that glittering formality and rich display. There were times when at her own Court at Treysa, at the military anniversary dinners that were so often held, she had been compelled to sit at table with her husband and the guests for four and five hours on end, without showing any sign of fatigue beyond taking her smelling-salts from the hand of her lady-in-waiting. Yet she never complained, though the eating, and more especially the drinking, disgusted her. It was a duty—one of the many wearisome, soul-killing duties which devolve upon a Crown Princess—of which the world at large is in utter ignorance. Therefore she accepted it in silence, yet bored always by meeting and speaking with the same circle of people day after day—a small circle which was ever intriguing, ever consumed by its own jealousies, ever striving for the favour of the aged king; the narrow-minded little world within the Palace who treated those outside as though of different flesh and blood to themselves.

Whether at a marriage, at a funeral, at the opera, at a review, or at a charity *fete*—everywhere where her Court duties called her—she met the same people, she heard the same interminable chatter and the same shameful scandals, until, unhappy in her own domestic life, she had grown to loathe it all, and to long for that liberty of which she had dreamed when a girl at her father's castle at Wartenstein, or at the great old Residenz-Schloss, or palace, at Pressburg.

Yet what liberty could she, heiress to a throne, obtain; what, indeed, within her husband's Court, a circle who dined at five o'clock and were iron-bound by etiquette?

The State dinner at the Imperial palace that night differed but little from any other State dinner—long, dull, and extremely uninteresting. Given in honour of a Swedish Prince who was at the moment the guest of the Emperor, there were present the usual circle of Imperial Archdukes and Archduchesses, who after dinner were joined in the great reception room by the Ministers of State, the British, French, and Italian Ambassadors, the Swedish Minister and the whole staff of the Swedish Embassy in the Schwindgasse. Every one was in uniform and wore his orders, the Emperor himself standing at the end of the room, chatting with his young guest in French.

The Crown Princess Claire, a striking figure in turquoise chiffon, was standing near, discussing Leoncavallo's new opera with her cousin, the Princess Marie of Bourbon, who had arrived only a few days before from Madrid. Suddenly her eye caught the figure she had all the evening been in Search of.

Count de Lindenau, Privy Councillor, Chamberlain, Minister of the Imperial Household, and Minister for Foreign Affairs of the Austrian Empire—a short, rather stout, bald-headed man, with heavy white moustache, with the crimson ribbon of the Order of Saint Stephen of Hungary across his shirt-front and the Grand Cross in brilliants upon his coat—stopped to bow low before the Crown Princess, who in an instant seized the opportunity to leave her cousin and speak with him.

"It is really quite a long time since we met, Count," she exclaimed pleasantly. "I met the Countess at Cannes in January, and was delighted to see her so much better. Is she quite well again?"

"I thank your Imperial Highness," responded the Minister. "The Countess has completely recovered. At present she is at Como. And you? Here for a long stay in Vienna, I hope. We always regret that you have left us, you know," he added, smiling, for she had, ever since a girl, been friendly with him, and had often visited his wife at their castle at Mauthhausen.

"No; I regret that I must return to Treysa in a few days," she said as she moved along and he strolled at her side down the great gilded room where the little groups were standing gossiping. Then, when his Excellency had asked after the health of the Crown Prince and of the little Princess Ignatia, she drew him aside to a spot where they could not be overheard, and halting, said in a lower tone,—

"I have wished to meet you, Count, because I want you to do me a favour."

"Your Imperial Highness knows quite well that if I can serve you in any way I am always only too delighted." And he bowed.

More than once she had asked favour of Lindenau, the stern Foreign Minister and favourite of the Emperor, and he had always acted as she wished. She had known him ever since her birth. He had, indeed, been present at her baptism.

"Well, it is this," she said. "I want to give my recommendation to you on behalf of Count Leitolf, who is at present chief of the King's private cabinet at Treysa, and who is strongly desirous of returning to the Austrian diplomatic service, and is anxious for a post abroad." Mention of Leitolf's name caused the wily old Minister to glance at her quickly. The rumour had reached his ears, and in an instant he recognised the situation—the Crown Princess wished to rid herself of him. But the old fellow was diplomatic, and said, as though compelled to recall the name,—

"Leitolf? Let me see. That is Count Carl, whom I sent to London a few years ago? He resigned his post to take service under your father-in-law the King. Ah yes, I quite recollect. And he now wishes to be appointed abroad again, eh? And you wish to recommend him?"

"Exactly, Count," she answered. "I think that Leitolf is tired of our Court; he finds it too dull. He would prefer Rome, he tells me."

"Your Imperial Highness is well aware that any recommendation of yours always has the most earnest attention," said the Minister, with a polite bow. His quick grey eyes were watching the beautiful woman sharply. He wondered what had occurred between her and Count Carl.

"Then you will send him to Rome?" she asked, unable to conceal her eagerness.

"If he will present himself at the Ministry, he will be at once appointed to the Embassy to the Quirinal," responded his Excellency quietly.

"But he will not present himself, I am afraid."

"Oh, why not?" inquired the great Austrian diplomatist, regarding her in surprise.

"Because—" and she hesitated, as a slight flush crossed her features—"because he is rather ashamed to ask for a second appointment, having resigned from London."

The old Minister smiled dubiously.

"Ah!" he exclaimed confidentially, "I quite understand. Your Imperial Highness wishes to get rid of him from your Court, eh?"

The Princess started, twisting her diamond bracelet nervously round her wrist.

"Why do you think that, Count?" she asked quickly, surprised that he should have thus divined her motive.

"Well, your Imperial Highness is rather unduly interested in the man—if you will permit me to say so," was his answer. "Besides, if I may speak frankly, as I know I may, I have regarded his presence in your Court as distinctly dangerous—for you. There are, you know, evil tongues ever ready to invent scandal, even against a Crown Princess."

"I know," she said, in a low, changed voice. "But let us walk; otherwise they will all wonder why I am talking with you so long," and the two moved slowly along side by side. "I know," she went on—"I know that I have enemies; and, to confess the truth, I wish, in order to show them that they lie, to send him from me."

"Then he shall go. To-morrow I will send him orders to rejoin the service, and to proceed to Rome immediately. And," he added in a kindly voice, "I can only congratulate your Imperial Highness upon your forethought. Leitolf is entirely without discretion. Only this evening I was actually told that he had followed you to Vienna, and—"

But he stopped abruptly, without concluding his sentence. "And what else?" she asked, turning pale. Even the Minister knew; therefore Leitolf had evidently allowed himself to be seen.

"Shall I tell you, Princess?"

"Certainly; you need not keep anything from me."

"I was also told that he is staying at the Hotel Imperial, and that you had called upon him this afternoon." She started, and looked him straight in the face.

"Who told you that?" she demanded.

"I learned it from the report of the secret agents of the Ministry."

"Then I am spied upon here!" she exclaimed, pale with anger. "Even in my own home watch is kept upon me."

"Not upon your Imperial Highness," was the great Minister's calm reply, "but upon the man we have recently been discussing. It was, I venture to think, rather indiscreet of you to go to the hotel; although, of course, the knowledge of your visit is confidential, and goes no further than myself. It is a secret of the Ministry."

"Indiscreet!" she echoed with a sigh. "In this polluted atmosphere, to breathe freely is to be indiscreet. Because I am an Archduchess I am fettered as a prisoner, and watched like a criminal under surveillance. My enemies, jealous of my position and power, have invented scandalous stories that have aroused suspicion, and for that reason you all believe ill of me."

"Pardon me, Princess," said the crafty old man, bowing, "I, for one, do not. Your anxiety to rid yourself of the fellow is proof to me that the scandal is a pure invention, and I am only too pleased to render you this service. Your real enemies are those around your husband, who have hinted and lied regarding you in order to estrange you from Court."

"Then you are really my friend, Count?" she asked anxiously. "You do not believe what they say regarding me?"

"I do not, Princess," he replied frankly; "and I trust you will still regard me, as I hope I have ever been, your Imperial Highness's friend. I know full well how Leitolf craved your favour for recommendation to your King; and you, with a woman's blindness to the grave eventualities of the future, secured him the appointment. Of late you have, I suppose, realised the fatal mistake?"

"Yes," she said in a low voice; "I have now foreseen my own peril. I have been very foolish; but I have halted, and Leitolf must go."

"Very wise—very wise indeed! Your Imperial Highness cannot afford to run any further risk. In a few months, or a couple of years at most, the poor King's disease must prove fatal, and you will find yourself Queen of a brilliant kingdom. Once Queen, your position will be assured, and you will make short work of all those who have conspired to secure your downfall. You will, perhaps, require assistance. If so, rely upon me to render you in secret whatever help lies in my power. With you, a Hapsbourg, as Queen, the influence of Austria must be paramount, remember. Therefore I beg of your Imperial Highness to exercise the greatest discretion not to imperil yourself. The Crown Prince must be allowed no loophole through which he can openly quarrel with you. Remain patient and forbearing until you are Queen."

They were in a corner of the great hall, standing behind one of the high marble columns and unobserved.

"I am always patient, Count," was her rather sad response, her chest heaving beneath her chiffon. "As you well know, my marriage has not been a happy one; but I strive to do my duty to both the Court and the people. I make no denial to you. You doubtless know the truth—that when a girl I loved Count Leitolf, and that it was an act prompted by foolish sentimentalism to have connived at his appointment at my husband's own Court. Betrayed, perhaps, by my own actions, my enemies have seized upon my embarrassing situation to lie about me. Ah," she added bitterly, "how little they know of my own dire unhappiness!"

"No, no," urged the Minister, seemingly full of sympathy for her, knowing the truth as he did. "Bear up; put a brave countenance always towards the world. When Leitolf has gone your Imperial Highness will have less embarrassment, and people cannot then place any misconstructions upon your actions. You will not have the foolish young man following you wherever you go, as he now does. At noon to-morrow I will sign the decree for his immediate appointment to Rome, and he will receive but little leave of absence, I can assure you. He will be as much a prisoner in the Palazzo Chigi as is his Holiness in the Vatican," he added.

"Thank you," she answered simply, glancing gratefully into his grey, deeply-lined face; and as he bowed to her she left him and swept up the room to where the Emperor was engaged in conversation with Lord Powerstock, the British Ambassador.

The old Minister's face had changed the instant he left her. The mask of the courtier had fallen from the wily old countenance, and glancing after her, he muttered some words that were inaudible.

If she had but seen the evil smile that played about the old diplomatist's lips, she would have detected that his intention was to play her false, and she might then have saved herself.

But, alas! in her ignorance she went on light-heartedly, her long train sweeping behind her, believing in De Lindenau's well-feigned sympathy, and congratulating herself that the all-powerful personage behind the Emperor was still her friend.

The Minister saw that she was satisfied; then turning on his heel, he gave vent to a short, hard laugh of triumph.

VI

The House of Her Enemies

Two days later the Crown Princess Claire returned to Marburg.

In the twilight the express from Vienna came to a standstill in the big, echoing station at Treysa, the bright and wealthy capital, and descending from her private saloon, she walked over the red carpet laid for her, bowing pleasantly to the line of bareheaded officials waiting to receive her; then, mounting into her open landau, she drove up the fine, tree-lined Klosterstrasse to the royal palace.

De Trauttenberg was with her—the woman whom she now knew to be a spy. Around her, on every side, the crowd at her side shouted a glad welcome to "their Claire," as they called her, and just before the royal carriage could move off, two or three of the less timorous ones managed to seize her hand and kiss it, though the police unceremoniously pushed them away.

She smiled upon the enthusiastic crowd; but, alas! she was heavy of heart. How little, she thought, did those people who welcomed her dream of her unhappiness! She loved the people, and, looking upon them, sighed to think that she was not free like them.

Behind her clattered the hoofs of her cavalry escort, and beside the carriage were two agents of police on bicycles. Wherever she moved in her husband's kingdom she was always under escort, because of anarchist threats and socialistic rumours.

Marburg was one of the most beautiful and wealthiest of the kingdoms and duchies comprised in the German Empire. The fine capital of Treysa was one of the show cities of Germany, always bright, gay, and brilliant, with splendid streets, wide, tree-lined promenades, a great opera house, numerous theatres, gay restaurants, and an ever-increasing commerce. Frequented much by English and Americans, there were fine hotels, delightful public gardens, and pleasant suburbs. In no other part of the Empire were the nobility so wealthy or so exclusive, and certainly no Court in Europe was so difficult of access as that of Marburg.

The kingdom, which possessed an area of nearly seven thousand square miles and a population of over fifteen millions, was rich in manufactures and in minerals, besides being a smiling country in a high state of cultivation, with beautiful mountainous and wooded districts, where in the valleys were situated many delightful summer resorts.

Through its length and breadth, and far beyond the frontiers, the name of the Crown Princess Claire was synonymous of all that was good and affable, generous to the poor, and ever interested in the welfare of the people.

The big electric globes were already shining white in the streets as she drove back to the beautiful royal palace that was, alas! to her a prison. Her few days of liberty in Vienna were over, and when presently, after traversing many great thoroughfares full of life and movement, the carriage swung out into a broader tree-lined avenue, at the end of which were the great gates of the royal gardens, her brave heart fell within her.

Beyond was the house of her enemies, the house in which she was compelled to live friendless, yet surrounded by those who were daily whispering of her overthrow.

The great gates swung open to allow the cavalcade to pass, then closed again with a clang that, reaching her ear, caused her to shudder.

The Countess noticed it, and asked whether she felt cold. To this she gave a negative reply, and still remained silent, until the carriage, passing up through the beautiful park, at last drew up before the magnificent palace.

Descending, she allowed the gorgeously-dressed man in the royal livery to take her cloak from her shoulders; and then, without a word, hastened along the great marble hall, up the grand staircase and along corridor after corridor—those richly-carpeted corridors of her prison that she knew so well—to her own splendid suite of apartments.

The servants she met at every turn bowed to her, until she opened the door of a large, airy, well-furnished room, where a middle-aged woman, in cap and apron, sat reading by a shaded lamp.

In an instant, on recognising the newcomer, she sprang to her feet. But at the same moment the Princess rushed to the dainty little cot in the corner and sank down beside the sleeping curly-haired child—her child—the little Princess Ignatia.

So passionately did she kiss the sweet chubby little face of the sleeping child that she awoke, and recognising who it was, put out her little hands around her mother's neck.

"Ah, my little pet!" cried the Princess. "And how are you? It seems so long, so very long, since we parted." And her voice trembled, for tears stood in her eyes. The child was all she had in the world to love and cherish. She was her first thought always. The glare and glitter of the brilliant Court were all hateful to her, and she spent all the time she dared in the nursery with little Ignatia.

The English nurse, Allen, standing at her side, said, with that formality which was bound to be observed within those walls,—

"The Princess is in most excellent health, your Imperial Highness. I have carried out your Highness's instructions, and taken her each day for a walk in the park."

"That's right, Allen," responded the mother, also in English. "Where is the Crown Prince?"

"I have not seen him, your Highness, since you left. He has not been in to see Ignatia."

Claire sighed within herself, but made no outward sign. "Ah, I expect he has been away—to Berlin, perhaps. Is there any function to-night, have you heard?"

"A State ball, your Highness. At least they said so in the servants' hall."

The Princess glanced at the little silver timepiece, for she feared that her presence was imperative, even though she detested all such functions, where she knew she would meet that brilliant crowd of men and women, all of them her sworn enemies. What Steinbach had told her in confidence had lifted the scales from her eyes. There was a wide and cleverly-contrived conspiracy against her.

She took her fair-haired child in her arms, while Allen, with deft fingers, took off her hat and veil. Her maids were awaiting her in her own room, but she preferred to see Ignatia before it was too late to disturb the little one's sleep. With the pretty, blue-eyed little thing clinging around her neck, she paced the room with it, speaking, in German, as every fond mother will speak to the one she adores.

Though born to the purple, an Imperial Princess, Claire was very human after all. She regretted always that she was not as other women were, allowed to be her own mistress, and to see and to tend to her child's wants instead of being compelled so often to leave her in the hands of others, who, though excellent servants, were never as a mother.

She sent Allen upon a message to the other end of the palace in order to be alone with the child, and when the door closed she kissed its soft little face fondly again and again, and then burst into tears. Those Court sycophants were conspiring, to drive her away—perhaps even to part her from the only one for whom she entertained a spark of affection. Many of her enemies were women. Could any of them really know all that was meant by a mother's heart?

Prince Ferdinand-Leopold-Joseph-Marie, her husband, seldom, if ever, saw the child. For weeks he never mentioned its existence, and when he did it was generally with an oath, in regret that it was not a son and an heir to the throne.

In his paroxysms of anger he had cursed her and his little daughter, and declared openly that he hated the sight of them both. But she was ever patient. Seldom she responded to his taunts or his sarcasm, or resented his brutal treatment. She was philosophic enough to know that she had a heavy burden to bear, and for the sake of her position as future Queen of Marburg she must bear it bravely.

Allen was absent fully a quarter of an hour, during which time she spoke continually to little Ignatia, pacing up and down the room with her.

The child, seeing her mother's tears, stared at her with her big, wide-open eyes.

"Why does mother cry?" she asked in her childish voice, stroking her cheek.

"Because mother is not happy, darling," was the Princess's sad answer. "But," she added, brightening up, "you are happy, aren't you? Allen has bought you such a beautiful doll, she tells me."

"Yes, mother," the child answered. "And to-morrow, Allen promises, if I am very good, that we will go to buy a perambulator for my dolly to ride in. Won't that be nice?"

"Oh, it will! But you must be very, very good—and never cry, like mother, will you?"

"No," answered the little one. "I'll never cry, like mother does."

And the unhappy woman, hearing the child's lisping words, swallowed the great lump that arose in her throat. It was surely pathetic, that admission of a heart-broken mother to her child. It showed that even though an Imperial Princess, she was still a womanly woman, just as any good woman of the people.

A few moments later Allen returned with the reply to the message she had sent to the aged King.

"His Majesty says that, though regretting your Imperial Highness is tired after her journey, yet your presence with the Crown Prince at the ball is imperative." Claire sighed with a heavy heart, saying,—

"Very well, Allen. Then we will put Ignatia to bed, for I must go at once and dress," and she passed her hand across her hot, wearied brow.

Again and again she kissed the child, and then, having put her back into her cot, over which was the royal crown of Marburg in gold, she bade the infant Princess goodnight, and went along to eat a hasty dinner—for she was hungry after her eighteen-hour journey—and afterwards to put herself in the charge of her quick-handed maids, to prepare her for the brilliant function of that evening.

Two hours later, when she swept into the magnificent Throne Room, a brilliant, beautiful figure in her Court gown of cream, and wearing her wonderful tiara, her face was as stern and haughty as any of those members of the royal family present. With her long train rustling behind her, and with her orders and ribbons giving the necessary touch of colour to her bodice, she took up her position beside her husband, a fair-headed, round-faced, slight-moustached man, in a dark-blue uniform, and wearing a number of orders. His face was flat and expressionless.

Though they had not met for a week, no word of greeting escaped him. They stood side by side, as though they were strangers. He eyed her quickly, and his countenance turned slightly pale, as though displeased at her presence.

Yet the whole assembly, even though hating her, could not but admire her neat waist, her splendid figure, and matchless beauty. In the whole of the Courts of Europe there was no prettier woman than the Crown Princess Claire; her figure was perfect, and her gait always free—the gait of a princess. Even when dressed in her maid's dresses, as she had done on occasion, her walk betrayed her. Imperial blood can seldom be disguised.

The hundred women, those German princesses, duchesses, countesses, baronesses, to each of whom attached their own particular scandal—the brilliant little world that circled around the throne—looked at her standing there with her husband, her hands clasped before her, and envied her looks, figure, position—everything. She was a marked woman.

The proud, haughty expression upon her face as she regarded the assembly was only assumed. It was the mask she was compelled to wear at Court at the old King's command. Her nature was the reverse of haughty, yet the artificiality of palace life made it necessary for the Crown Princess to be as unapproachable as the Queen herself.

The guests were filing before the white-haired King, the hide-bound old martyr to etiquette, when the Crown Prince spoke to his wife in an undertone, saying roughly, with bitter sarcasm,—

"So you are back? Couldn't stay away from us longer, I suppose?"

"I remained in Vienna as long as I said I should," was the sweet-faced woman's calm reply.

"A pity you didn't stay there altogether," he muttered. "You are neither use nor ornament here."

"You have told me that several times before. Much as I regret it, Ferdinand, my place is here."

"Yes, at my side—to annoy me," he said, frowning.

"I regret to cause you any annoyance," she answered. "It is not intentional, I assure you."

A foul oath escaped him, and he turned from her to speak with Count Graesal, grand-marechal of the Court. Her face, however, betrayed nothing of his insult. At Court her countenance was always sphinx-like. Only in her private life, in that gorgeous suite of apartments on the opposite side of the palace, did she give way to her own bitter unhappiness and blank despair.

VII

A Shameful Truth

When at last the brilliant company moved on into the great ballroom she had an opportunity of walking among those men and women who, though they bent before her, cringing and servile, were, she knew, eagerly seeking her ruin. The Ministers, Stuhlmann, Hoepfner, and Meyer, all three creatures of the King, bowed low to her, but she knew they were her worst enemies. The Countess Hupertz, a stout, fair-haired, masculine-looking woman, also bent before her and smiled—yet this woman had invented the foulest lies concerning her, and spread them everywhere. In all that brilliant assembly she had scarcely one single person whom she could term a friend. And for a very simple reason. Friendliness with the Crown Princess meant disfavour with the King, and none of those place-seekers and sycophants could afford to risk that.

Yet, knowing that they were like a pack of hungry wolves about her, seeking to tear her reputation to shreds and cast her out of the kingdom, she walked among them, speaking with them, and smiling as though she were perfectly happy.

Presently, when the splendid orchestra struck up and dancing commenced, she came across Hinckeldeym, the wily old President of the Council of Ministers, who, on many occasions, had showed that, unlike the others, he regarded her as an ill-used wife. A short, rather podgy, dark-haired man, in Court dress, he bowed, welcomed her back to Treysa, and inquired after her family in Vienna.

Then, as she strolled with him to the farther end of the room, lazily fanning herself with her great ostrich-feather fan, she said in a low voice,—

"Hinckeldeym, as you know, I have few friends here. I wonder whether you are one?"

The flabby-faced old Minister pursed his lips, and glanced at her quickly, for he was a wily man. Then, after a moment's pause, he said,—

"I think that ever since your Imperial Highness came here as Crown Princess I have been your partisan. Indeed, I thought I had the honour of reckoning myself among your Highness's friends."

"Yes, yes," she exclaimed quickly. "But I have so many enemies here," and she glanced quickly around, "that it is really difficult for me to distinguish my friends."

"Enemies!" echoed the tactful Minister in surprise. "What causes your Highness to suspect such a thing?"

"I do not suspect—I know," was her firm answer as she stood aside with him. "I have learnt what these people are doing. Why? Tell me, Hinckeldeym—why is this struggling crowd plotting against me?"

He looked at her for a moment in silence. He was surprised that she knew the truth.

"Because, your Imperial Highness—because they fear you. They know too well what will probably occur when you are Queen."

"Yes," she said in a hard, determined voice. "When I am Queen I will sweep clear this Augean stable. There will be a change, depend upon it. This Court shall be an upright and honourable one, and not, as it now is, a replica of that of King Charles the Second of England. They hate me, Hinckeldeym—they hate me because I am a Hapsbourg; because I try and live uprightly and love my child, and when I am Queen I will show them that even a Court may be conducted with gaiety coupled with decorum."

The Minister—who, though unknown to her, was, perhaps, her worst enemy, mainly through fear of the future—listened to all she said in discreet silence. It was a pity, he thought, that the conspiracy had been betrayed to her, for although posing as her friend he would have been the first to exult over her downfall. It would place him in a position of safety.

He noted her threat. It only confirmed what the Court had anticipated—namely, that upon the death of the infirm old monarch, all would be changed, and that brilliant aristocratic circle would be sent forth into obscurity—and by an Austrian Archduchess, too!

The Princess Claire unfortunately believed the crafty Hinckeldeym to be her friend, therefore she told him all that she had learnt; of course, not betraying the informer.

"From to-day," she went on in a hard voice, "my attitude is changed. I will defend myself. Against those who have lied about me, and invented their vile scandals, I will stand as an enemy, and a bitter one. Hitherto I have been complacent and patient, suffering in silence, as so many defenceless women suffer. But for the sake of this kingdom, over which I shall one day be Queen, I will stand firm; and you, Hinckeldeym, must remain my friend."

"Your Imperial Highness has but to command me," replied the false old courtier, bowing low with the lie ever ready upon his lips. "I hope to continue as your friend."

"From the day I first set foot in Treysa, these people have libelled me and plotted my ruin," she went on. "I know it all. I can give the names of each of my enemies, and I am kept informed of all the scandalous tales whispered into my husband's ears. Depend upon it that those liars and scandalmongers will in due time reap their reward."

"I know very little of it," the Minister declared in a low voice, so that he could not be overheard. "Perhaps, however, your Highness has been indiscreet—has, I mean, allowed these people some loophole through which to cast their shafts?"

"They speak of Leitolf," she said quite frankly. "And they libel me, I know."

"I hear to-day that Leitolf is recalled to Vienna, and is being sent as attache to Rome," he remarked. "Perhaps it is as well in the present circumstances."

She looked him straight in the face as the amazing truth suddenly dawned upon her.

"Then you, too, Hinckeldeym, believe that what is said about us is true!" she exclaimed hoarsely, suspecting, for the first time, that the man with the heavy, flabby face might play her false.

And she had confessed to him, of all men, her intention of changing the whole Court entourage the instant her husband ascended the throne! She saw how terribly injudicious she had been.

But the cringing courtier exhibited his white palms, and with that clever exhibition of sympathy which had hitherto misled her, said,—

"Surely your Imperial Highness knows me sufficiently well to be aware that in addition to being a faithful servant to his Majesty the King, I am also a strong and staunch friend of yours. There may be a plot," he said; "a vile, dastardly plot to cast you out from Marburg. Yet if you are only firm and judicious, you must vanquish them, for they are all cowards—all of them." She believed him, little dreaming that the words she had spoken that night had sealed her fate. Heinrich Hinckeldeym was a far-seeing man, the friend of anybody who had future power in his hands—a man who was utterly unscrupulous, and who would betray his closest friend when necessity demanded. And yet, with his courtly manner, his fat yet serious face, his clever speech, and his marvellous tact, he had deceived more than one of the most eminent diplomatists in Europe, including even Bismarck himself.

He looked at her with his bright, ferret-like eyes, debating within himself when the end of her should be. He and his friends had already decided that the blow was soon to be struck, for every day's delay increased their peril. The old King's malady might terminate fatally at any moment, and once Queen, then to remove her would be impossible.

She had revealed to him openly her intention, therefore he was determined to use in secret her own words as a weapon against her, for he was utterly unscrupulous.

The intrigues of Court had a hundred different undercurrents, but it was part of his policy to keep well versed in them all. His finger was ever upon the pulse of that circle about the throne, while he was also one of the few men in Marburg who had the ear of the aristocratic old monarch with whom etiquette was as a religion.

"Your Imperial Highness is quite right in contemplating the Crown Prince's accession to the throne," he said ingeniously, in order to further humour her. "The doctors see the King daily, and the confidential reports made to us Ministers are the reverse of reassuring. In a few months at most the end must come—suddenly in all probability. Therefore the Crown Prince should prepare himself for the responsibilities of the throne, when your Highness will be able to repay your enemies for all their ill-nature."

"I shall know the way, never fear," she answered in a low, firm voice. "To-day their power is paramount, but to-morrow mine shall be. I shall then live only for my husband and my child. At present I am living for a third reason—to vindicate myself."

"Then your Imperial Highness contemplates changing everything?" he asked simply, but with the ingenuity of a great diplomatist. Every word of her reply he determined to use in order to secure her overthrow.

"I shall change all Ministers of State, Chamberlains, every one, from the Chancellor of the Orders down to the Grand Master of the Ceremonies. They shall all go, and first of all the *dames du palais*—those women who have so cleverly plotted against me, but of whose conspiracy I am now quite well aware." And she mentioned one or two names—names that had been revealed to her by the obscure functionary Steinbach.

The Minister saw that the situation was a grave, even desperate one. He was uncertain how much she knew concerning the plot, and was therefore undecided as to what line he should adopt. In order to speak in private they left the room, pacing the long, green-carpeted corridor that, enclosed in glass, ran the whole length of that wing of the palace. He tried by artful means to obtain from her further details, but she refused to satisfy him. She knew the truth, and that, she declared, was all sufficient.

Old Hinckeldeym was a power in Marburg. For eighteen years he had been the confidant of the King, and now fearing his favour on the wane, had wheedled himself into the good graces of the Crown Prince, who had given him to understand, by broad hints, that he would be only too pleased to rid himself of the Crown Princess. Therefore, if he could effect this, his future was assured. And what greater weapon could he have against her than her own declaration of her intention to sweep clear the Court of its present entourage?

He had assuredly played his cards wonderfully well. He was a past master in deception and double-dealing. The Princess, believing that he was at least her friend, had spoken frankly to him, never for one moment expecting a foul betrayal.

Yet, if the truth were told, it was that fat-faced, black-eyed man who had first started the wicked calumny which had coupled her name with Leitolf; he who had dropped scandalous hints to the Crown Prince of his beautiful wife's *penchant* for the good-looking *chef du cabinet*; he who had secretly stirred up the hostility against the daughter of the Austrian Archduke, and whose fertile brain had invented lies which were so ingeniously concocted that they possessed every semblance of truth.

A woman of Imperial birth may be a diplomatist, versed in all the intricacies of Court etiquette and Court usages, but she can never be at the same time a woman of the world. Her education is not that of ordinary beings; therefore, as in the case of the Princess Claire, though shrewd and tactful, she was no match for the crafty old Minister who for eighteen years had directed the destiny of that most important kingdom of the German Empire.

The yellow-haired Countess Hupertz, one of Hinckeldeym's puppets, watched the Princess and Minister walking in the corridor, and smiled grimly. While the orchestra played those dreamy waltzes, the tragedy of a throne was being enacted, and a woman—a sweet, good, lovable woman, upright and honest—was being condemned to her fate by those fierce, relentless enemies by which she was, alas! surrounded.

As she moved, her splendid diamonds flashed and glittered with a thousand fires, for no woman in all the Court could compare with her, either for beauty or for figure. And yet her husband, his mind poisoned by those place-hunters—a man whose birth was but as a mushroom as compared with that of Claire, who possessed an ancestry dating back a thousand years—blindly believed that which they told him to be the truth.

De Trauttenberg, in fear lest she might lose her own position, was in Hinckeldeym's pay, and what she revealed was always exaggerated—most of it, indeed, absolutely false.

The Court of Marburg had condemned the Crown Princess Claire, and from their judgment there was no appeal. She was alone, defenceless—doomed as the victim of the jealousies and fears of others.

Returning to the ballroom, she left the Minister's side; and, by reason of etiquette, returned to join that man in the dark-blue uniform who cursed her—the man who was her husband, and who ere long was to reign as sovereign.

Stories of his actions, many of them the reverse of creditable, had reached her ears, but she never gave credence to any of them. When people discussed him she refused to listen. He was her husband, the father of her little Ignatia, therefore she would hear nothing to his discredit.

Yes. Her disposition was quiet and sweet, and she was always loyal to him. He, however, entirely misjudged her.

An hour later, when she had gone to her room, her husband burst in angrily and ordered the two maids out, telling them that they would not be wanted further that night. Then, when the door was closed, he strode up to where she sat before the great mirror, lit by its waxen candles, for Henriette had been arranging her hair for the night.

"Well, woman!" he cried, standing before her, his brows knit, his eyes full of fire, "and what is your excuse to me this time?"

"Excuse?" she echoed, looking at him in surprise and very calmly. "For what, Ferdinand?"

"For your escapade in Vienna!" he said between his teeth. "The instant you had left, Leitolf received a telegram calling him to Wiesbaden, but instead of going there he followed you."

"Not with my knowledge, I assure you," she said quickly. "Why do you think so ill of me—why do you always suspect me?" she asked in a low, trembling voice of reproach.

"Why do I suspect you? You ask me that, woman, when you wrote to the man at his hotel, made an appointment, and actually visited him there? One of our agents watched you. Do you deny it?"

"No," she answered boldly. "I do not deny going to the Count's hotel. I had a reason for doing so."

He laughed in her face.

"Of course you had—you, who pretend to be such a good and faithful wife, and such a model mother," he sneered. "I suppose you would not have returned to Treysa so soon had he not have come back."

"You insult me!" she cried, rising from her chair, her Imperial blood asserting itself.

"Ah!" he laughed, taunting her. "You don't like to hear the truth, do you? It seems that the scandal concerning you has been discovered in Vienna, for De Lindenau has ordered the fellow to return to the diplomatic service, and is sending him away to Rome."

She was silent. She saw how every word and every action of hers was being misconstrued.

"Speak, woman!" he cried, advancing towards her. "Confess to me that you love the fellow."

"Why, Ferdinand, do you wish me to say what is untrue?" she asked in a low voice, quite calm again, notwithstanding his threatening attitude.

"Ah, you deny it! You lie to me, even when I know the truth—when all the Court discuss your affection for the fellow whom you yourself introduced among us. You have been with him in Paris. Deny that!"

"I deny nothing that is true," she answered. "I only deny your right to charge me with what is false."

"Oh yes," he cried. "You and your brat are a pretty pair. You believe we are all blind; but, on the contrary, everything is known. Confess!" he muttered between his teeth. "Confess that you love that man."

She was silent, standing before him, her beautiful eyes fixed upon the carpet.

He repeated his question in a harder tone than before, but still she uttered no word. She was determined not to repeat the denial she had already given, and she recognised that he had some ulterior motive in wringing from her a confession which was untrue.

"You refuse to speak!" he cried in a quick paroxysm of anger. "Then take that!" and he struck her with his fist a heavy blow full in the face, with such force, indeed, that she reeled, and fell backwards upon the floor.

"Another time perhaps you'll speak when I order you to," he said through his set teeth, as with his foot he kicked her savagely twice, the dull blows sounding through the big, gilt-ceilinged room.

Then with a hard laugh of scorn upon his evil lips the brute that was a Crown Prince, and heir to a European throne, turned and left with an oath upon his lips, as he slammed the door after him.

In the big, gorgeous room, where the silence was broken by the low ticking of the ormolu clock, poor, unhappy Claire lay there where she had fallen, motionless as one dead. Her beautiful face was white as death, yet horribly disfigured by the cowardly blow, while from the corner of her mouth there slowly trickled a thin red stream.

VIII

Is Mainly About the Count

Next morning, when she saw her reflection in the mirror, she sighed heavily, and hot tears sprang to her eyes.

Her beautiful countenance, bruised and swollen, was an ugly sight; her mouth was cut, and one of her even, pretty teeth had been broken by the cowardly blow.

Henriette, the faithful Frenchwoman, had crept back to her mistress's room an hour after the Crown Prince had gone, in order to see if her Highness wanted anything, when to her horror she discovered her lying insensible where she had been struck down.

The woman was discreet. She had often overheard the Prince's torrents of angry abuse, and in an instant grasped the situation. Instead of alarming the other servants, she quickly applied restoratives, bathed her mistress's face tenderly in eau de Cologne, washing away the blood from the mouth, and after half an hour succeeded in getting her comfortably to bed.

She said nothing to any one, but locked the door and spent the remainder of the night upon the sofa near her Princess.

While Claire was seated in her wrap, taking her chocolate at eight o'clock next morning, the Countess de Trauttenberg, her husband's spy, who probably knew all that had transpired, entered with the engagement-book.

She saw what a terrible sight the unhappy woman presented, yet affected not to notice it.

"Well, Trauttenberg?" asked the Princess in a soft, weary voice, hardly looking up at her, "what are our engagements to-day?"

The lady-in-waiting consulted the book, which upon its cover bore the royal crown above the cipher "C," and replied,—

"At eleven, the unveiling of the monument to Schilling the sculptor in the Albert-Platz; at one, luncheon with the Princess Alexandrine, to meet the Duchess of Brunswick-Lunebourg; at four, the drive; and to-night, 'Faust,' at the Opera."

Her Highness sighed. The people, the enthusiastic crowd who applauded her, little knew how wearying was that round of daily duties, how soul-killing to a woman with a broken heart. She was "their Claire," the woman who was to be their Queen, and they believed her to be happy!

"Cancel all my engagements," she said. "I shall not go out to-day. Tell the Court newsman that I am indisposed—a bad cold—anything."

"As your Imperial Highness commands," responded De Trauttenberg, bowing, and yet showing no sign that she observed the disfiguration of her poor face.

The woman's cold formality irritated her.

"You see the reason?" she asked meaningly, looking into her face.

"I note that your Imperial Highness has—has met with a slight accident," she said. "I trust it is not painful."

That reply aroused the fire of the Hapsbourg blood within her veins. The woman was her bitter enemy. She had lied about her, and had poisoned her husband's mind against her. And yet she was helpless. To dismiss her from her duties would only be a confirmation of what the woman had, no doubt, alleged.

It was upon the tip of her tongue to charge her openly as an enemy and a liar. It was that woman, no doubt, who had spied upon her when she had called upon Count Leitolf, and who on her return to Treysa had gone straight to the Crown Prince with a story that was full of vile and scandalous inventions.

"Oh, dear, no," she said, managing to control her anger by dint of great effort. "It is not at all painful, I assure you. Perhaps, Trauttenberg, you had better go at once and tell the newsman, so that my absence at the Schilling unveiling will be accounted for."

Thus dismissed, the woman, with her false smiles and pretended sympathy, went forth, and the journals through Germany that day reported, with regret, that the Crown Princess Claire of Marburg was confined to her room, having caught a severe chill on her journey from Vienna, and that she would probably remain indisposed for a week.

When her maids had dressed her she passed on into her gorgeous little blue-and-gold boudoir, her own sanctum, for in it were all the little nick-nacks, odds and ends which on her marriage she had brought from her own home at Wartenstein. Every object reminded her of those happy days of her youth, before she was called upon to assume the shams of royal place and power; before she entered that palace that was to her but a gilded prison.

The long windows of the room looked out upon the beautiful gardens and the great lake, with its playing fountains beyond, while the spring sunlight streaming in gave it an air of cheerfulness even though she was so despondent and heavy of heart. The apartment was gorgeously furnished, as indeed was the whole of the great palace. Upon the backs of the chairs, embroidered in gold upon the damask, was the royal crown and cipher, while the rich carpet was of pale pastel blue. For a long time she stood at the window, looking out across the park.

She saw her husband in his cavalry uniform riding out with an escort clattering behind him, and watched him sadly until he was out of sight. Then she turned and glanced around the cosy room which everywhere bore traces of her artistic taste and refinement. Upon the side-tables were many photographs, signed portraits of her friends, reigning sovereigns, and royal princes; upon the little centre-table a great old porcelain bowl of fresh tea-roses from the royal hot-houses. Her little buhl escritoire was littered with her private correspondence—most of it being in connection with charities in various parts of the kingdom in which she was interested, or was patroness.

Of money, or of the value of it, she knew scarcely anything. She was very wealthy, of course, for her family were one of the richest in Europe, while the royal house of Marburg was noted for its great wealth; yet she had never in her life held in her possession more than a few hundred marks at a time. Her bills all went to the official of the household whose duty it was to examine and pay them, and to charities she sent drafts through that same gold-spectacled official.

She often wondered what it was like to be poor, to work for a daily wage like the people she saw in the street and in the theatres. They seemed bright, contented, happy, and at least they had their freedom, and loved and married whom they chose.

Only the previous night, when she had entered her carriage at the station, a working-man had held his little child up to her for her to pat its head. She had done so, and then sighed to compare the difference between the royal father and that proud father of the people.

Little Ignatia, sweet and fresh, in her white frock and pale pink sash, was presently brought in by Allen to salute her mother, and the latter snatched up the child gladly in her arms and smothered its chubby face with fond kisses.

But the child noticed the disfigured countenance, and drew herself back to look at it.

"Mother is hurt," she said in English, in her childish speech. "Poor mother!"

"Yes, I fell down, darling," she answered. "Wasn't that very unfortunate? Are you sorry?"

"Very sorry poor mother is hurt," answered the child. "And, why!—one of poor mother's tooths have gone." The Princess saw that Allen was looking at her very hard, therefore she turned to her and explained,—

"It is nothing—nothing; a slight accident. I struck myself."

But the child stroked its mother's face tenderly with the soft, chubby little hand, saying,—

"Poor mother must be more careful another time or I shall scold her. And Allen will scold her too."

"Mother will promise to be more careful," she assured the little one, smiling. And then, seating herself, listened for half an hour to the child's amusing prattle, and her joyous anticipation of the purchase of a perambulator for her dolly.

With tender hands the Crown Princess retied the broad pink ribbon of the sash, and presently produced some chocolates from the silver bon-bon box which she kept there on purpose for her little one.

And Allen, the rather plain-faced Englishwoman, who was the best of nurses, stood by in silence, wondering how such an accident could have happened to her Imperial mistress, but, of course, unable to put any question to her.

"You may take Ignatia to buy the perambulator, Allen," said she at last in English. "Get a good one; the best you can. And after luncheon let me see it. I shall not go out to-day, so you can bring the Princess back to me at two o'clock."

"Very well, your Highness."

And both she and the child withdrew, the latter receiving the maternal kiss and caramels in each hand.

Again alone, Claire sat for a long time in deep thought. The recollection of those cruel, bitter accusations which her husband had uttered was still uppermost in her mind. What her humble friend Steinbach had told her was, alas! only too true. At Court it was said that she loved Leitolf, and the Crown Prince believed the scandalous libel.

"Ah, if Ferdinand only knew!" she murmured to herself. "If he could only read my heart! Then he would know the truth. Perhaps, instead of hating me as he does, he would be as forbearing as I try to be. He might even try to love me. Yet, alas!" she added bitterly, "such a thing cannot be. The Court of Marburg have decided that, in the interests of their own future, I must be ruined and disgraced. It is destiny, I suppose," she sighed; "my destiny!"

Then she was silent, staring straight before her at Bronzino's beautiful portrait of the Duchess Eleanor on the wall opposite. The sound of a bugle reached her, followed by the roll of the drums as the palace guard was changed. The love of truth, the conscientiousness which formed so distinct a feature in Claire's character, and mingled with its picturesque delicacy a certain firmness and dignity, she maintained consistently always.

The Trauttenberg returned, but she dismissed her for the day, and when she had left the boudoir the solitary woman murmured bitterly aloud,—

"A day's leave will perhaps allow you to plot and conspire further against the woman to whom you owe everything, and upon whose charity your family exist. Go and report to my husband my appearance this morning, and laugh with your friends at my unhappiness!" She rose and paced the room, her white hands clasped before her in desperation.

"Carl! Carl!" she cried in a hoarse, low voice. "I have only your indiscretion to thank for all this! And yet have I not been quite as indiscreet? Why, therefore, should I blame you? No," she said in a whisper, after a pause, "it is more my own fault than yours. I was blind, and you loved me. I foolishly permitted you to come here, because your presence recalled all the happiness of the past—of those sweet, idyllic days at Wartenstein, when we—when we loved each other, and our love was but a day-dream never to be realised. I wonder whether you still recollect those days, as I remember them—those long rambles over the mountains alone by the by-paths that I knew from my childhood days, and how we used to stand together hand in hand and watch the sinking sun flashing upon the windows of the castle far away. Nine years have gone since those days of our boy-and-girl love—nine long, dark years that have, I verily believe, transformed my very soul. One by one have all my ideals been broken and swept away, and now I can only sit and weep over the dead ashes of the past. The past—ah! what that means to me—life and love and freedom. And the future?" she sighed. "Alas! only black despair, ignominy, and shame." Again she halted at the window, and hot tears coursed down her pale cheeks. Those words, uttered almost without consciousness on her own part, contained the revelation of a life of love, and disclosed the secret burden of a heart bursting with its own unuttered grief. She was repulsed, she was forsaken, she was outraged where she had bestowed her young heart with all its hopes and wishes. She was entangled inextricably in a web of horrors which she could not even comprehend, yet the result seemed inevitable.

"These people condemn me! They utter their foul calumnies, and cast me from them unjustly," she cried, pushing her wealth of fair hair from her brow in her desperation. "Is there no justice for me? Can a woman not retain within her heart the fond remembrance of the holy passion of her youth—the only time she has loved—without it being condemned as a sin? without—"

The words died on her dry lips, for at that moment there was a tap at the door, and she gave permission to enter.

One of the royal servants in gorgeous livery bowed and advanced, presenting to her a small packet upon a silver salver, saying,—

"The person who brought this desired that it should be given into your Imperial Highness's hands at once."

She took the packet, and the man withdrew.

A single glance was sufficient to show her that the gummed address label had been penned by Count Carl Leitolf's own hand. Her heart beat quickly as she cut the string and opened the packet, to find within a book—a dull, uninteresting, philosophical treatise in German. There was no note or writing of any kind.

She ran through the leaves quickly, and then stood wondering. Why had he sent her that? The book was one that she certainly could never read to understand. Published some fifteen years before, it bore signs of not being new. She was much puzzled.

That Leitolf had a motive in sending it to her she had no doubt. But what could it denote? Again and again she searched in it to find some words or letters underlined—some communication meant for her eye alone.

Presently, utterly at a loss to understand, she took up the brown-paper wrapping, and looked again at the address. Yes, she was not mistaken. It was from Carl.

For a few moments she held the paper in her hand, when suddenly she detected that the gummed address label had only been stuck on lightly by being wetted around the edge, and a thought occurred to her to take it off and keep it, together with the book.

Taking up the large ivory paper-knife, she quickly slipped it beneath the label and removed it, when to her astonished eyes there were presented some written words penned across the centre, where the gum had apparently been previously removed.

The words, for her eye alone, were in Carl's handwriting, lightly written, so that they should not show through the label.

The message—the last message from the man who loved her so fondly, and whose heart bled for her in her gilded unhappiness—read:—

"Adieu, my Princess. I leave at noon to-day, because you have willed it so. I have heard of what occurred last night. It is common knowledge in the palace. Be brave, dear heart. May God now be your comforter. Recollect, though we shall never again meet, that I shall think ever and eternally of you, my Princess, the sweet-faced woman who was once my own, but who is now, alas! lost to me for ever. Adieu, adieu. I kiss your hand, dear heart, adieu!"

It was his last message. His gentle yet manly resignation, the deep pathos of his farewell, told her how full of agony was his own heart. How bitter for her, too, that parting, for now she would stand alone and unprotected, without a soul in whom to confide, or of whom to seek advice.

As she reread those faintly-traced words slowly and aloud the light died from her face.

"I kiss your hand, dear heart, adieu!" she murmured, and then, her heart overburdened by grief, she burst into a flood of emotion.

IX

The Three Strangers

By noon all Treysa knew, through the papers, of the indisposition of the Crown Princess; and during the afternoon many smart carriages called at the gates of the royal palace to inquire after her Imperial Highness's health.

The pompous, scarlet-liveried porters told every one that the Princess had, unfortunately, caught a severe chill on her journey from Vienna, and her medical advisers, although they did not consider it serious, thought, as a precaution, it was best that for a few days she should remain confined to her room.

Meanwhile the Princess, in her silent, stunning, overwhelming sorrow, was wondering how she might call Steinbach. She was unapproachable to any but the Court set, therefore to call a commoner would be an unheard-of breach of etiquette. And yet she desired to see him and obtain his advice. In all that gay, scheming circle about her he was the only person whom she could trust. He was devoted to her service because of the little charitable actions she had rendered him. She knew that he would if necessary lay down his very life in order to serve her, for he was one of the very few who did not misjudge her.

The long day dragged by. She wrote many letters—mostly to her family and friends in Vienna. Then taking a sheet of the royal notepaper from the rack, she again settled herself, after pacing the boudoir in thought for some time, and penned a long letter, which when finished she reread and carefully corrected, afterwards addressing it in German to "His Imperial Majesty the Emperor, Vienna," and sealing it with her own private seal.

"He misjudges me," she said to herself very gravely; "therefore it is only right that I should defend myself."

Then she rang, and in answer to her summons one of the royal footmen appeared.

"I want a special messenger to carry a letter for me to Vienna. Go at once to the Ministry of Foreign Affairs and ask the Under-Secretary, Fischer, whether Steinbach may be placed at my service," she commanded.

"Yes, your Imperial Highness," answered the clean-shaven, grave-faced man, who bowed and then withdrew.

Allen soon afterwards brought in little Ignatia to show the doll's perambulator, with which the child was delighted, wheeling it up and down the boudoir. With the little one her mother played for upwards of an hour. The bright little chatterbox caused her to forget the tragedy of her own young life, and Allen's kindly English ways were to her so much more sympathetic than the stiff formalities of her treacherous lady-in-waiting.

The little one in her pretty speeches told her mother of her adventures in the toy-shops of Treysa, where she was, of course, recognised, and where the shopkeepers often presented her little Royal Highness with dolls and games. In the capital the tiny Ignatia was a very important and popular personage everywhere; certainly more popular with the people than the parrot-faced, hard-hearted old King himself.

Presently, while the Crown Princess was carrying her little one pick-a-pack up and down the room, the child crowing with delight at its mother's romping and caresses, there came a loud summons at the door, the rap that announced a visitor, and the same grave-faced manservant opened the long white doors, saying,—

"Your Imperial Highness. Will it please you to receive Herr Steinbach of the Department of Foreign Affairs?"

"Bring Herr Steinbach here," she commanded, and then, kissing the child quickly, dismissed both her and her nurse.

A few moments later the clean-shaven, dark-haired man in sombre black was ushered in, and bending, kissed the Crown Princess's hand with reverent formality.

As soon as they were alone she turned to him, and, taking up the letter, said,—

"I wish you, Steinbach, to travel to Vienna by the express to-night, obtain audience of the Emperor, and hand this to him. Into no other hand must you deliver it, remember. In order to obtain your audience you may say that I have sent you; otherwise you will probably be refused. If there is a reply, you will bring it; if not—well, it does not matter."

The quick-eyed man, bowing again, took the letter, glanced at the superscription, and placing it in the inner pocket of his coat, said,—

"I will carry out your Imperial Highness's directions."

The Princess crossed to the door and opened it in order to satisfy herself that there were no eavesdroppers outside. Then returning to where the man stood, she said in a low voice,—

"I see that you are puzzled by the injury to my face when the papers are saying I have a chill. I met with a slight accident last night." Then in the next breath she asked, "What is the latest phase of this conspiracy against me, Steinbach? Tell me. You need conceal nothing for fear of hurting my feelings."

The man hesitated a moment; then he replied,—

"Well, your Imperial Highness, a great deal of chatter has been circulated regarding Count Leitolf. They now say that, having grown tired of him, you have contrived to have him transferred to Rome."

"Well?"

"They also say that you visited Leitolf while you were in Vienna. And I regret," he added, "that your enemies are now spreading evil reports of you among the people. Certain journalists are being bribed to print articles which contain hints against your Highness's honour."

"This is outrageous!" she cried. "Having ruined me in the eyes of my husband and the King, they now seek to turn the people against me! It is infamous!"

"Exactly. That really seems their intention. They know that your Highness is the most popular person in the whole Kingdom, and they intend that your popularity shall wane."

"And I am helpless, Steinbach, utterly helpless," she cried in desperation. "I have no friend except yourself."

The man sighed, for he was full of sympathy for the beautiful but unjustly-treated woman, whose brave heart he knew was broken. He was aware of the love-story of long ago between the Count and herself, but he knew her too well to believe any of those scandalous tales concerning her. He knew well how, from the very first days of her married life, she had been compelled to endure sneers, insult, and libellous report. The King and Queen themselves had been so harsh and unbending that she had always held aloof from them. Her every action, either in private or in public, they criticised adversely. She even wore her tiaras, her jewels, and her decorations in a manner with which they found fault; and whatever dress she assumed at the various functions, the sharp-tongued old Queen, merely in order to annoy her, would declare that she looked absolutely hideous. And all this to a bride of twenty-one, and one of the most beautiful girls in Europe!

All, from the King himself down to the veriest palace lackey, had apparently united to crush her, to break her spirit, and drive her to despair.

"I hope, as I declared when we last met, Princess, that I shall ever remain your friend," said the humble employe of the Foreign Ministry. "I only wish that I could serve you to some good purpose—I mean, to do something that might increase your happiness. Forgive me, your Highness, for saying so."

"The only way to give me happiness, Steinbach, is to give me freedom," she said sadly, as though speaking to herself. "Freedom—ah, how I long for it! How I long to escape from this accursed palace, and live as the people live! I tell you," she added in a low, half-whisper, her pale, disfigured face assuming a deadly earnest look—"I tell you that sometimes I feel—well, I feel that I can't endure it much longer, and that I'm slowly being driven insane."

He started at her words, and looked her straight in the face. Should he tell her the truth of an amazing discovery he had made only on the previous day; or was it really kinder to her to hold his tongue?

His very heart bled for her. To her influence he owed all—everything.

No; he could not tell her of that new and dastardly plot against her—at least not yet. Surely it was not yet matured! When he returned from Vienna would be quite time enough to warn her against her increased peril. Now that Leitolf had left her, life might perhaps be a trifle more happy; therefore why should he, of all men, arouse her suspicions and cause her increased anxiety?

Steinbach was a cautious man; his chief fault perhaps was his over-cautiousness. In this affair he might well have spoken frankly; yet his desire always was to avoid hurting the feelings of the woman with whom he so deeply sympathised—the Imperial Princess, to whom he acted as humble, devoted, and secret friend.

"You must not allow such fears to take possession of you," he urged. "Do not heed what is said regarding you. Remember only that your own conscience is clear, even though your life is, alas, a martyrdom! Let them see that you are heedless and defiant, and ere long they will grow tired of their efforts, and you will assume a power at Court far greater than hitherto."

"Ah no—never!" she sighed. "They are all against me—all. If they do not crush me by force, they will do so by subterfuge," declared the unhappy woman. "But," she added quickly with an effort, "do not let us speak of it further. I can only thank you for telling me the truth. Go to-night to Vienna, and if there is a reply, bring it to me immediately. And stay—what can I do to give you recompense? You have no decoration! I will write at once a recommendation for you for the cross of St. Michael, and whenever you wear it you will, I hope, remember the grateful woman who conferred it upon you."

"I thank your Highness most truly," he said. "I have coveted the high honour for many years, and I can in turn only reassure you that any mission you may entrust to me will always be carried out in secret and faithfully."

"Then adieu, Steinbach," she said, dismissing him. "*Bon voyage*, and a quick return from Vienna—my own dear Vienna, where once I was so very happy."

The man in black bent low and again kissed the back of the soft white hand, then, backing out of the door, bowed again and withdrew.

When Henriette came that evening to change her dress the woman said in French,—

"I ask your Imperial Highness's pardon, but the Prince, who returned half an hour ago, commanded me to say that he would dine with you this evening, and that there would be three men guests."

"Guests!" she cried. "But the Prince must be mad! How can I receive guests in this state, Henriette?"

"I explained that your Imperial Highness was not in a fit state to dine in public," said the maid quietly; "but the Prince replied that he commanded it."

What fresh insult had her husband in store for her? Did he wish to exhibit her poor bruised face publicly before her friends? It was monstrous!

Yet he had commanded; therefore she allowed Henriette to brush her fair hair and dress her in a black net dinner-gown, one that she often wore when dining in the privacy of her own apartments. Henriette cleverly contrived, by the aid of powder and a few touches of make-up, to half conceal her mistress's disfiguration; therefore at eight o'clock the Princess Claire entered the fine white-and-gold reception-room, lit by its hundreds of small electric lamps, and there found her husband in uniform, speaking earnestly with three elderly and rather distinguished-looking men in plain evening dress.

Turning, he smiled at her as though nothing had occurred between them, and then introduced his friends by name; but of their names she took no notice. They were strangers, and to her quite uninteresting.

Yet she bowed, smiled, and put on that air of graciousness that, on account of her Court training, she could now assume at will.

The men were from somewhere in North Germany, she detected by their speech, and at the dinner-table the conversation was mostly upon the advance of science; therefore she concluded, from their spectacled appearance and the technical terms they used, that they were scientists from Berlin to whom her husband wished to be kind, and had invited them quite without formality.

Their conversation did not interest her in the least; therefore she remained almost silent throughout the meal, except now and then to address a remark to one or other of her guests. She noticed that once or twice they exchanged strange glances. What could it mean?

At last she rose, and after they had bowed her out they reseated themselves, and all four began conversing in a lower tone in English, lest any servant should enter unexpectedly.

Then ten minutes later, at a signal from the Prince, they rose and passed into the *fumoir*, a pretty room panelled with cedar-wood, and with great palms and plashing fountains, where coffee was served and cigars were lit.

There the conversation in an undertone in English was again resumed, the Prince being apparently very interested in something which his guests were explaining. Though the door was closed and they believed themselves in perfect privacy, there was a listener standing in the adjoining room, where the cedar panelling only acted as a partition.

It was the Princess Claire. Her curiosity had been aroused as to who the strangers really were.

She could hear them speaking in English at first with difficulty, but presently her husband spoke. The words he uttered were clear. In an instant they revealed to her an awful, unexpected truth.

She held her breath, her left hand upon her bare chest above her corsage, her mouth open, her white face drawn and haggard.

Scarce believing her own ears, she again listened. Could it really be true?

Her husband again spoke. Ah yes! of the words he uttered there could be not the slightest doubt. She was doomed.

With uneven steps she staggered from her hiding-place along the corridor to her own room, and on opening the door she fell forward senseless upon the carpet.

X

The Peril of the Princess

That night, six hours later, when the great palace was silent save for the tramping of the sentries, the Princess sat in the big chair at her window, looking out upon the park, white beneath the bright moonbeams.

The room was in darkness, save for the tiny silver lamp burning before the picture of the Madonna. The Trauttenberg had found her lying insensible, and with Henriette's aid had restored her to consciousness and put her to bed. Then the Countess had gone along to the Crown Prince and told him that his wife had been seized with a fainting fit, and was indisposed.

And the three guests, when he told them, exchanged significant glances, and were silent.

In the darkness, with the moonlight falling across the room, the Princess, in her white silk dressing-gown, sat staring straight before her out upon the fairy-like scene presented below. No word escaped her pale lips, yet she shuddered, and drew her laces about her as though she were chilled.

She was recalling those hard words of her husband's which she had overheard—the words that revealed to her the ghastly truth. If ever she had suffered during her married life, she suffered at that moment. It was cruel, unjust, dastardly. Was there no love or justice for her?

The truth was a ghastly one. Those three strangers whom her husband had introduced to her table as guests were doctors, two from Berlin and the third from Cologne—specialists in mental disease. They had come there for the purpose of adding their testimony and certificates to that of Veltman, the crafty, thin-nosed Court physician, to declare that she was insane!

What fees were promised those men, or how that plot had been matured, she could only imagine. Yet the grim fact remained that her enemies, with the old King and her husband at their head, intended to confine her in an asylum.

She had heard her husband himself suggest that on the morrow they should meet Veltman, a white-bearded, bald-headed old charlatan whom she detested, and add their testimony to his that she was not responsible for her actions. Could anything be more cold-blooded, more absolutely outrageous? Those words of her husband showed her plainly that in his heart there now remained not one single spark either of affection or of sentiment. He was anxious, at all hazards and at whatever cost, by fair means or foul, to rid himself of her.

Her enemies were now playing their trump card. They had no doubt bribed those three men to certify what was a direct untruth. A royal sovereign can, alas I command the services of any one; for everybody, more or less, likes to render to royalty a service in the hope of decoration or of substantial reward. Most men are at heart place-seekers. Men who are most honest and upright in their daily lives will not hesitate to perjure themselves, or "stretch a point" as they would doubtless put it, where royalty is concerned.

Gazing out into the brilliant moonlight mirrored upon the smooth surface of the lake, she calmly reviewed the situation.

She was in grave peril—so grave, indeed, that she was now utterly bewildered as to what her next step should be. Once certified as a lunatic and shut up in an asylum somewhere away in the heart of the country, all hope of the future would be cut off. She would be entirely at the mercy of those who so persistently and unscrupulously sought her end. Having failed in their other plot against, her, they intended to consign her to a living tomb.

Yet by good fortune had her curiosity been aroused, and she had overheard sufficient to reveal to her the truth. Her face was now hard, her teeth firmly set. Whatever affection she had borne her husband was crushed within her now that she realised how ingeniously he was conspiring against her, and to what length he was actually prepared to go in order to rid himself of her.

She thought of Ignatia, poor, innocent little Ignatia, the child whom its father had cursed from the very hour of its birth, the royal Princess who one day might be crowned a reigning sovereign. What would become of her? Would her own Imperial family stand by and see their daughter incarcerated in a madhouse when she was as sane as they themselves—more sane, perhaps?

She sat bewildered.

With the Emperor against her, however, she had but little to hope for in that quarter. His Majesty actually believed the scandal that had been circulated concerning Leitolf, and had himself declared to her face that she must be mad.

Was it possible that those hot words of the Emperor's had been seized upon by her husband to obtain a declaration that she was really insane?

Insane? She laughed bitterly to herself at such a thought.

"Ah!" she sighed sadly, speaking hoarsely to herself. "What I have suffered and endured here in this awful place are surely sufficient to send any woman mad. Yet God has been very good to me, and has allowed me still to preserve all my faculties intact. Why don't they have some assassin to kill me?" she added desperately. "It would surely be more humane than what they now intend."

Steinbach, her faithful but secret friend, was on his way to Vienna. She wondered whether, after reading the letter, the Emperor would relent towards her? Surely the whole world could not unite as her enemy. There must be human pity and sympathy in the hearts of some, as there was in the heart of the humble Steinbach.

Not one of the thirty millions over whom she would shortly rule was so unhappy as she that night. Beyond the park shone the myriad lights of the splendid capital, and she wondered whether any one living away there so very far from the world ever guessed how lonely and wretched was her life amid all that gorgeous pomp and regal splendour.

Those three grave, spectacled men who had dined at her table and talked their scientific jargon intended to denounce her. They had been quick to recognise that a future king is a friend not to be despised, while the bankers' drafts that certain persons had promised them in exchange for their signatures as experts would no doubt be very acceptable.

Calmly she reviewed the situation, and saw that, so clearly had her enemies estranged her from every one, she was without one single friend.

For her child's sake it was imperative for her to save herself. And she could only save herself by flight. But whither? The only course open to her was to leave secretly, taking little Ignatia with her, return to her father, and lay before him the dastardly plot now in progress.

Each hour she remained at the palace increased her peril. Once pronounced insane by those three specialists there would be no hope for her. Her enemies would take good care that she was consigned to an asylum, and that her actions were misconstrued into those of a person insane.

Her heart beat quickly as she thought out the best means of secret escape.

To leave that night was quite impossible. Allen was sleeping with Ignatia; and besides, the guards at the palace gate, on seeing her make her exit at that hour, would chatter among themselves, in addition to which there were no express trains to Vienna in the night. The best train was at seven o'clock in the evening, for upon it was a *wagon-lit* and dining-car that went through to the Austrian capital, *via* Eger.

About six o'clock in the evening would be the best time to secure the child, for Allen and Henriette would then both be at dinner, and little Ignatia would be in charge of the under-nurse, whom she could easily send away upon some pretext. Besides, at that hour she could secure some of Henriette's clothes, and with her veil down might pass the sentries, who would probably take her for the French maid herself.

She calculated that her absence would not be noted by her servants till nearly eight; for there was a Court ball on the morrow, and on nights of the balls she always dressed later.

And so, determined to leave the great palace which to her was a prison, she carefully thought over all the details of her flight. On the morrow she would send to the royal treasurer for a sum of money, ostensibly to make a donation to one of her charities.

Presently rising, she closed the shutters, and switching on the electric light, opened the safe in the wall where her jewels were kept—mostly royal heirlooms that were worth nearly a million sterling.

Case after case she drew out and opened. Her two magnificent tiaras, her emerald and diamond necklet, the great emerald pendant, once the property of Catherine di Medici, six wonderful collars of perfect pearls and some other miscellaneous jewels, all of them magnificent, she replaced in the safe, as they were heirlooms of the Kingdom. Those royal tiaras as Crown Princess she placed in their cases and put them away with a sigh, for she knew she was renouncing her crown for ever. Her own jewels, quite equal in magnificence, she took from their cases and placed together upon the bed. There was her magnificent long rope of pearls, that when worn twice twisted around her neck hung to below the knees, and was declared to be one of the finest in the world; her two diamond collars, her wonderful diamond bodice ornaments, her many pairs of earrings, antique brooches, and other jewels—she took them all from their cases until they lay together, a brilliant, scintillating heap, the magnificent gems flashing with a thousand fires.

At last she drew forth a leather case about six inches square, and opening it, gazed upon it in hesitancy. Within was a large true-lover's knot in splendid diamonds, and attached to it was the black ribbon and the jewelled cross—her decoration as Dame de la Croix Etoilee of Austria, the order bestowed upon the Imperial Archduchesses.

She looked at it wistfully. Sight of it brought to her mind the fact that in renouncing her position she must also renounce that mark of her Imperial birth. Yet she was determined, and with trembling fingers detached the ribbon and cross from the diamond ornament, threw the latter on to the heap upon the bed, and replaced the former with the jewels she intended to leave behind.

The beautiful cross had been bestowed upon her by her uncle the Emperor upon her marriage, and would now be sent back to him.

She took two large silk handkerchiefs from a drawer, and made two bundles of the precious gems. Then she hid them away until the morrow, and reclosing the safe, locked it; and taking the key off the bunch, placed it in the drawer of her little escritoire.

Thus she had taken the first step towards her emancipation.

Her eye caught the Madonna, with its silver lamp, and she halted before it, her head bowed, her lips moving in silent prayer as she sought help, protection, and guidance in the act of renunciation she was about to commit.

Then, after ten minutes or so, she again moved slowly across the room, opening the great inlaid wardrobe where hung a few of her many dresses. She looked upon them in silence. All must be left behind, she decided. She could only take what she could carry in her hand. She would leave her personal belongings to be divided up by that crowd of human wolves who hungered to destroy her. The Trauttenberg might have them as her perquisites—in payment for her treachery.

By that hour to-morrow she would have left Treysa for ever. She would begin a new life—a life of simplicity and of freedom, with her darling child.

Presently she slept again, but it was a restless, fevered sleep. Constantly she wondered whether it would be possible for her to pass those palace guards with little Ignatia. If they recognised the child they might stop her, for only Allen herself was permitted to take her outside the palace.

Yet she must risk it; her only means of escape was that upon which she had decided.

Next day passed very slowly. The hours dragged by as she tried to occupy herself in her boudoir, first with playing with the child, and afterwards attending to her correspondence. She wrote no letter of farewell, as she deemed it wiser to take her leave without a word. Yet even in those last hours of her dignity as Crown Princess her thoughts were with the many charitable institutions of which she was patroness, and of how best she could benefit them by writing orders to the royal treasurer to give them handsome donations in her name.

She saw nothing of her husband. For aught she knew, those three grave-faced doctors might have already consulted with Veltman; they might have already declared her insane.

The afternoon passed, and alone she took her tea in English fashion, little Ignatia being brought to her for half an hour, as was the rule when she was without visitors. She had already been to Henriette's room in secret, and had secured a black-stuff dress and packet, a long black travelling-coat and a felt canotte, all of which she had taken to her own room and hidden in her wardrobe.

When Allen took the child's hand in order to lead her out, her mother glanced anxiously at the clock, and saw that it was half-past five.

"You can leave Ignatia here while you go to dinner," she said in English; "she will be company for me. Tell the servants that I am not to be disturbed, even by the Countess de Trauttenberg."

"Very well, your Highness," was the Englishwoman's answer, as bowing she left the room.

For another quarter of an hour she laughed and played with the child, then said,—

"Come, darling, let us go along to my room." And taking her tiny hand, led her gently along the corridor to her own chamber. Once within she locked the door, and quickly throwing off her own things, assumed those of the maid which she took from the wardrobe. Then upon Ignatia she put a cheap dark coat of grey material and a dark-blue woollen cap which at once concealed the child's golden curls. This concluded, she assumed a thick black lace veil, which well concealed her features, and around her throat she twisted a silken scarf. The collar of her coat, turned up, hid the colour of her hair, and her appearance was in a few moments well transformed. Indeed, she presented the exact prototype of her maid Henriette.

The jewels were in a cheap leather hand-bag, also the maid's property. This she placed in her dressing-bag, and with it in her hand she took up little Ignatia, saying,—

"Hush, darling! don't speak a word. You'll promise mother, won't you?"

The child, surprised at all this preparation, gave her promise, but still remained inquisitive.

Then the Crown Princess Claire gave a final glance around the room, the scene of so much of her bitter domestic unhappiness. Sighing heavily, she crossed herself before the Madonna, uttered a few low words in prayer, and unlocking the door stole out into the long, empty corridor.

Those were exciting moments—the most exciting in all her life.

With her heart beating quickly she sped onward to the head of the great marble gilt staircase. Along one of the side corridors a royal valet was approaching, and the man nodded to her familiarly, believing her to be Henriette.

At the head of the staircase she looked down, but saw nobody. It was the hour when all the servants were at their evening meal. Therefore, descending quickly, she passed through the great winter garden, a beautiful place where, among the palms and flowers, were cunningly placed tiny electric lamps. Across a large courtyard she went—as it was a short cut from that wing of the palace in which her apartments were situated—and at last she reached the main entrance, where stood the head concierge in his cocked hat and scarlet livery, and where idled an agent of police in plain clothes, reading the evening paper.

At her approach they both glanced at her.

She held her breath. What if they stopped her on account of the child?

But summoning all her courage she went forward, compelled to pass them quite closely.

Then as she advanced she nodded familiarly to the gold-laced janitor, who to her relief wished her good-evening, and she passed out into the park.

She had successfully passed through one peril, but there was yet a second—those carefully-guarded gilded gates which gave entrance to the royal demesne. Day and night they were watched by palace servants and the agents of police entrusted with his Majesty's personal safety.

She sped on down the broad gravelled drive, scarce daring to breathe, and on arrival at the gatehouse passed in it, compelled to make her exit through the small iron turnstile where sat two men, the faithful white-bearded old gatekeeper, who had been fifty years in the royal service, and a dark-faced brigadier of police. Recognition would mean her incarceration in an asylum as insane.

Both men looked up as she entered. It was the supreme moment of her peril. She saw that the detective was puzzled by her veil. But she boldly passed by them, saying in French, in a voice in imitation of Henriette's,—

"*Bon soir, messieurs*!"

The old gatekeeper, in his low, gruff German, wished her good-night unsuspiciously, drew the lever which released the turnstile, and next moment the Crown Princess Claire stepped out into the world beyond—a free woman.

XI

Doom or Destiny

With quickened footsteps she clasped the child to her, and hurrying on in the falling gloom, skirted the long, high walls of the royal park, where at equal distances stood the sentries.

More than one, believing her to be Mademoiselle, saluted her.

She was free, it is true; but she had yet to face many perils, the greatest of them all being that of recognition by the police at the station, or by any of the people, to whom her countenance was so well known.

Presently she gained the broad Klosterstrasse, where the big electric lamps were already shining; and finding a fiacre at the stand, entered it and drove to a small outfitter's shop, where she purchased two travelling-rugs and a shawl for little Ignatia. Thence she went to a pastrycook's and bought some cakes, and then drove up the wide Wolbeckerstrasse to the central railway station.

The streets were alive with life, for most of the shops were closed, the main thoroughfares were illuminated, and all Treysa was out at the cafes or restaurants, or promenading the streets, for the day was a national festival. The national colours were displayed everywhere, and the band of the 116th Regiment was playing a selection from "La Boheme" as she crossed the great Domplatz.

Hers was indeed a strange position.

Unknown and unrecognised, she drove in the open cab, with the tiny, wondering Princess at her side, through the great crowds of holiday-makers—those people who had they known of her unhappiness would in all probability have risen in a body and revolted.

She remembered that she had been "their Claire," yet after that night she would be theirs no longer. It was a sad and silent leave-taking. She had renounced her crown and imperial privileges for ever.

Many men and women stared at her as she passed under the bright electric street lamps, and once or twice she half feared that they might have penetrated her disguise. Yet no cheer was raised; none rushed forward to kiss her hand.

She gave the cabman orders to drive up and down several of the principal thoroughfares, for there was still plenty of time for the train;

and, reluctant to take leave of the people of Treysa whom she loved so well, and who were her only friends, she gazed upon them from behind her veil and sighed.

At the busy, echoing station she arrived ten minutes before the express was due, and took her tickets; but when she went to the *wagon-lit* office, the official, not recognising her, sharply replied that the places had all been taken by an American tourist party. Therefore she was compelled to enter an ordinary first-class compartment. The train was crowded, and all the corner seats were taken. Fearing to call a porter to her assistance lest she should be recognised—when the royal saloon would at once be attached to the train for her—she was compelled to elbow her way through the crowd and take an uncomfortable seat in the centre of a compartment, where all through the night she tried to sleep, but in vain.

Little Ignatia soon closed her eyes and was asleep, but Claire, full of regrets at being compelled to renounce husband, crown, everything, as she had done, and in wonder of what the future had in store for her, sat silent, nursing her child through the long night hours. Her fellow-travellers, two fat Germans of Jewish cast, and three women, slept heavily, the men snoring.

The grey dawn showed at last over the low green hills. Had her absence been discovered? Most certainly it had, but they had now passed the confines of the kingdom, and she was certain that the people at the palace would not telegraph news of her disappearance for fear of creating undue scandal.

At last she had frustrated their dastardly plot to incarcerate her in an asylum. She sat there, a figure of sweet loveliness combined with exceeding delicacy and even fragility—one of the most refined elegance and the most exquisite modesty.

At a small wayside station where they stopped about seven o'clock she bought a glass of coffee, and then they continued until the Austrian frontier at Voitersreuth was reached; and at Eger, a few miles farther on, she was compelled to descend and change carriages, for only the *wagon-lit* went through to the capital.

It was then eleven o'clock in the morning, and feeling hungry, she took little Ignatia into the buffet and had some luncheon, the child delighted at the novel experience of travelling.

"We are going to see grandfather," her mother told her. "You went to see him when you were such a wee, wee thing, so you don't remember him."

"No," declared the child with wide-open, wondering eyes; "I don't remember. Will Allen be there?"

"No, darling, I don't think so," was the evasive reply to a question which struck deep into the heart of the woman fleeing from her persecutors.

While Ignatia had her milk, her mother ate her cutlet at the long table among the other hasty travellers, gobbling up their meal and shouting orders to waiters with their mouths full.

Hitherto, when she passed there in the royal saloon, the railway officials had come forward, cap in hand, to salute her as an Imperial Archduchess of Austria; but now, unknown and unrecognised, she passed as an ordinary traveller. Presently, when the Vienna express drew up to the platform, she fortunately found an empty first-class compartment, and continued her journey alone, taking off her hat and settling herself for the remaining nine hours between there and the capital. Little Ignatia was still very sleepy, therefore she made a cushion for her with her cape and laid her full length, while she herself sat in a corner watching the picturesque landscape, and thinking—thinking deeply over all the grim tragedy of the past.

After travelling for three hours, the train stopped at a small station called Protovin, the junction of the line from Prague, whence a train had arrived in connection with the express. Here there seemed quite a number of people waiting upon the platform.

She was looking out carelessly upon them when from among the crowd a man's eyes met hers. He stared open-mouthed, turned pale, and next instant was at the door. She drew back, but, alas! it was too late. She was without hat or veil, and he had recognised her.

She gave vent to a low cry, half of surprise, half of despair.

Next second the door opened, and the man stood before her, hat in hand.

"Princess!" he gasped in a low, excited voice. "What does this mean? You—alone—going to Vienna?"

"Carl!" she cried, "why are *you* here? Where have you come from?"

"I have been to my estate up at Rakonitz, before going to Rome," was his answer. "Is it Destiny that again brings us together like this?"

And entering the carriage, he bent and kissed her hand.

Was it Destiny, or was it Doom?

"You with Ignatia, and no lady-in-waiting? What does this mean?" he inquired, utterly puzzled.

The porter behind him placed his bag in the carriage, while he, in his travelling-ulster and cap, begged permission to remain there.

What could she say? She was very lonely, and she wanted to tell him what had occurred since her return to Treysa and of the crisis of it all. So she nodded in the affirmative.

Then he gave the porter his tip, and the man departed. Presently, before the train moved off, the sleeping child opened her eyes, shyly at first, in the presence of a stranger; but a moment later, recognising him, she got up, and rushing gladly towards him, cried in her pretty, childish way,—

"Leitolf! Good Leitolf to come with us! We are so very tired!"

"Are you, little Highness?" exclaimed the man laughing, and taking her upon his knee. "But you will soon be at your destination."

"Yes," she pouted, "but I would not mind if mother did not cry so much."

The Princess pressed her lips together. She was a little annoyed that her child should reveal the secret of her grief. If she did so to Leitolf she might do so to others.

After a little while, however, the motion of the train lulled the child off to sleep again, and the man laid her down as before. Then, turning to the sorrowing woman at his side, he asked,—

"You had my message—I mean you found it?"

She nodded, but made no reply. She recollected each of those finely-penned words, and knew that they came from the heart of as honest and upright a man as there was in the whole empire.

"And now tell me, Princess, the reason of this second journey to Vienna?" he asked, looking at her with his calm, serious face.

For a moment she held her breath. There were tears welling in her eyes, and she feared lest he might detect them—feared that she might break down in explaining to him the bitter truth.

"I have left Treysa for ever," she said simply.

He started from his seat and stared at her.

"Left Treysa!" he gasped. "Left the Court—left your husband! Is this really true?"

"It is the truth, Carl," was her answer in a low, tremulous tone. "I could bear it no longer."

He was silent. He recognised the extreme gravity of the step she had taken. He recognised, too, that, more serious than all, her unscrupulous enemies who had conspired to drive her from Court had now triumphed.

His brows were knit as he realised all that she was suffering—this pure, beautiful woman, whom he had once loved so fondly, and whose champion he still remained. He knew that the Crown Prince was a man of brutal instinct, and utterly unsuited as husband of a sweet, refined, gentle woman such as Claire. It was, indeed, a tragedy—a dark tragedy.

In a low voice he inquired what had occurred, but she made no mention of the brutal, cowardly blow which had felled her insensible, cut her lip, and broken her white teeth. She only explained very briefly the incident of the three guests at dinner, and the amazing conversation she had afterwards overheard.

"It is a dastardly plot!" he cried in quick anger. "Why, you are as sane as I am, and yet the Crown Prince, in order to get rid of you, will allow these doctors to certify you as a lunatic! The conspiracy shall be exposed in the press. I will myself expose it!" he declared, clenching his fists.

"No, Carl," she exclaimed quickly. "I have never done anything against my husband's interest, nor have I ever made complaint against him. I shall not do so now. Remember, what I have just told you is in strict confidence. The public must not know of it."

"Then will you actually remain a victim and keep silence, allowing these people to thus misjudge you?" he asked in a tone of reproach.

"To bring opprobrium upon my husband is to bring scandal upon the Court and nation," was her answer. "I am still Crown Princess, and I have still my duty to perform towards the people."

"You are a woman of such high ideals, Princess," he said, accepting her reproof. "Most other wives who have been treated as you have would have sought to retaliate."

"Why should I? My husband is but the weak-principled puppet of a scandalous Court. It is not his own fault. He is goaded on by those who fear that I may reign as Queen."

"Few women would regard him in such a very generous light," Leitolf remarked, still stunned by the latest plot which she had revealed. If there was an ingenious conspiracy to confine her in an asylum, then surely it would be an easy matter for the very fact of her flight to be misconstrued into insanity. They would tear her child from her, and imprison her, despairing and brokenhearted. The thought of it goaded him to desperation. She told him of her intention of returning to her father, the Archduke Charles, and of living in future in her old home at Wartenstein—that magnificent castle of which they both had such pleasant recollections.

"And I shall be in Rome," he sighed. "Ah, Princess, I shall often think of you, often and often."

"Never write to me, I beg of you, Carl," she said apprehensively. "Your letter might fall into other hands, and certainly would be misunderstood. The world at large does not believe in platonic friendship between man and woman, remember."

"True," he murmured. "That is why they say that you and I are still lovers, which is a foul and abominable lie." Their eyes met, and she saw a deep, earnest look in his face that told her that he was thinking still of those days long ago, and of that giddy intoxication of heart and sense which belongs to the novelty of passion which we feel once, and but once, in our lives.

At that moment the train came to a standstill at the little station of Gratzen, and, unnoticed by them, a man passed the carriage and peered in inquisitively. He was a thick-set, grey-bearded, hard-faced German, somewhat round-shouldered, rather badly dressed, who, leaning heavily upon his stick, walked with the air of an invalid.

He afterwards turned quickly upon his heel and again limped past, gazing in, so as to satisfy himself that he was not mistaken.

Then entering a compartment at the rear of the train the old fellow resumed his journey, smiling to himself, and stroking his beard with his thin, bony hand, as though he had made a very valuable discovery and yet was puzzled.

XII

"An Open Scandal!"

At Klosterneuberg, six miles from Vienna, Leitolf kissed her hand in deep reverence, taking sad leave of her, for on arrival at the capital she would probably be recognised, and they both deemed it judicious that she should be alone.

"Good-bye," he said earnestly, holding her hand as the train ran into the suburban station. "This meeting of ours has been a strange and unexpected one, and this is, I suppose, our last leave-taking. I have nothing to add," he sighed. "You know that I am ever your servant, ever ready to serve your Imperial Highness in whatsoever manner you may command. May God bless and comfort you. Adieu."

"Good-bye, Carl," she said brokenly. It was all she could say. She restrained her tears by dint of great effort.

Then, when he had gone and closed the carriage door, she burst into a fit of sobbing. By his absence it seemed to her that the light of her life had been extinguished. She was alone, in hopeless despair.

Darkness had now fallen, and as the train rushed on its final run along the precipitous slopes of the Kahlenberg, little Ignatia placed her arms around her mother's neck and said,—

"Mother, don't cry, or I shall tell Allen, and she'll scold you. Poor, dear mother!"

The Princess kissed the child's soft arms, and at length managed to dry her own eyes, assuming her hat and veil in preparation for arrival at the capital. And none too soon, for ere she had dressed Ignatia and assumed her own disguise the train slowed down and stopped, while the door was thrown open and a porter stood ready to take her wraps.

She took Ignatia in her arms and descended in the great station, bright beneath its electric lamps, and full of bustle and movement. She saw nothing more of Leitolf, who had disappeared into the crowd. He had wished her farewell for ever.

A fiacre conveyed her to her father's magnificent palace in the Parkring, where on arrival the gorgeous concierge, mistaking her for a domestic, treated her with scant courtesy.

"His Imperial Highness the Archduke is not in Vienna," was his answer. "What's your business with him, pray?"

The Princess, laughing, raised her veil, whereupon the gruff old fellow, a highly-trusted servant, stammered deep apologies, took off his hat, and bent to kiss the hand of the daughter of the Imperial house.

"My father is away, Franz? Where is he?"

"At Wartenstein, your Imperial Highness. He left yesterday," and he rang the electric bell to summon the major-domo.

She resolved to remain the night, and then resume her journey to the castle. Therefore, with little Ignatia still in her arms, she ascended the grand staircase, preceded by the pompous servitor, until she reached the small green-and-gilt salon which she always used when she came there.

Two maids were quickly in attendance, electric lights were switched on everywhere, and the bustle of servants commenced as soon as the news spread that the Archduchess Claire had returned.

Several of the officials of the Archducal Court came to salute her, and the housekeeper came to her to receive orders, which, being simple, were quickly given.

She retired to her room with little Ignatia, and after putting the child to bed, removed the dust of travel and went to one of the smaller dining-rooms, where two men in the Imperial livery served her dinner in stiff silence.

Her father being absent, many of the rooms were closed, the furniture swathed in holland, and the quiet of the great, gorgeous place was to her distinctly depressing. She was anxious to know how her father would take her flight—whether he would approve of it or blame her.

She sent distinct orders to Franz that no notice was to be given to the journals of her unexpected return, remarking at the same time that he need not send to the station, as she had arrived without baggage. If it were known in Vienna that she had returned, the news would quickly be telegraphed back to Treysa. Besides, when the fact of her presence in the Austrian capital was known, she would, as Crown Princess, be compelled by Court etiquette to go at once and salute her uncle the Emperor. This she had no desire to do just at present. His hard, unjust words at her last interview with him still rankled in her memory.

His Majesty was not her friend. That had recently been made entirely plain.

So, after dining, she chatted for a short time with De Bothmer, her father's private secretary, who came to pay his respects to her, and then retired to her own room—the room with the old ivory crucifix where the oil light burnt dimly in its red glass.

She crossed herself before it, and her lips moved in silent prayer.

A maid came to her and reported that little Ignatia was sleeping soundly, but that was not sufficient. She went herself along the corridor to the child's room and saw that she was comfortable, giving certain instructions with maternal anxiety.

Then she returned to her room accompanied by the woman, who, inquisitive regarding her young mistress's return, began to chat to her while she brushed and plaited her hair, telling her all the latest gossip of the palace.

The Archduke, her father, had, it appeared, gone to Wartenstein for a fortnight, and had arranged to go afterwards to Vichy for the cure, and thence to Paris; therefore, next morning, taking the maid with her to look after little Ignatia, she left Vienna again for the Tyrol, travelling by Linz and Salsburg to Rosenheim, and then changing on to the Innsbruck line and alighting, about six o'clock in the evening, at the little station of Rattenberg. There she took a hired carriage along the post road into the beautiful Zillerthal Alps, where, high up in a commanding position ten miles away, her old home was situated—one of the finest and best-preserved mediaeval castles in Europe.

It was already dark, and rain was falling as the four horses, with their jingling bells, toiled up the steep, winding road, the driver cracking his whip, proud to have the honour of driving her Imperial Highness, who until four years ago had spent the greater part of her life there. Little Ignatia, tired out by so much travelling, slept upon her mother's knee, and the Crown Princess herself dozed for a time, waking to find that they were still toiling up through the little village of Fugen, which was her own property.

Presently, three miles farther on, she looked out of the carriage window, and there, high up in the darkness, she saw the lighted windows of the great, grim stronghold which, nearly a thousand years ago, had been the fortress of the ancient Kings of Carinthia, those warlike ancestors of hers whose valiant deeds are still recorded in song and story.

Half an hour later the horses clattered into the great courtyard of the castle, and the old castellan came forth in utter amazement to bow before her.

Electric bells were rung, servants came forward quickly, the Archduke's chamberlain appeared in surprise, and the news spread in an instant through the servants' quarters that the Archduchess Claire—whom the whole household worshipped—had returned and had brought with her the tiny Princess Ignatia.

Everywhere men and women bowed low before her as, preceded by the black-coated chamberlain, she went through those great, old vaulted halls she knew so well, and up the old stone winding stairs to the room which was still reserved for her, and which had not been disturbed since she had left it to marry.

On entering she glanced around, and sighed in relief. At last she was back at home again in dear old Wartenstein. Her dream of liberty was actually realised!

Little Ignatia and the nurse were given an adjoining room which she had used as a dressing-room, and as she stood there alone every object in the apartment brought back to her sweet memories of her girlhood, with all its peaceful hours of bliss, happiness, and high ideals.

It was not a large room, but extremely cosy. The windows in the ponderous walls allowed deep alcoves, where she loved to sit and read on summer evenings, and upon one wall was the wonderful old fourteenth-century tapestry representing a tournament, which had been a scene always before her ever since she could remember. The bed, too, was gilded, quaint and old-fashioned, with hangings of rich crimson silk brocade of three centuries ago. Indeed, the only modern innovations there were the big toilet-table with its ancient silver bowl and ewer, and the two electric lights suspended above.

Old Adelheid, her maid when she was a girl, came quickly to her, and almost shed tears of joy at her young mistress's return. Adelheid, a stout, round-faced, grey-haired woman, had nursed her as a child, and it was she who had served her until the day when she had left Vienna for Treysa after her unfortunate marriage.

"My sweet Princess!" cried the old serving-woman as she entered, and, bending, kissed her hand, "only this moment I heard that you had come back to us. This is really a most delightful surprise. I heard that you were in Vienna the other day, and wondered whether you would come to see us all at old Wartenstein—or whether at your Court so far away you had forgotten us all."

"Forgotten you, Adelheid!" she exclaimed quickly, pushing her fair hair from her brow, for her head ached after her fatiguing journey; "why,

I am always thinking of the dear old place, and of you—who used to scold me so."

"When you deserved it, my Princess," laughed the pleasant old woman. "Ah!" she added, "those were happy times, weren't they? But you were often really incorrigible, you know, especially when you used to go down into the valley and meet young Carl Leitolf in secret. You remember—eh? And how I found you out?"

Claire held her breath for a moment at mention of that name.

"Yes, Adelheid," she said in a somewhat changed tone. "And you were very good. You never betrayed our secret."

"No. Because I believed that you both loved each other—that boy-and-girl love which is so very sweet while it lasts, but is no more durable than the thistledown. But let us talk of the present now. I'll go and order dinner for you, and see that you have everything comfortable. I hope you will stay with us a long, long time. This is your first return since your marriage, remember."

"Where is my father?" her Highness asked, taking off her hat, and rearranging her hair before the mirror.

"In the green salon. He was with the secretary, Wernhardt, but I passed the latter going out as I came up the stairs. The Archduke is therefore alone."

"Then I will go and see him before I dine," she said; so, summoning all her courage, she gave a final touch to her hair and went out, and down the winding stairs, afterwards making her way to the opposite side of the ponderous stronghold, where her father's study—called the green salon on account of the old green silk hangings and upholstery—was situated.

She halted at the door, but for an instant only; then, pale-faced and determined, she entered the fine room with the groined roof, where, at a table at the farther end, her father, in plain evening dress, was writing beneath a shaded lamp.

He raised his bald head and glanced round to see who was the intruder who entered there without knocking. Then, recognising his daughter, he turned slowly in his writing-chair, his brows knit, exclaiming coldly the single inquiry,—

"Well?"

His displeasure at her appearance was apparent. He did not even welcome her, or inquire the reason of her return. The expression upon his thin, grey face showed her that he was annoyed.

She rushed across to kiss him, but he put out his hand coldly, and held her at arm's length.

"There is time for that later, Claire," he said in a hard voice. "I understand that you have left Treysa?"

"Yes, I have. Who told you?"

"The Crown Prince, your husband, has informed me by telegraph of your scandalous action."

"Scandalous action!" she cried quickly, while in self-defence she began to implore the sympathy of the hard-hearted old Archduke, a man of iron will and a bigot as regarded religion. In a few quick sentences, as she stood before him in the centre of the room, she told him of all she had suffered; of her tragic life in her gilded prison at Treysa; of the insults heaped upon her by the King and Queen; of her husband's ill-treatment; and finally, of the ingenious plot to certify her as demented.

"And I have come to you, father, for protection for myself and my child," she added earnestly. "If I remain longer at Treysa my enemies will drive me really insane. I have tried to do my duty, God knows, but those who seek my downfall are, alas! too strong. I am a woman, alone and helpless. Surely you, my own father, will not refuse to assist your daughter, who is the victim of a foul and dastardly plot?" she cried in tears, advancing towards him. "I have come back to live here with my child in seclusion and in peace—to obtain the freedom for which I have longed ever since I entered that scandalous and unscrupulous Court of Treysa. I implore of you, father, for my dear, dead mother's sake, to have pity upon me, to at least stand by me as my one friend in all the world—you—my own father!"

He remained perfectly unmoved. His thin, bloodless face only relaxed into a dubious smile, and he responded in a hard voice,—

"You have another friend, Claire," Then he rose from his chair, his eyes suddenly aflame with anger as he asked, "Why do you come here with such lies as these upon your lips? To ask my assistance is utterly useless. I have done with you. It is too late to-night for you to leave Wartenstein, but recollect that you go from here before ten o'clock to-morrow morning, and that during my lifetime you never enter again beneath this roof!"

"But, father—why?" she gasped, staring at him amazed.

"Why? Why, because the whole world is scandalised by your conduct! Every one knows that the reason of your unhappiness with the Crown Prince is because you have a lover—that low-bred fellow

Leitolf—a man of the people," he sneered. "Your conduct at Treysa was an open scandal, and in Vienna you actually visited him at his hotel. The Emperor called me, and told me so. He is highly indignant that you should bring such an outrageous scandal upon our house, and—"

"Father, I deny that Count Leitolf is my lover!" she cried, interrupting him. "Even you, my own father, defame me," she added bitterly.

"Defame you!" he sneered. "Bah! you cannot deceive me when you have actually eloped from Treysa with the fellow. See," he cried, taking a telegram from the table and holding it before her, "do you deny what is here reported—that you and he travelled together, and that he descended from the train just before reaching Vienna, in fear of recognition. No," he went on, while she stood before him utterly stunned and rendered speechless by his words, which, alas! showed the terrible misconstruction placed upon their injudicious companionship upon the journey. "No, you cannot deny it! You will leave Wartenstein tomorrow, for you have grown tired of your husband; you have invented the story of the plot to declare you insane; and you have renounced your crown and position in order to elope with Leitolf! From to-night I no longer regard you as my daughter. Go!" and he pointed imperiously to the door. "Go back to the people—the common herd of whom you are so very fond—go back to your miserable lover if you wish. To me your future is quite immaterial, and understand perfectly that I forbid you ever to return beneath my roof. You have scandalised the whole of Europe, and you and your lover may now act just as you may think proper."

"But, father!" she protested, heartbroken, bursting into bitter tears. "Leitolf is not my lover! I swear to you it is all untrue!"

"Go!" he shouted, his face red with anger. "I have said all I need say. Go! Leave me. I will never see you again—never—*never*!"

XIII

The Man with the Red Cravat

A secret service agent—one of the spies of the crafty old Minister Minckeldeym—had followed Claire from Treysa. Her accidental meeting with Leitolf had, he declared, been prearranged.

It was now said that she, a Crown Princess of the Imperial blood, had eloped with her lover! The Court scandal was complete.

Alone in her room that night she sat for hours sobbing, while the great castle was silent. She was now both homeless and friendless. All the desperate appeals she had made to her father had been entirely unavailing. He was a hard man always. She had, he declared, brought a shameful scandal upon this Imperial house, and he would have nothing further to do with her. Time after time she stoutly denied the false and abominable charge, trying to explain the dastardly plot against her, and the combination of circumstances which led to her meeting with the Count at Protovin. But he would hear no explanation. Leitolf was her lover, he declared, and all her excuses were utterly useless. He refused her his protection, and cast her out as no child of his.

After long hours of tears and ceaseless sobbing, a strange thought crossed her mind. True, she was unjustly condemned as having eloped with Carl; yet, after all, was not even that preferable to the fate to which her husband had conspired to relegate her? The whole of Europe would say that she left the Court in company with a lover, and she bit her lip when she thought of the cruel libel. Yet, supposing that they had no ground for this gossip, was it not more than likely that her enemies would seek to follow her and confine her in an asylum?

The strange combination of circumstances had, however, given them good ground for declaring that she had eloped, and if such report got abroad, as it apparently had done, then her husband would be compelled to sue for a divorce.

She held her breath. Her fingers clenched themselves into her palms at thought of it—a divorce on account of the man who had always, from her girlhood, been her true, loyal, and platonic friend! And if it was sought to prove what was untrue? Should she defend herself, and establish her innocence? Or would she, by refusing to make defence, obtain the freedom from Court which she sought?

She had been utterly dumbfounded by her father's allegations that she had eloped. Until he had denounced her she had never for one moment seen the grave peril in which his presence at Protovin had placed her. He had compromised her quite unintentionally. Her own pure nature and open mind had never suspected for one moment that those who wished her ill would declare that she had eloped.

Now, as she sat there in the dead silence, she saw plainly, when too late, how injudicious she had been—how, indeed, she had played into the hands of those who sought her downfall. It was a false step to go to Leitolf at the hotel in Vienna, and a worse action still to ask that he should be recalled from her Court and sent away as attache to Rome. The very fact that she showed interest in him had, of course, lent colour to the grave scandals that were being everywhere whispered. Now the report that she, an Imperial Archduchess, had eloped with him would set the empires of Austria and Germany agog.

What the future was to be she did not attempt to contemplate. She was plunged in despair, utterly hopeless, broken, and without a friend except Steinbach. Was it destiny that she should be so utterly misjudged? Even her own father had sent her forth as an outcast!

Early next morning, taking little Ignatia and the bag containing her jewels, but leaving the maid behind, she drove from the castle, glancing back at it with heavy heart as the carriage descended into the green, fertile valley, gazing for the last time upon that old home she loved so well. It was her last sight of it. She would never again look upon it, she sadly told herself.

She, an Imperial Archduchess of Austria, Crown Princess of a great German kingdom, a Dame of the Croix Etoilee, a woman who might any day become a reigning queen, had renounced her crown and her position, and was now an outcast! Hers was a curious position—stranger, perhaps, than that in which any woman had before found herself. Many a royalty is to-day unhappy in her domestic life, suffering in silence, yet making a brave show towards the world. She had tried to do the same. She had suffered without complaint for more than three long, dark years—until her husband had not only struck her and disfigured her, but had contemplated ridding himself of her by the foulest and most cowardly means his devilish ingenuity could devise.

As she drove through those clean, prosperous villages which were on her own private property, the people came forth, cheering with enthusiasm and rushing to the carriage to kiss her hand. But she only smiled upon them sadly—not, they said, shaking their heads after she had passed, not the same smile as in the old days, before she married the German Prince and went to far-off Treysa.

The stationmaster at Rattenberg came forward to make his obeisance, and as certain military manoeuvres were in progress and some troops were drawn up before the station, both officers and men drew up and saluted. An old colonel whom she had known well before her marriage came forward, and bowing, offered to see her to her compartment, expressing delight at having met her again.

"Your Imperial Highness will never be forgotten here," declared the gallant, red-faced old fellow, who wore fierce white moustaches. "The poor are always wondering whether you are ever coming back. And at last your Highness is here! And going—where?"

She hesitated. Truth to tell, she had never thought of her destination.

"I go now to Lucerne, incognito," she replied, for want of something else to say; and they both walked on to the platform, he carrying Henriette's cheap little leather bag containing her jewels.

"So this," he said, "is our little Princess Ignatia, about whom we have heard so much." And laughingly he touched the shy child's soft cheek caressingly.

"And who are you?" inquired the child wonderingly, examining his bright uniform from head to foot.

The Princess joined in the Colonel's laughter. Usually the child was shy, but, strangely enough, always talkative with any one who wore a uniform, even though he might be a private soldier on sentry duty at the palace.

The Colonel was not alone in remarking within himself the plainness and cheapness of her Imperial Highness's costume. It had been remarked everywhere, but was supposed that she wore that very ordinary costume in order to pass incognito.

The train took her to Innsbruck, and after luncheon at the buffet she continued her journey to Lucerne, arriving there late in the evening, and taking the hotel omnibus of the Schweizerhof. There she gave her name as the Baroness Deitel, and declared that her luggage had been mis-sent—a fact which, of course, aroused some suspicion within the mind of the shrewd clerk in the bureau. Visitors without luggage are never appreciated by hotel-keepers.

Next day, however, she purchased a trunk and a number of necessaries, *lingerie* for herself and for the little Princess, all of which was sent to the hotel—a fact that quickly re-established confidence.

A good many people were staying in the place as usual, and very quickly, on account of her uncommon beauty and natural grace, people began to inquire who she was. But the reply was that she was Baroness Deitel of Frankfort—that was all. From her funereal black they took her for a young widow, and many of the idle young men in the hotel endeavoured to make her acquaintance. But she spoke to no one. She occupied herself with her child, and if alone in the hall she always read a book or newspaper.

The fact was that she was watching the newspapers eagerly, wondering if they would give currency to the false report of her elopement. But as day after day went by and nothing appeared, she grew more assured, hoping that at least the Court at Treysa had suppressed from the press the foul lie that had spread from mouth to mouth.

One paragraph she read, however, in a Vienna paper was very significant, for it stated that the Crown Prince Ferdinand of Marburg had arrived in Vienna at the invitation of the Emperor, who had driven to the station to meet him, and who had embraced him with marked cordiality.

She read between the lines. The Emperor had called him to Vienna in order to hear his side of the story—in order to condemn her without giving her a chance to explain the truth. The Emperor would no doubt decide whether the fact of her leaving the Court should be announced to the public or not.

Her surmise was not far wrong, for while sitting in the big hall of the hotel after luncheon four days later, she saw in the *Daily Mail* the following telegram, headed, "A German Court Scandal: Startling Revelations."

Holding her breath, and knowing that, two young Englishmen, seated together and smoking, were watching her, she read as follows:—

"Reuter's correspondent at Treysa telegraphs it has just transpired that a very grave and astounding scandal has occurred at Court. According to the rumour—which he gives under all reserve—late one night a week ago the Crown Princess Ferdinand escaped from the palace, and taking with her her child, the little Princess Ignatia, eloped to Austria with Count Charles-Leitolf, an official of the Court. A great sensation has been caused in Court circles in both Germany and Austria. The Crown Princess before her marriage was, it will be remembered, the Archduchess Claire, only daughter of the Archduke Charles of Austria, and notable at the Court of Vienna on account of her extreme beauty. It appears that for some time past at the Court of Treysa there have been rumours regarding the intimate friendship between the Crown Princess and the Count, who was for some time attache at the Austrian Embassy in London. Matters culminated a short time ago when it became known that the Count had followed the Princess to Vienna, where she had gone to visit her father. She returned to Treysa for a few days, still followed by Leitolf, and then left again under his escort, and has not since been seen.

"In Treysa the sensation caused is enormous. It is the sole topic of conversation. The Crown Princess was greatly beloved by the people, but her elopement has entirely negatived her popularity, as the scandal is considered utterly unpardonable. The Crown Prince has left hurriedly for Vienna in order to confer with the Emperor, who, it is rumoured, has issued an edict withdrawing from the Princess her title, and all her rights as an Imperial Archduchess, and her decorations, as well as forbidding her to use the Imperial arms. The excitement in the city of Treysa is intense, but in the Court circle everything is, of course, denied, the King having forbidden the press to mention or comment upon the matter in any way. Reuter's correspondent, however, has, from private sources within the palace, been able to substantiate the above report, which, vague though it may be, is no doubt true, and the details of which are already known in all the Courts of Europe. It is thought probable in Treysa that the Crown Prince Ferdinand will at once seek a divorce, for certain of the palace servants, notably the lady-in-waiting, the Countess de Trauttenberg, have come forward and made some amazing statements. A Council of Ministers is convened for to-morrow, at which his Majesty will preside."

"De Trauttenberg!" exclaimed the Princess bitterly between her teeth. "The spy! I wonder what lies she has invented."

She saw the two Englishmen with their eyes still upon her, therefore she tried to control her feelings. What she had read was surely sufficient to rouse her blood. She returned to her room. "I am no longer popular with the people!" she thought to herself. "They too believe ill of me! My enemies have, alas! triumphed." She re-read the telegram with its bold heading—the announcement which had startled Europe two days before—and then with a low sigh replaced the paper upon the table.

This crisis she had foreseen. The Court had given those facts to the press correspondent because they intended to hound her down as an infamous and worthless woman, because they had conspired to drive her out of Treysa; and victory was now theirs.

But none of the tourist crowd in the Schweizerhof ever dreamed that the cheaply-dressed, demure little widow was the notorious woman whom all; the world was at that moment discussing—the royal Ionian who had boldly cast aside a crown.

What she read caused her to bite her lips till they bled. She returned to her room, and sat for an hour plunged in bitter tears. All the world was against her, and she had no single person in whom to confide, or of whom to seek assistance.

That night, acting upon a sudden impulse, she took little Ignatia with her, and left by the mail by way of Bale for Paris, where she might the better conceal herself and the grief that was slowly consuming her brave young heart.

The journey was long and tedious. There was no *wagon-lit*, and the child, tired out, grew peevish and restless. Nevertheless, half an hour before noon next day the express ran at last into the Gare de l'Est, and an elderly, good-natured, grave-looking man in black, with a bright red tie, took her dressing-bag and gallantly assisted her to alight. She was unused to travelling with the public, for a royal saloon with bowing servants and attendants had always been at her disposal; therefore, when the courteous old fellow held out his hand for her bag, she quite mechanically gave it to him.

Next instant, however, even before she had realised it, the man had disappeared into the crowd of alighting passengers.

The truth flashed upon her in a second.

All her magnificent jewels had been stolen!

XIV

In Secret

Realising her loss, the Princess quickly informed one of the station officials, who shouted loudly to the police at the exit barrier that a theft had been committed, and next moment all was confusion.

Half a dozen police agents, as well as some gardes in uniform, appeared as though by magic, and while the exit was closed, preventing the weary travellers who had just arrived from leaving, an inspector of police came up and made sharp inquiry as to her loss.

In a moment a knot of inquisitive travellers gathered around her.

"A man wearing a bright red cravat has taken my dressing-bag, and made off with it. All my jewels are in it!" Claire exclaimed excitedly.

"Pardon, madame," exclaimed the police official, a shrewd-looking functionary with fair, pointed beard, "what was the dressing-bag like?"

"A crocodile one, covered with a black waterproof cover."

"And the man wore a red tie?"

"Yes. He was dressed in black, and rather elderly. His red tie attracted me."

For fully a quarter of an hour the iron gate was kept closed while, accompanied by the inspector and two agents, she went among the crowd trying to recognise the gallant old fellow who had assisted her to alight. But she was unable. Perhaps she was too agitated, for misfortune seemed now to follow upon misfortune. She had at the first moment of setting foot in Paris lost the whole of her splendid jewels!

With the police agents she stood at the barrier when it was reopened, and watched each person pass out; but, alas! she saw neither the man with the red tie nor her dressing-bag.

And yet the man actually passed her unrecognised. He was wearing a neat black tie and a soft black felt hat in place of the grey one he had worn when he had taken the bag from her hand. He had the precious dressing-case, but it was concealed within the serviceable pigskin kit-bag which he carried.

She was looking for the grey hat, the red tie, and her own bag, but, of course, saw none of them.

And so the thief, once outside the station, mounted into a fiacre and drove away entirely unsuspected.

"Madame," exclaimed the inspector regretfully, when the platform had at last emptied, "I fear you have been the victim of some clever international thief. It is one of the tricks of jewel-thieves to wear a bright-coloured tie by which the person robbed is naturally attracted. Yet in a second, so deft are they, they can change both cravat and hat, and consequently the person robbed fails to recognise them in the excitement of the moment. This is, I fear, what has happened in your case. But if you will accompany me to the office I will take a full description of the missing property."

She went with him to the police-office on the opposite side of the great station, and there gave, as far as she was able, a description of some of the stolen jewels. She, however, did not know exactly how many ornaments there were, and as for describing them all, she was utterly unable to do so.

"And Madame's name?" inquired the polite functionary.

She hesitated. If she gave her real name the papers would at once be full of her loss.

"Deitel," she answered. "Baroness Deitel of Frankfort."

"And to what hotel is Madame going?"

She reflected a moment. If she went to Ritz's or the Bristol she would surely be recognised. She had heard that the Terminus, at the Gare St. Lazare, was a large and cosmopolitan place, where tourists stayed, so she would go there.

"To the Terminus," was her reply.

Then, promising to report to her if any information were forthcoming after the circulation of the description of the thief and of the stolen property, he assisted her in obtaining her trunk, called a fiacre for her, apologised that she should have suffered such loss, and then bowed her away.

She pressed the child close to her, and staring straight before her, held her breath.

Was it not a bad augury for the future? With the exception of a French bank-note for a thousand francs in her purse and a little loose change, she was penniless as well as friendless.

At the hotel she engaged a single room, and remained in to rest after her long, tiring journey. With a mother's tender care her first thought was for little Ignatia, who had stood wondering at the scene at the station, and who, when her mother afterwards explained that the thief had run away with her bag, declared that he was "a nasty, bad man."

On gaining her room at the hotel the Princess put her to bed, but she remained very talkative, watching her mother unpack the things she had purchased in Lucerne.

"Go to sleep, darling," said her mother, bending down and kissing her soft little face. "If you are very good Allen will come and see you soon."

"Will she? Then I'll be ever so good," was the child's reply; and thus satisfied, she dropped off to sleep.

Having arranged the things in the wardrobe, the Princess stood at the window gazing down upon the traffic in the busy Rue Saint Lazare, and the cafes, crowded at the hour of the absinthe. Men were crying "*La Presse*" in strident voices below. Paris is Paris always—bright, gay, careless, with endless variety, a phantasmagoria of movement, the very cinematograph of human life. Yet how heavy a heart can be, and how lonely is life, amid that busy throng, only those who have found themselves in the gay city alone can justly know.

Her slim figure in neat black was a tragic one. Her sweet face was blanched and drawn. She leaned her elbows upon the window-ledge, and looking straight before her, reflected deeply.

"Is there any further misfortune to fall upon me, I wonder?" she asked herself. "The loss of my jewels means to me the loss of everything. On the money I could have raised upon them I could have lived in comfort in some quiet place for years, without any application to my own lawyers. Fate, indeed, seems against me," she sighed. "Because I have lived an honest, upright life, and have spoken frankly of my intention to sweep clean the scandalous Court of Treysa, I am now outcast by both my husband and by my father, homeless, and without money. Many of the people would help me, I know, but it must never be said that a Hapsbourg sought financial aid of a commoner. No, that would be breaking the family tradition; and whatever evil the future may have in store for me I will never do that."

"I wonder," she continued after a pause—"I wonder if the thief who took my jewels knew of my present position, my great domestic grief and unhappiness, whether he would not regret? I believe he would. Even a thief is chivalrous to a woman in distress. He evidently thinks me a wealthy foreigner, however, and by to-night all the stones will be knocked from their settings and the gold flung into the melting-pot. With some of them I would not have parted for a hundred times their worth—the small pearl necklace which my poor mother gave me when I was a child, and my husband's first gift, and the Easter egg in diamonds. Yet I shall never see them again. They are gone for ever. Even the police agent held out but little hope. The man, he said, was no doubt an international thief, and would in an hour be on his way to the Belgian or Italian frontier."

That was true. Jewel-thieves, and especially the international gangs, are the most difficult to trace. They are past masters of their art, excellent linguists, live expensively, and always pass as gentlemen whose very title and position cause the victim to be unsuspicious. The French and Italian railways are the happy hunting-ground of these wily gentry. The night expresses to the Riviera, Rome, and Florence in winter, and the "Luxe" services from Paris to Arcachon, Vichy, Lausanne, or Trouville in summer, are well watched by them, and frequent hauls are made, one of the favourite tricks being that of making feint to assist a lady to descend and take her bag from her hand.

"I don't suppose," she sighed, "that I shall ever see or hear of my ornaments again. Yet I think that if the thief but knew the truth concerning me he would regret. Perhaps he is without means, just as I am. Probably he became a thief of sheer necessity, as I have heard many men have become. Criminal instinct is not always responsible for an evil life. Many persons try to live honestly, but fate is ever contrary. Indeed, is it not so with my own self?"

She turned, and her eyes fell upon the sleeping child. She was all she had now to care for in the whole wide world.

Recollections of her last visit to Paris haunted her—that visit when Carl had so very indiscreetly followed her there, and taken her about incognito in open cabs to see the sights. There had been no harm in it whatsoever, no more harm than if he had been her equerry, yet her enemies had, alas! hurled against her their bitter denunciations, and whispered their lies so glibly that they were believed as truth. Major Scheel, the attache at the Embassy, had recognised them, and being Leitolf's enemy, had spread the report. It had been a foolish caprice of hers to take train from Aix-les-Bains to Paris to see her old French nurse Marie, who had been almost as a mother to her. The poor old woman, a pensioned servant of the Archducal family, had, unfortunately, died a month ago, otherwise she would have had a faithful, good friend in Paris. Marie, who knew Count Leitolf well, could have refuted their allegations had she lived; but an attack of pneumonia had proved fatal, and she had been buried with a beautiful wreath bearing the simple words "From Claire" upon her coffin.

As the sunset haze fell over Paris she still sat beside the sleeping child. If her enemies condemned her, then she would not defend herself. God, in whom she placed her fervent trust, should judge her. She had no fear of man's prejudices or misjudgment. She placed her faith entirely in her Maker. To His will she bowed, for in His sight the pauper and the princess are equal.

That evening she had a little soup sent to her room, and when Ignatia was again sleeping soundly she went forth upon the balcony leading from the corridor, and sitting there, amused herself by looking down upon the life and movement of the great salon below. To leave the hotel was impossible because of Ignatia, and she now began to regret that she had not brought the maid with her from Wartenstein.

Time after time the misfortune of the loss of her jewels recurred to her. It had destroyed her independence, and it had negatived all her plans. Money was necessary, even though she were an Imperial Archduchess. She was incognito, and therefore had no credit.

The gay, after-dinner scene of the hotel was presented below—the flirtations, the heated conversations, and the lazy, studied attitudes of the bloused English girl, who lolls about in cane lounge-chairs after dining, and discusses plays and literature. From her chair on the balcony above she looked down upon that strange, changeful world—the world of tourist Paris. Born and bred at Court as she had been, it was a new sensation to her to have her freedom. The life was entirely fresh to her, and would have been pleasant if there were not behind it all that tragedy of her marriage.

Several days went by, and in order to kill time she took little Ignatia daily in a cab and drove in the Bois and around the boulevards, revisiting all the "sights" which Leitolf had shown her. Each morning she went out driving till the luncheon-hour, and having once lunched with old Marie upstairs at the Brasserie Universelle in the Avenue de l'Opera, she went there daily.

You probably know the place. Downstairs it is an ordinary *brasserie* with a few chairs out upon the pavement, but above is a smart restaurant peculiarly Parisian, where the *hors d'oeuvres* are the finest in Eurorie and the *vin gris* a speciality. The windows whereat one sits overlook the Avenue, and from eleven o'clock till three it is crowded.

She went there for two reasons—because it was small, and because the life amused her. Little Ignatia would sit at her side, and the pair generally attracted the admiration of every one on account of their remarkably good looks. The habitues began inquiring of the waiters as to who was the beautiful lady in black, but the men only elevated their shoulders and exhibited their palms. "A German," was all they could answer. "A great lady evidently."

That she attracted attention everywhere she was quite well aware, yet she was not in the least annoyed. As a royalty she was used to being gazed upon. Only when men smiled at her, as they did sometimes, she met them with a haughty stare. The superiority of her Imperial blood would on such occasions assert itself, much to the confusion of would-be gallants.

Thus passed those spring days with Paris at her gayest and best. The woman who had renounced a crown lived amid all that bright life, lonely, silent, and unrecognised, her one anxiety being for the future of her little one, who was ever asking when Allen would return.

XV

The Shy Englishman

One afternoon about four o'clock, as the Princess, leading little Ignatia, who was daintily dressed in white, was crossing the great hall of the Hotel Terminus on her way out to drive in the Bois, a rather slim, dark-haired man, a little under forty, well dressed in a blue-serge suit, by which it required no second glance to tell that he was an Englishman, rose shyly from a chair and bowed deeply before her.

At that hour there were only two or three elderly persons in the great hall, all absorbed in newspapers.

She glanced at the stranger quickly and drew back. At first she did not recognise him, but an instant later his features became somehow familiar, although she was puzzled to know where she had met him before.

Where he had bowed to her was at a safe distance from the few other people in the hall; therefore, noticing her hesitation, the man exclaimed in English with a smile,—

"I fear that your Imperial Highness does not recollect me, and I trust that by paying my respects I am not intruding. May I be permitted to introduce myself? My name is Bourne. We met once in Treysa. Do you not recollect?"

In an instant the truth recurred to her, and she stood before him open-mouthed.

"Why, of course!" she exclaimed. "Am I ever likely to forget? And yet I saw so little of your face on that occasion that I failed now to recognise you! I am most delighted to meet you again, Mr. Bourne, and to thank you."

"Thanks are quite unnecessary, Princess," he declared; whereupon in a low voice she explained that she was there incognito, under the title of the Baroness Deitel, and urged him not to refer to her true station lest some might overhear.

"I know quite well that you are here incognito," he said. "And this is little Ignatia, is it?" and he patted the child's cheeks. Then he added, "Do you know I have had a very great difficulty in finding you. I have searched everywhere, and was only successful this morning, when I saw you driving in the Rue Rivoli and followed you here."

Was this man a secret agent from Treysa, she wondered. In any case, what did he want with her? She treated him with courtesy, but was at the same time suspicious of his motive. At heart she was annoyed that she had been recognised. And yet was she not very deeply indebted to him?

"Well, Mr. Bourne," said the Princess, drawing herself up, and taking the child's hand again to go out, "I am very pleased to embrace this opportunity of thanking you for the great service you rendered me. You must, however, pardon my failure to recognise you."

"It was only natural," the man exclaimed quickly. "It is I who have to apologise, your Highness," he whispered. "I have sought you because I have something of urgent importance to tell you. I beg of you to grant me an interview somewhere, where we are not seen and where we cannot be overheard."

She looked at him in surprise. The Englishman's request was a strange one, yet from his manner she saw that he was in earnest. Why, she wondered, did he fear being seen with her?

"Cannot you speak here?" she inquired.

"Not in this room, among these people. Are there not any smaller salons upstairs? they would be empty at this hour. If I recollect aright, there is a small writing-room at the top of the stairs yonder. I would beg of your Highness to allow me to speak to you there."

"But what is this secret you have to tell me?" she inquired curiously. "It surely cannot be of such a nature that you may not explain it in an undertone here?"

"I must not be seen with you, Princess," he exclaimed quickly. "I run great risk in speaking with you here in public. I will explain all if you will only allow me to accompany you to that room."

She hesitated. So ingenious had been the plots formed against her that she had now grown suspicious of every one. Yet this man was after all a mystery, and mystery always attracted her, as it always attracts both women and men equally.

So with some reluctance she turned upon her heel and ascended the stairs, he following her at a respectful distance.

Their previous meeting had indeed been a strange one.

Fond of horses from her girlhood, she had in Treysa made a point of driving daily in her high English dogcart, sometimes a single cob, and sometimes tandem. She was an excellent whip, one of the best in all Germany, and had even driven her husband's coach on many occasions. On the summer's afternoon in question, however, she was driving a cob in one of the main thoroughfares of Treysa, when of a sudden a motor car had darted past, and the animal, taking fright, had rushed away into the line of smart carriages approaching on the opposite side of the road.

She saw her peril, but was helpless. The groom sprang out, but so hurriedly that he fell upon his head, severely injuring himself; while at that moment, when within an ace of disaster, a man in a grey flannel suit sprang out from nowhere and seized the bridle, without, however, at once stopping the horse, which reared, and turning, pinned the stranger against a tree with the end of one of the shafts.

In an instant a dozen men, recognising who was driving, were upon the animal, and held it; but the next moment she saw that the man who had saved her had fallen terribly injured, the shaft having penetrated his chest, and he was lying unconscious.

Descending, she gazed upon the white face, from the mouth of which blood was oozing; and having given directions for his immediate conveyance to the hospital and for report to be made to her as soon as possible, she returned to the palace in a cab, and telephoned herself to the Court surgeon, commanding him to do all in his power to aid the sufferer.

Next day she asked permission of the surgeon that she might see the patient, to thank him and express her sympathy. But over the telephone came back the reply that the patient was not yet fit to see any one, and, moreover, had expressed a desire that nobody should come near him until he had quite recovered.

In the fortnight that went by she inquired after him time after time, but all that she was able to gather was that his name was Guy Bourne, and that he was an English banker's clerk from London, spending his summer holiday in Treysa. She sent him beautiful flowers from the royal hothouses, and in reply received his thanks for her anxious inquiries. He told the doctor that he hoped the Princess would not visit him until he had quite recovered. And this wish of his she had of course respected. His gallant action had, without a doubt, saved her from a very serious accident, or she might even have lost her life.

Gradually he recovered from his injuries, which were so severe that for several days his life was despaired of, and then when convalescent a curious thing happened.

He one day got up, and without a word of thanks or farewell to doctors, staff, or to the Crown Princess herself, he went out, and from that moment all trace had been lost of him.

Her Highness, when she heard of this, was amazed. It seemed to her as though for some unexplained reason he had no wish to receive her thanks; or else he was intent on concealing his real identity with some mysterious motive or other.

She had given orders for inquiry to be made as to who the gallant Englishman was; but although the secret agents of the Government had made inquiry in London, their efforts had been futile.

It happened over two years ago. The accident had slipped from her memory, though more than once she had wondered who might be the man who had risked his life to save hers, and had then escaped from Treysa rather than be presented to her.

And now at the moment when she was in sore need of a friend he had suddenly recognised her, and come forward to reveal himself!

Naturally she had not recognised in the dark, rather handsome face of the well-dressed Englishman the white, bloodless countenance of the insensible man with a brass-tipped cart-shaft through his chest. And he wanted to speak to her in secret? What had he, a perfect stranger, to tell her?

The small writing-room at the top of the stairs was fortunately empty, and a moment later he followed her into it, and closed the door.

Little Ignatia looked with big, wondering eyes at the stranger. The Princess seated herself in a chair, and invited the Englishman to take one.

"Princess," he said in a refined voice, "I desire most humbly to apologise for making myself known to you, but it is unfortunately necessary."

"Unfortunately?" she echoed. "Why unfortunately, Mr. Bourne, when you risked your life for mine? At that moment you only saw a woman in grave peril; you were not aware of my station."

"That is perfectly true," he said quietly. "When they told me at the hospital who you were, and when you sent me those lovely flowers and fruit, I was filled with—well, with shame."

"Why with shame?" she asked. "You surely had no need to be ashamed of your action? On the contrary, the King's intention was to decorate you on account of your brave action, and had already given orders for a letter to be sent to your own King in London, asking his

Majesty to allow you as a British subject to receive and wear the insignia of the Order of the Crown and Sword."

"And I escaped from Treysa just in time," he laughed. Then he added, "To tell you the truth, Princess, it is very fortunate that I left before—well, before you could see me, and before his Majesty could confer the decoration."

"But why?" she asked. "I must confess that your action in escaping as you did entirely mystified me."

"You were annoyed that I was ungentlemanly enough to run away without thanking your Highness for all your solicitude on my behalf, and for sending the surgeon of the royal household to attend to my injuries. But, believe me, I am most deeply and sincerely grateful. It was not ingratitude which caused me to leave Treysa in secret as I did, but my flight was necessary."

"Necessary? I don't understand you."

"Well, I had a motive in leaving without telling any one."

"Ah, a private motive!" she said—"something concerning your own private affairs, I suppose?"

He nodded in the affirmative. How could he tell her the truth?

His disinclination to explain the reason puzzled her sorely. That he was a gallant man who had saved a woman without thought of praise or of reward was proved beyond doubt, yet there was something curiously mysterious about him which attracted her. Other men would have at least been proud to receive the thanks and decoration of a reigning sovereign, while he had utterly ignored them. Was he an anarchist?

"Princess," he said at last, rising from his chair and flushing slightly, "the reason I have sought you to-day is not because of the past, but is on account of the present."

"The present! why?"

"I—I hardly know what to say, Princess," he said confusedly. "Two years ago I fled from you because you should not know the truth—because I was in fear. And now Fate brings me again in your path in a manner which condemns me."

"Mr. Bourne, why don't you speak more plainly? These enigmas I really cannot understand. You saved my life, or at least saved me from a very serious accident, and yet you escaped before I could thank you personally. To-day you have met me, and you tell me that you escaped because you feared to meet me."

"It is the truth, your Highness. I feared to meet you," he said, "and, believe me, I should not have sought you to-day were it not of most urgent necessity."

"But why did you fear to meet me?"

"I did not wish you to discover what I really am," he said, his face flushing with shame.

"Are you so very timid?" she asked with a light laugh.

But in an instant she grew serious. She saw that she had approached some sore subject, and regretted. The Englishman was a strange person, to say the least, she thought.

"I have nothing to say in self-defence, Princess," he said very simply. "The trammels of our narrow world are so hypocritical, our laws so farcical and full of incongruities, and our civilisation so fraught with the snortings of Mother Grundy, that I can only tell you the truth and offer no defence. I know from the newspapers of your present perilous position, and of what is said against you. If you will permit me to say so, you have all my sympathy." And he paused and looked straight into her face, while little Ignatia gazed at him in wonder.

"I wonder if your Highness will forgive me if I tell you the truth?" he went on, as though speaking to himself.

"Forgive you? Why, of course," she laughed. "What is there to forgive?"

"Very much, Princess," he said gravely. "I—I'm ashamed to stand here before you and confess; yet I beg of you to forgive me, and to accept my declaration that the fault is not entirely my own."

"The fault of what?" she inquired, not understanding him.

"I will speak plainly, because I know that your good nature and your self-avowed indebtedness to me—little as that indebtedness is—will not allow you to betray me," he said in a low, earnest tone. "You will recollect that on your Highness's arrival at the Gare de l'Est your dressing-bag was stolen, and within it were your jewels—your most precious possession at this critical moment of your life?"

"Yes," she said in a hard voice of surprise, her brows contracting, for she was not yet satisfied as to the stranger's *bona fides*. "My bag was stolen."

"Princess," he continued, "let me, in all humility, speak the truth. The reason of my escape from Treysa was because your police held a photograph of me, and I feared that I might be identified. I am a thief—one of an international gang. And—and I pray you to forgive me, and to preserve my secret," he faltered, his cheeks again colouring. "Your jewels are intact, and in my possession. You can now realise quite plainly why—why I escaped from Treysa!"

She held her breath, staring at him utterly stupefied. This man who had saved her, and so nearly lost his own life in the attempt, was a thief!

XVI

Light Fingers

Her Highness was face to face with one of those clever international criminals whose *coups* were so constantly being reported in the Continental press.

She looked straight into his countenance, a long, intense look, half of reproach, half of surprise, and then, in a firm voice, said,—

"Mr. Bourne, I owe you a very great debt. To-day I will endeavour to repay it. Your secret, and the secret of the theft, shall remain mine."

"And you will give no information to the police?" he exclaimed quickly—"you promise that?"

"I promise," she said. "I admire you for your frankness. But, tell me—it was not you who took my bag at the station?"

"No. But it was one of us," he explained. "When the bag containing the jewels was opened I found, very fortunately, several letters addressed to you—letters which you evidently brought with you from Treysa. Then I knew that the jewels were yours, and determined, if I could find you, to restore them to you with our apologies."

"Why?" she asked. "You surely do not get possession of jewels of that value every day?"

"No, Princess. But the reason is, that although my companions are thieves, they are not entirely devoid of the respect due to a woman. They have read in the newspapers of your domestic unhappiness, and of your flight with the little Princess, and have decided that to rob a defenceless woman, as you are at this moment, is a cowardly act. Though we are thieves, we still have left some vestige of chivalry."

"And your intention is really to restore them to me?" she remarked, much puzzled at this unexpected turn of fortune.

"Yes, had I not found those letters among them, I quite admit that, by this time, the stones would have been in Amsterdam and re-cut out of all recognition," he said, rather shamefacedly. Then, taking from his pocket the three letters addressed to her—letters which she had carried away from Treysa with her as souvenirs—he handed them to her, saying,—

"I beg of you to accept these back again. They are better in your Imperial Highness's hands than my own."

Her countenance went a trifle pale as she took them, and a sudden serious thought flashed through her mind.

"Your companions have, I presume, read what is contained in these?"

"No, Princess; they have not. I read them, and seeing to whom they were addressed, at once took possession of them. I only showed my companions the addresses."

She breathed more freely.

"Then, Mr. Bourne, I am still more deeply in your debt," she declared; "you realised that those letters contained a woman's secret, and you withheld it from the others. How can I sufficiently thank you?"

"By forgiving me," he said. "Remember, I am a thief, and if you wished you could call the hotel manager and have me arrested."

"I could hardly treat in that way a man who has acted so nobly and gallantly as you have," she remarked, with perfect frankness. "If those letters had fallen into other hands they might, have found their way back to the Court, and to the King."

"I understand perfectly," he said, in a low voice. "I saw by the dates, and gathered from the tenor in which they were written that they concealed some hidden romance. To expose what was written there would have surely been a most cowardly act—meaner even than stealing a helpless, ill-judged woman's jewels. No, Princess," he went on; "I beg that although I stand before you a thief, to whom the inside of a gaol is no new experience, a man who lives by his wits and his agility and ingenuity in committing theft, you will not entirely condemn me. I still, I hope, retain a sense of honour."

"You speak like a gentleman," she said. "Who were your parents?"

"My father, Princess, was a landed proprietor in Norfolk. After college I went to Sandhurst, and then entered the British Army; but gambling proved my ruin, and I was dismissed in disgrace for the forgery of a bill in the name of a brother officer. As a consequence, my father left me nothing, as I was a second son; and for years I drifted about England, an actor in a small travelling company; but gradually I fell lower and lower, until one day in London I met a well-known card-sharper, who took me as his partner, and together we lived well in the elegant rooms to which we inveigled men and there cheated them. The inevitable came at last—arrest and imprisonment. I got three years, and after serving it, came abroad and joined Roddy Redmayne's gang, with whom I am at present connected."

The career of the man before her was certainly a strangely adventurous one. He had not told her one tithe of the remarkable romance of his life. He had been a gentleman, and though now a jewel thief, he still adhered to the traditions of his family whenever a woman was concerned. He was acute, ingenious beyond degree, and a man of endless resource, yet he scorned to rob a woman who was poor.

The Princess Claire, a quick reader of character, saw in him a man who was a criminal, not by choice, but by force of circumstance. He was now still suffering from that false step he had taken in imitating his brother officer's signature and raising money upon the bill. However she might view his actions, the truth remained that he had saved her from a terrible accident.

"Yours has been an unfortunate career, Mr. Bourne," she remarked. "Can you not abandon this very perilous profession of yours? Is there no way by which you can leave your companions and lead an honest life?"

When she spoke she made others feel how completely the purely natural and the purely ideal can blend into each other, yet she was a woman breathing thoughtful breath, walking in all her natural loveliness with a heart as frail-strung, as passion-touched, as ever fluttered in a female bosom.

"Ah, Princess!" he cried earnestly, "I beg of you not to reproach me; willingly I would leave it all. I would welcome work and an honest life; but, alas! nowadays it is too late. Besides, who would take me in any position of trust, with my black record behind me? Nobody." And he shook his head. "In books one reads of reformed thieves, but there are none in real life. A thief, when once a thief, must remain so till the end of his days—of liberty."

"But is it not a great sacrifice to your companions to give up my jewellery?" she asked in a soft, very kindly voice. "They, of course, recognise its great value?"

"Yes," he smiled. "Roddy, our chief, is a good judge of stones—as good, probably, as the experts at Spink's or Streeter's. One has to be able to tell good stuff from rubbish when one deals in diamonds, as we do. Such a quantity of fake is worn now, and, as you may imagine, we don't care to risk stealing paste."

"But how cleverly my bag was taken!" she said. "Who took it? He was an elderly man."

"Roddy Redmayne," was Bourne's reply. "The man who, if your Highness will consent to meet him, will hand it back to you intact."

"You knew, I suppose, that it contained jewels?"

"We knew that it contained something of value. Roddy was advised of it by telegraph from Lucerne."

"From Lucerne? Then one of your companions was there?"

"Yes, at your hotel. An attempt was made to get it while you were on the platform awaiting the train for Paris, but you kept too close a watch. Therefore, Roddy received a telegram to meet you upon your arrival in Paris, and he met you."

What he told her surprised her. She had been quite ignorant of any thief making an attempt to steal the bag at Lucerne, and she now saw how cleverly she had been watched and met.

"And when am I to meet Mr. Redmayne?" she asked.

"At any place and hour your Imperial Highness will appoint," was his reply. "But, of course, I need not add that you will first give your pledge of absolute secrecy—that you will say nothing to the police of the way your jewels have been returned to you."

"I have already given my promise. Mr. Redmayne may rely upon my silence. Where shall we fix the meeting? Here?"

"No, no," he laughed—"not in the hotel. There is an agent of police always about the hall. Indeed, I run great risk of being recognised, for I fear that the fact of your having reported your loss to the police at the station has set Monsieur Hamard and his friends to watch for us. You see, they unfortunately possess our photographs. No. It must be outside—say at some small, quiet cafe at ten o'clock to-night, if it will not disturb your Highness too much."

"Disturb me?" she laughed. "I ought to be only too thankful to you both for restoring my jewels to me."

"And we, on our part, are heartily ashamed of having stolen them from you. Well, let us say at the Cafe Vachette, a little place on the left-hand side of the Rue de Seine. You cross the Pont des Arts, and find it immediately; or better, take a cab. Remember, the Vachette, in the Rue de Seine, at ten o'clock. You will find us both sitting at one of the little tables outside, and perhaps your Highness will wear a thick veil, for a pretty woman in that quarter is so quickly noticed."

She smiled at his final words, but promised to carry out his directions. Surely it was a situation unheard of—an escaped princess making a rendezvous with two expert thieves in order to receive back her own property.

"Then we shall be there awaiting you," he said. "And now I fear that I've kept you far too long, Princess. Allow me to take my leave."

She gave him her hand, and thanked him warmly, saying—

"Though your profession is a dishonourable one, Mr. Bourne, you have, nevertheless, proved to me that you are at heart still a gentleman."

"I am gratified that your Imperial Highness should think so," he replied, and bowing, withdrew, and stepped out of the hotel by the restaurant entrance at the rear. He knew that the agent of police was idling in the hall that led out into the Rue St. Lazare, and he had no desire to run any further risk of detection, especially while that bag with its precious contents remained in the shabby upstairs room in the Rue Lafayette.

Her Highness took little Ignatia and drove in a cab along the Avenue des Champs Elysees, almost unable to realise the amazing truth of what her mysterious rescuer of two years ago had revealed to her. She now saw plainly the reason he had left Treysa in secret. He was wanted by the police, and feared that they would recognise him by the photograph sent from the Prefecture in Paris. And now, on a second occasion, he was serving her against his own interests, and without any thought of reward!

With little Ignatia prattling at her side, she drove along, her mind filled with that strange interview and the curious appointment that she had made for that evening.

Later that day, after dining in the restaurant, she put Ignatia to bed and sat with her till nine o'clock, when, leaving her asleep, she put on a jacket, hat, and thick veil—the one she had worn when she escaped from the palace—and locking the door, went out.

In the Rue St. Lazare she entered a cab and drove across the Pont des Arts, alighting at the corner of the Rue de Seine, that long, straight thoroughfare that leads up to the Arcade of the Luxembourg, and walked along on the left-hand side in search of the Cafe Vachette.

At that hour the street was almost deserted, for the night was chilly, with a boisterous wind, and the small tables outside the several uninviting cafes and *brasseries* were mostly deserted. Suddenly, however, as she approached a dingy little place where four tables stood out upon the pavement, two on either side of the doorway, a man's figure rose, and with hat in hand, came forward to meet her.

She saw that it was Bourne, and with scarcely a word, allowed herself to be conducted to the table where an elderly, grey-haired man had risen to meet her.

"This is Mr. Redmayne," explained Bourne, "if I may be permitted to present him to you."

The Princess smiled behind her veil, and extended her hand. She recognised him in an instant as the gallant old gentleman in the bright red cravat, who, on pretence of assisting her to alight, had made off with her bag.

She, an Imperial Archduchess, seated herself there between the pair of thieves.

XVII

In Which "The Mute" is Revealed

When, in order to save appearances, Bourne had ordered her a *bock*, Roddy Redmayne bent to her, and in a low whisper said,—

"I beg, Princess, that you will first accept my most humble apologies for what I did the other day. As to your Highness's secrecy, I place myself entirely in your hands."

"I have already forgiven both Mr. Bourne and yourself," was her quiet answer, lifting her veil and sipping the *bock*, in order that her hidden face should not puzzle the waiter too much. "Your friend has told me that, finding certain letters in the bag, you discovered that it belonged to me."

"Exactly, and we were all filled with regret," said the old thief. "We have heard from the newspapers of your flight from Treysa, owing to your domestic unhappiness, and we decided that it would be a coward's action to take a woman's jewels in such circumstances. Therefore we resolved to try and discover you and to hand them back intact."

"I am very grateful," was her reply. "But is it not a considerable sacrifice on your part? Had you disposed of them you would surely have obtained a good round sum?"

The man smiled.

"We will not speak of sacrifice, your Highness," the old fellow said. "If you forgive us and accept back your property, it is all that we ask. I am ashamed, and yet at the same time gratified, that you, an Imperial Princess, should offer me your hand, knowing who and what I am."

"Whatever you may be, Mr. Redmayne," she said, "you have shown yourself my friend."

"And I am your friend; I'll stand your friend, Princess, in whatever service you may command me," declared the keen-eyed old man, who was acknowledged by the Continental police to be one of the cleverest criminals in the length and breadth of Europe. "We have discovered that you are alone here; but remember that you are not friendless. We are your friends, even though the world would call us by a very ugly name—a gang of thieves."

"I can only thank you," she sighed. "You are extremely good to speak like this. It is true that misfortune has fallen upon me, and being friendless, it is reassuring to know that I have at least two persons in Paris ready to perform any service I require. Mr. Bourne once rendered me a very great service, but refused to accept any reward." And she added, laughing, "He has already explained the reason of his hurried departure from Treysa."

"Our departures are often hurried ones, your Highness," he said. "Had we not discovered that the jewels were yours, we should in an hour have dispersed, one to England, one to Germany, and one to Amsterdam. But in order to discover you we remained here, and risked being recognised by the police, who know me, and are aware of my profession. To-morrow we leave Paris, for already Hamard's agents, suspecting me of the theft, are searching everywhere to discover me."

"But you must not leave before I make you some reward," she said. "Where are the jewels?"

"In that closed cab. Can you see it away yonder?" and he pointed to the lights of a vehicle standing some distance up the street. "Kinder, one of our friends, has it with him. Shall we get into the cab and drive away? Then I will restore the bag to you, and if I may advise your Highness, I would deposit it in the Credit Lyonnais to-morrow. It is not safe for a woman alone to carry about such articles of great value. There are certain people in Paris who would not hesitate to take your life for half the sum they represent."

"Thank you for your advice, Mr. Redmayne," she said. "I will most certainly take it."

"Will your Highness walk to the cab with me?" Bourne asked, after he had paid the waiter. "You are not afraid to trust yourself with us?" he added.

"Not at all," she laughed. "Are you not my friends?" And she rose and walked along the street to where the cab was in waiting. Within the vehicle was a man whom he introduced to her as Mr. Kinder, and when all four were seated within, Bourne beside her and Redmayne opposite her, the elder man took the precious bag from Kinder's hand and gave it to her, saying,—

"We beg of your Highness to accept this, with our most humble apologies. You may open it and look within. You will not, I think, find anything missing," he added.

She took the dressing-bag, and opening it, found within it the cheap leather bag she had brought from Treysa. A glance inside showed her that the jewels were still there, although there were so many that she, of course, did not count them.

For a few moments she remained in silence; then thanking the two for their generosity, she said,—

"I cannot accept their return without giving you some reward, Mr. Redmayne. I am, unfortunately, without very much money, but I desire you to accept these—if they are really worth your acceptance," and taking from the bag a magnificent pair of diamond earrings she gave them into his hand. "You, no doubt, can turn them into money," she added.

The old fellow, usually so cool and imperturbable, became at once confused.

"Really, Princess," he declared, "we could not think of accepting these. You, perhaps, do not realise that they are worth at least seven hundred pounds."

"No; I have no idea of their value. I only command you to accept them as a slight acknowledgment of my heartfelt gratitude."

"But—"

"There are no buts. Place them in your pocket, and say nothing further."

A silence again fell between them, while the cab rolled along the asphalte of the boulevard.

Suddenly Bourne said,—

"Princess, you cannot know what a weight of anxiety your generous gift has lifted off our minds. Roddy will not tell you, but it is right that you should know. The fact is that at this moment we are all three almost penniless—without the means of escape from Paris. The money we shall get for those diamonds will enable us to get away from here in safety."

She turned and peered into his face, lit by the uncertain light of the street lamps. In his countenance she saw a deep, earnest look.

"Then the truth is that without money to provide means of escape you have even sacrificed your chances of liberty, in order to return my jewels to me!" she exclaimed, for the first time realising the true position.

He made no response; his silence was an affirmative. Kinder, who had spoken no word, sat looking at her, entirely absorbed by her grace and beauty.

"Well," she exclaimed at last, "I wonder if you would all three do me another small favour?"

"We shall be only too delighted," was Bourne's quick reply. "Only please understand, your Highness, that we accept these earrings out of pure necessity. If we were not so sorely in need of money, we should most certainly refuse."

"Do not let us mention them again," she said quickly. "Listen. The fact is this. I have very little ready money, and do not wish at this moment to reveal my whereabouts by applying to my lawyers in Vienna or in Treysa. Therefore it will be best to sell some of my jewellery—say one thousand pounds' worth. Could you arrange this for me?"

"Certainly," Roddy replied, "with the greatest pleasure. For that single row diamond necklet we could get from a thousand to twelve hundred pounds—if that amount is sufficient."

She reopened the bag, and after searching in the fickle light shed by the street lamps she at length pulled out the necklet in question—one of the least valuable of the heap of jewels that had been restored to her in so curious and romantic a manner.

The old jewel thief took it, weighed it in his hand, and examined it critically under the feeble light. He had already valued it on the day when he had secured it. It was worth in the market about four thousand pounds, but in the secret channel where he would sell it he would not obtain more than twelve hundred for it, as, whatever he said, the purchaser would still believe it to be stolen property, and would therefore have the stones recut and reset.

"You might try Pere Perrin," Guy remarked. "It would be quicker to take it to him than to send it to Amsterdam or Leyden."

"Or why not old Lestocard, in Brussels? He always gives decent prices, and is as safe as anybody," suggested Kinder.

"Is time of great importance to your Highness?" asked the head of the association, speaking with his decidedly Cockney twang.

"A week or ten days—not longer," she replied.

"Then we will try Pere Perrin to-morrow, and let you know the result. Of course, I shall not tell him whose property it is. He will believe that we have obtained it in the ordinary way of our profession. Perrin is an old Jew who lives over at Batignolles, and who asks no questions. The stuff he buys goes to Russia or to Italy."

"Very well. I leave it to you to do your best for me, Mr. Redmayne," was her reply. "I put my trust in you implicitly."

"Your Imperial Highness is one of the few persons—beyond our own friends here—who do. To most people Roddy Redmayne is a man not to be trusted, even as far as you can see him!" and he grinned, adding, "But here we are at the Pont d'Austerlitz. Harry and I will descend, and you, Bourne, will accompany the Princess to her hotel."

Then he shouted an order to the man to stop, and after again receiving her Highness's warmest thanks, the expert thief and his companion alighted, and, bowing to her, disappeared.

When the cab moved on again towards the Place de la Bastille, she turned to the Englishman beside her, saying—

"I owe all this to you, Mr. Bourne, and I assure you I feel most deeply grateful. One day I hope I may be of some service to you, if," and she paused and looked at him—"well, if only to secure your withdrawal from a criminal life."

"Ah, Princess," he sighed wistfully, "if I only could see my way clear to live honestly! But to do so requires money, money—and I have none. The gentlemanly dress which you see me wearing is only an imposture and a fraud—like all my life, alas! nowadays."

She realised that this man, a gentleman by birth, was eager to extricate himself from the low position into which he had, by force of adverse circumstances, fallen. He was a cosmopolitan of cosmopolitans, a quiet, slow-speaking, slightly built, high-browed, genial-souled man, with his slight, dark moustache, shrewd dark eyes, and a mouth that had humour smiling at the corners; a man of middle height, his dark hair showing the first sign of changing early to grey, and a countenance bitten and scarred by all the winds and suns of the round globe; a wise and quiet man, able to keep his own counsel, able to get his own end with few words, and yet unable to shape his own destiny; a marvellous impostor, the friend of men and women of the *haut monde*, who all thought him a gentleman, and never for one instant suspected his true occupation.

Such was the man who had once risked his life for hers, the man who had now returned her stolen jewels to her, and who was at that moment seated at her side escorting her to her hotel on terms of intimate friendship.

She thought deeply over his bitter words of regret that he was what he was. Could she assist him, she wondered. But how?

"Remain patient," she urged, in a calm, kindly tone. "I shall never forget my great indebtedness to you, and I will do my utmost in order that you may yet realise your wish to lead an honest life. At this moment I am, like yourself, an outcast, wondering what the future may have in store for me. But be patient and hope, for it shall be my most strenuous endeavour to assist you to realise your commendable desire."

"Ah! really your Highness is far too kind," he answered, in a voice that seemed to her to falter in emotion. "I only hope that some way will open out to me. I would welcome any appointment, however menial, that took me out of my present shameful profession—that of a thief."

"I really believe you," she said. "I can quite understand that it is against the nature of a man of honour to find himself in your position."

"I assure you, Princess, that I hate myself," he declared in earnest confidence. "What greater humility can befall a man than to be compelled to admit that he is a thief—as I admitted to you this afternoon? I might have concealed the fact, it is true, and have returned the jewels anonymously; yet an explanation of the reason of my sudden flight from Treysa after all your kindness was surely due to you. And—well, I was forced to tell you the whole truth, and allow you to judge me as you will."

"As I have already said, Mr. Bourne, your profession does not concern me. Many a man of note and of high position and power in the Ministries of Europe commits far greater peculations than you do, yet is regarded as a great man, and holds the favour of his sovereign until he commits the unpardonable sin of being found out. No, a man is not always what his profession is."

"I thank you for regarding me in such a lenient light, your Highness, and I only look forward with hope to the day when, by some turn of Fortune's wheel, I gain the liberty to be honest," he answered.

"Remember, Mr. Bourne, that I am your friend; and I hope you are still mine in return," she said, for the cab had now stopped at the corner of the Rue d'Amsterdam, as he had ordered it, for it was running unnecessary risk for him to drive with her up to the hotel.

"Thank you, Princess," he said earnestly, raising his hat, his dark, serious eyes meeting hers. "Let us be mutual friends, and perhaps we can help each other. Who knows? When I lay in the hospital with my chest broken in I often used to wonder what you would say if you knew my real identity. You, an Imperial Princess, were sending flowers and fruit from the royal table to a criminal for whom half the police in Europe were in active search!"

"Even an Imperial Princess is not devoid of gratitude," she said, when he was out upon the pavement and had closed the door of the cab.

The vehicle moved forward to the hotel, and he was left there, bowing in silence before her, his hat in his hand.

To the hall porter she gave the precious bag, with orders to send it at once to her room, and then turned to pay the cabman.

But the man merely raised his white hat respectfully, saying,—

"Pardon, Madame, but I have already been paid."

Therefore she gave him a couple of francs as tip.

Then she ascended in the lift to her room, where a porter with the bag was awaiting her, and unlocking the door, found that little Ignatia, tired out by her afternoon drive, had not stirred.

Locking the door and throwing off her things, she opened the bag and took out the magnificent ornaments one by one. She had not counted them before leaving the palace, therefore could not possibly tell if all were intact. In handfuls she took them out and laid them in a glittering heap upon the dressing-table, when of a sudden she found among them a small envelope containing something hard to the touch.

This she opened eagerly, and took out a cheap, tiny little brooch, about half an inch long, representing a beetle, scarlet, with black spots—the innocent little insect which has so interested all of us back in our youthful days—a ladybird.

The ornament was a very cheap one, costing one franc at the outside, but in the envelope with it was a letter. This she opened, scanned the few brief lines quickly, then re-read it very carefully, and stood staring at the little brooch in her hand, puzzled and mystified.

The words written there revealed to her the existence of a secret.

XVIII

The Ladybird

The note enclosed with the cheap little brooch ran,—

"If your Imperial Highness will wear this always in a prominent position, so that it can be seen, she will receive the assistance of unknown friends."

That was all. Yet it was surely a curious request, for her to wear that cheap little ornament.

She turned it over in her hand, then placing it upon a black dress, saw how very prominently the scarlet insect showed.

Then she replaced all the jewels in her bag and retired, full of reflections upon her meeting with the friendly thieves and her curious adventure.

Next morning she took the bag to the Credit Lyonnais, as Roddy Redmayne had suggested, where it was sealed and a receipt for it was given her. After that she breathed more freely, for the recovery of her jewels now obviated the necessity of her applying either to her father or to Treysa.

The little ladybird she wore, as old Roddy and his companions suggested, and at the bank and in the shops a number of people glanced at it curiously, without, of course, being aware that it was a secret symbol—of what? Claire wondered.

Both Roddy and Guy had told her that they feared to come to her at the Terminus, as a detective was always lurking in the hall; therefore she was not surprised to receive, about four o'clock, a note from Roddy asking her to meet him at the Vachette at nine.

When Ignatia was asleep she took a cab to the dingy little place, where she found Roddy smoking alone at the same table set out upon the pavement, and joined him there. She shook hands with him, and then was compelled to sip the *bock* he ordered.

"We will go in a moment," he whispered, so that a man seated near should not overhear. "I thought it best to meet you here rather than risk your hotel. Our friend Bourne asked me to present his best compliments. He left this morning for London."

"For London! Why?"

"Because—well," he added, with a mysterious smile, "there were two agents of police taking an undue interest in him, you know."

"Ah!" she laughed; "I understand perfectly."

The old thief, who wore evening dress beneath his light black overcoat, smoked his cigar with an easy, nonchalant air. He passed with every one as an elderly Englishman of comfortable means; yet if one watched closely his quick eyes and the cunning look which sometimes showed in them, they would betray to the observer that he was a sly, ingenious old fellow—a perfect past master of his craft.

Presently they rose, and after she had dismissed her cab, walked in company along the narrow street, at that hour almost deserted.

"The reason I asked you here, your Highness, was to give you the proceeds of the necklet. I sold it to-day to old Perrin for twelve hundred and sixty pounds. A small price, but it was all he would give, as, of course, he believed that I could never have come by it honestly," and he grinned broadly, taking from his pocket an envelope bulky with French thousand-franc bank-notes and handing it to her.

"I am really very much obliged," she answered, transferring the envelope to her pocket. "You have rendered me another very great service, Mr. Redmayne; for as a matter of fact I was almost at the end of my money, and to apply for any would have at once betrayed my whereabouts."

"Ah, your Highness," replied the old thief, "you also have rendered me a service; for with what you gave us last night we shall be able to leave Paris at once. And it is highly necessary, I can tell you, if we are to retain our liberty."

"Oh! then you also are leaving," she exclaimed, surprised, as they walked slowly side by side. She almost regretted, for he had acted with such friendliness towards her.

"Yes; it is imperative. I go to Brussels, and Kinder to Ostend. Are you making a long stay here?"

"To-morrow I too may go; but I don't know where."

"Why not to London, Princess?" he suggested. "My daughter Leucha is there, and would be delighted to be of any service to you—act as your maid or nurse to the little Princess. She's a good girl, is Leucha."

"Is she married?" asked her Highness.

"No. I trained her, and she's as shrewd and clever a young woman as there is in all London. She's a lady's maid," he added, "and to tell you the truth—for you may as well know it at first as at last—she supplies us with much valuable information. She takes a place, for instance, in London or in the country, takes note of where her lady's jewels are kept, and if they are accessible, gives us all the details how best to secure them, and then, on ground of ill-health, or an afflicted mother, or some such excuse, she leaves. And after a week or two we just look in and see what we can pick up. So clever is she that never once has she been suspected," he added, with paternal pride. "Of course, it isn't a nice profession for a girl," he added apologetically, "and I'd like to see her doing something honest. Yet how can she? we couldn't get on without her."

The Princess remained silent for a few moments. Surely her life now was a strange contrast to that at Treysa, mixing with criminals and becoming the confidante of their secrets!

"I should like to meet your daughter," she remarked simply.

"If your Imperial Highness would accept her services, I'm sure she might be of service to you. She's a perfect maid, all the ladies have said; and besides, she knows the world, and would protect you in your present dangerous and lonely position. You want a female companion—if your Highness will permit me to say so—and if you do not object to my Leucha on account of her profession, you are entirely welcome to her services, which to you will be faithful and honest, if nothing else."

"You are very fond of her!" the Princess exclaimed. "Very, your Highness. She is my only child. My poor wife died when she was twelve, and ever since that she has been with us, living upon her wits—and living well too. To confess all this to you I am ashamed; yet now you know who and what I am, and you are our friend, it is only right that you should be made aware of everything," the old fellow said frankly.

"Quite right. I admire you for telling me the truth. In a few days I shall cross to London, and shall be extremely glad of your daughter's services if you will kindly write to her."

"When do you think of leaving?"

"Well, probably the day after to-morrow, by the first service *via* Calais."

"Then Leucha shall meet that train on arrival at Charing Cross. She will be dressed as a maid, in black, with a black straw sailor hat and a white lace cravat. She will at once enter your service. The question of salary will not be discussed. You have assisted us, and it is our duty to help you in return, especially at this most perilous moment, when you are believed to have eloped with a lover."

"I'm sure you are very, very kind, Mr. Redmayne," she declared. "Truth to tell, it is so very difficult for me to know in whom to trust; I have been betrayed so often. But I have every confidence in both you and your daughter; therefore I most gladly accept your offer, for, as you say, I am sadly in need of some one to look after the child—some one, indeed, in whom I can trust." An exalted charm seemed to invest her always.

"Well, your Highness," exclaimed the pleasant-faced old fellow, "you have been kind and tolerant to us unfortunates, and I hope to prove to you that even a thief can show his gratitude."

"You have already done so, Mr. Redmayne; and believe me, I am very much touched by all that you have done—your actions are those of an honest man, not those of an outlaw."

"Don't let us discuss the past, your Highness," he said, somewhat confused by her kindly words; "let's think of the future—your own future, I mean. You can trust Leucha implicitly, and as the police, fortunately, have no suspicion of her, she will be perfectly free to serve you. Hitherto she has always obtained employment with an ulterior motive, but this fact, I hope, will not prejudice her in your eyes. I can only assure you that for her father's sake she will do anything, and that for his sake she will serve you both loyally and well." He halted beneath a street lamp, and tearing a leaf from a small notebook, wrote an address in Granville Gardens, Shepherd's Bush, which he gave to her, saying: "This is in case you miss her at Charing Cross. Send her a letter, and she will at once come to you."

Again she thanked him, and they walked to the corner of the Boulevard Saint Germain, where they halted to part.

"Remember, Princess, command me in any way," said the old man, raising his hat politely. "I am always at your service. I have not concealed anything from you. Take me as I am, your servant."

"Thank you, Mr. Redmayne. I assure you I deeply appreciate and am much touched by your kindness to a defenceless woman. *Au revoir*." And giving him her hand again, she mounted into a fiacre and drove straight back to her hotel.

Her friendship with this gang of adventurers was surely giving a curious turn to the current of strange events. She, a woman of imperial birth, had at last found friends, and among the class where one would hesitate to look for them—the outcasts of society! The more she reflected upon the situation, the more utterly bewildering it was to her. She was unused as a child to the ways of the world. Her life had always been spent within the narrow confines of the glittering Courts of Europe, and she had only known of "the people" vaguely. Every hour she now lived more deeply impressed her that "the people" possessed a great and loving heart for the ill-judged and the oppressed.

At the hotel she counted the notes Roddy had given her, and found the sum that he had named. The calm, smiling old fellow was actually an honest thief!

The following day she occupied herself in making some purchases, and in the evening a police agent called in order to inform her that up to the present nothing had been ascertained regarding her stolen jewels. They had knowledge of a gang of expert English jewel thieves being in Paris, and were endeavouring to discover them.

The Princess heard what the man said, but, keeping her own counsel, thanked him for his endeavours and dismissed him. She congratulated herself that Roddy and his two associates were already out of France.

On the following afternoon, about half-past four, when the Continental express drew slowly into Charing Cross Station, where a knot of eager persons as usual awaited its arrival, the Princess, leading little Ignatia and wearing the ladybird as a brooch, descended from a first-class compartment and looked about her in the bustling crowd of arrivals. A porter took her wraps and placed them in a four-wheeled cab for her, and then taking her baggage ticket said,—

"You'll meet me yonder at the Custom 'ouse, mum," leaving her standing by the cab, gazing around for the woman in black who was to be her maid. For fully ten minutes, while the baggage was being taken out of the train, she saw no one answering to Roddy's description of his daughter; but at last from out of the crowd came a tall, slim, dark-haired, rather handsome young woman, with black eyes and refined, regular features, neatly dressed in black, wearing a sailor hat, a white lace cravat, and black kid gloves.

As she approached the Princess smiled at her; whereupon the girl, blushing in confusion, asked simply,—

"Is it the Crown Princess Claire? or am I mistaken?"

"Yes. And you are Leucha Redmayne," answered her Highness, shaking hands with her, for from the first moment she became favourably impressed.

"Oh, your Highness, I really hope I have not kept you waiting," she exclaimed concernedly. "But father's letter describing you was rather hurried and vague, and I've seen several ladies alone with little girls, though none of them seemed to be—well, not one of them seemed to be a Princess—only yourself. Besides, you are wearing the little ladybird."

Her Highness smiled, explained that she was very friendly with her father, who had suggested that she should enter her service as maid, and expressed a hope that she was willing.

"My father has entrusted to me a duty, Princess," was the dark-eyed girl's serious reply. "And I hope that you will not find me wanting in the fulfilment of it."

And then they went together within the Customs barrier and claimed the baggage.

The way in which she did this showed the Princess at once that Leucha Redmayne was a perfectly trained maid.

How many ladies, she wondered, had lost their jewels after employing her?

XIX

Leucha Makes Confession

Leucha Redmayne was, as her father had declared, a very clever young woman.

She was known as "the Ladybird" on account of her habit of flitting from place to place, constantly taking situations in likely families. Most of the ladies in whose service she had been had regretted when she left, and many of them actually offered her higher wages to remain. She was quick and neat, had taken lessons in hairdressing and dressmaking in Paris, could speak French fluently, and possessed that quiet, dignified demeanour so essential to the maid of an aristocratic woman.

Her references were excellent. A well-known Duchess—whose jewels, however, had been too carefully guarded—and half a dozen other titled ladies testified to her honesty and good character, and also to their regret on account of her being compelled to leave their service; therefore, armed with such credentials, she never had difficulty in obtaining any situation that was vacant.

So ingenious was she, and so cleverly did she contrive to make her excuses for leaving the service of her various mistresses, that nobody, not even the most astute officers from Scotland Yard, ever suspected her.

The case of Lady Harefield's jewels, which readers of the present narrative of a royal scandal will well remember, was a typical one. Leucha, who saw in the *Morning Post* that Lady Harefield wanted a maid to travel, applied, and at once obtained the situation. She soon discovered that her Ladyship possessed some extremely valuable diamonds; but they were in the bank at Derby, near which town the country place was situated. She accompanied her Ladyship to the Riviera for the season, and then returning to England found out that her mistress intended to go to Court upon a certain evening, and that she would have the diamonds brought up from Derby on the preceding day. His Lordship's secretary was to be sent for them. As soon as she obtained this information she was taken suddenly ill, and left Lady Harefield's service to go back to her fictitious home in the country. At once she called her father and Bourne, with the result that on the day in question, when Lord Harefield's secretary arrived at St. Pancras

Station, the bag containing the jewels disappeared, and was never again seen.

More than once too, she had, by pre-arrangement with her father, left her mistress's bedroom window open and the jewel-case unlocked while the family were dining, with the result that the precious ornaments had been mysteriously abstracted. Many a time, after taking a situation, and finding that her mistress's jewels were paste, she had calmly left at the end of the week, feigning to be ill-tempered and dissatisfied, and not troubling about wages. If there were no jewels she never remained. And wherever she chanced to be—in London, in the country, or up in Scotland—either one or other of her father's companions was generally lurking near to receive her secret communications.

Hers had from childhood been a life full of strange adventures, of ingenious deceptions, and of clever subterfuge. So closely did she keep her own counsel that not a single friend was aware of her motive in so constantly changing her employment; indeed, the majority of them put it down to her own fickleness, and blamed her for not "settling down."

Such was the woman whom the Crown Princess Claire had taken into her service.

At the Savoy, where she took up a temporary abode under the title of Baroness Deitel of Frankfort, Leucha quickly exhibited her skill as lady's maid. Indeed, even Henriette was not so quick or deft as was this dark-eyed young woman who was the spy of a gang of thieves.

While she dressed the Princess's hair, her Highness explained how her valuable jewels had been stolen, and how her father had so generously restored them to her.

"Guy—Mr. Bourne, I mean—has already told me. He is back in London, and is lying low because of the police. They suspect him on account of a little affair up in Edinburgh about three months ago."

"Where is he?" asked the Princess; "I would so like to see him."

"He is living in secret over at Hammersmith. He dare not come here, I think."

"But we might perhaps pay him a visit—eh?"

From the manner in which the girl inadvertently referred to Bourne by his Christian name, her Highness suspected that they were fond of each other. But she said nothing, resolving to remain watchful and observe for herself.

That same evening, after dinner, when Ignatia was sleeping, and they sat together in her Highness's room overlooking the dark Thames and the long lines of lights of the Embankment, "the Ladybird," at the Princess's invitation, related one or two of her adventures, confessing openly to the part she had played as her father's spy. She would certainly have said nothing had not her Highness declared that she was interested, and urged her to tell her something of her life. Though trained as an assistant to these men ever since she had left the cheap boarding-school at Weymouth, she hated herself for the despicable part she had played, and yet, as she had often told herself, it had been of sheer necessity.

"Yes," she sighed, "I have had several narrow escapes of being suspected of the thefts. Once, when in Lady Milborne's service, down at Lyme Regis, I discovered that she kept the Milborne heirlooms, among which were some very fine old rubies—which are just now worth more than diamonds in the market—in a secret cupboard in the wall of her bedroom, behind an old family portrait. My father, with Guy, Kinder, and two others, were in the vicinity of the house ready to make the *coup*; and I arranged with them that on a certain evening, while her Ladyship was at dinner, I would put the best of the jewels into a wash-leather bag and lower them from the window to where Guy was to be in waiting for them in the park. He was to cut the string and disappear with the bag, while I would draw up the string and put it upon the fire. Her Ladyship seldom went to the secret cupboard, and some days might elapse before the theft was discovered. Well, on the evening in question I slipped up to the bedroom, obtained the rubies and let them out of the window. I felt the string being cut, and hauling it back again quickly burnt it, and then got away to another part of the house, hoping that her Ladyship would not go to her jewels for a day or two. In the meantime I dare not leave her service, or suspicion might fall upon me. Besides, the Honourable George, her eldest son—a fellow with a rather bad reputation for gambling and racing—was about to be married to the daughter of a wealthy landowner in the neighbourhood; a most excellent match for him, as the Milbornes had become poor owing to the depreciation in the value of land.

"About two hours after I had let down the precious little bag I chanced to be looking out into the park from my own window, and saw a man in the public footway strike three matches in order to light his pipe—the signal that my friends wanted to speak to me. In surprise I slipped out, and there found Guy, who, to my utter amazement, told me that they had not received the bag; they had been forestalled by a tall man in evening dress who had emerged from the Hall, and who chanced to be walking up and down smoking when the bag dangled in front of him! Imagine my feelings!

"Unfortunately I had not looked out, for fear of betraying myself; and as it was the exact hour appointed, I felt certain that my friend would be there. The presence of the man in evening dress, however, deterred them from emerging from the bushes, and they were compelled to remain concealed and watch my peril. The man looked up, and though the room was in darkness, he could see my white apron. Then in surprise he cut the string, and having opened the bag in the light, saw what it contained, placed it in his pocket, and re-entered the house. Guy described him, and I at once knew that it was the Honourable George, my mistress's son. He would no doubt denounce me as a thief.

"I saw the extreme peril of the situation. I had acted clumsily in not first ascertaining that the way was clear. To fly at once was to condemn myself. I reflected for a moment, and then, resolving upon a desperate course of action, returned to the house, in spite of Bourne's counsel to get away as quickly as possible. I went straight to her Ladyship's room, but from the way she spoke to me saw that up to the present her son had told her nothing. This was fortunate for me. He was keeping the secret in order, no doubt, to call the police on the morrow and accuse me in their presence. I saw that the only way was to bluff him; therefore I went very carefully to work.

"Just before midnight I slipped into his sitting-room, which adjoined his bedroom, and secreted myself behind the heavy plush curtains that were drawn; then when he was asleep I took the rubies from the drawer in which he had placed them, but in doing so the lock of the drawer clicked, and he awoke. He saw me, and sprang up, openly accusing me of theft. Whereupon I faced him boldly, declaring that if he did not keep his mouth closed I would alarm the household, who would find me alone in his room at that hour. He would then be compromised in the eyes of the woman whom in two days he was about to marry. Instantly he recognised that I held the whip-hand. He endeavoured, however, to argue; but I declared that if he did not allow me to have the rubies to replace in the cupboard and maintain silence, I would arouse the household. Then he laughed, saying, 'You're a fool, Leucha. I'm very hard up, and you quite providentially lowered them down to me. I intend to raise money on them to-morrow.' 'And to accuse me!' I said. 'No, you don't. I shall put them back, and we will both remain silent. Both of us have much to lose—you a wife, and I my liberty. Why should either of us risk it? Is it really worth while?' This argument decided him. I replaced the jewels, and next day left Lady Milborne's service.

"That was, however, one of the narrowest escapes I ever had, and it required all my courage to extricate myself, I can tell you."

"So your plots were not always successful," remarked the Princess, smiling and looking at her wonderingly. She was surely a girl of great resource and ingenuity.

"Not always, your Highness. One, which father had planned here a couple of months ago, and which was to be effected in Paris, has just failed in a peculiar way. The lady went to Paris, and, unknown to her husband, suddenly sold all her jewels *en masse* in order to pay her debts at bridge."

"She forestalled him!"

"Exactly," laughed the girl. "But it was a curious *contretemps*, was it not?"

Next day proved an eventful one to the Crown Princess, for soon after eleven o'clock, when with Leucha and Ignatia she went out of the hotel into the Strand, a man selling the *Evening News* held a poster before her, bearing in large capitals the words:—

EVENING NEWS, FRIDAY, JUNE 26th.
DEATH OF THE KING OF MARBURG.
EVENING NEWS.

She halted, staring at the words.

Then she bought a newspaper, and opening it at once upon the pavement, amid the busy throng, learnt that the aged King had died suddenly at Treysa, on the previous evening, of senile decay.

The news staggered her. Her husband had succeeded, and she was now Queen—a reigning sovereign!

In the cruelly wronged woman there still remained all the fervour of youthful tenderness, all the romance of youthful fancy, all the enchantment of ideal grace—the bloom of beauty, the brightness of intellect, and the dignity of rank, taking the peculiar hue from the conjugal character which shed over all like a consecration and a holy charm. Thoughts of her husband, the man who had so cruelly ill-judged her, were in her recollections, acting on her mind with the force of a habitual feeling, heightened by enthusiastic passion, and hallowed by a sense of duty. Her duty to her husband and to her people was to return at once to Treysa. As she walked with Leucha towards Trafalgar Square she reflected deeply. How could she go back now that her enemies had so openly condemned her? No; she saw that for her own happiness it was far better that she still remain away from Court—the Court over which at last she now reigned as Queen.

"My worst enemies will bow to me in adulation," she thought to herself. "They fear my retaliation, and if I went back I verily believe that I should show them no mercy. And yet, after all, it would be uncharitable. One should always repay evil with good. If I do not return, I shall not be tempted to revenge."

That day she remained very silent and pensive, full of an acute sense of the injustice inflicted upon her. Her husband the King was no doubt trying to discover her whereabouts, but up to the present had been unsuccessful. The papers, which spoke of her almost daily, stated that it was believed she was still in Germany, at one or other of the quieter spas, on account of little Ignatia's health. In one journal she had read that she had been recognised in New York, and in another it was cruelly suggested that she was in hiding in Rome, so as to be near her lover Leitolf.

The truth was that her enemies at Court were actually paying the more scurrilous of the Continental papers—those which will publish any libel for a hundred francs, and the present writer could name dozens of such rags on the Continent—to print all sorts of cruel, unfounded scandals concerning her.

During the past few days she had scarcely taken up a single foreign paper without finding the heading, "The Great Court Scandal," and something outrageously against her; for her enemies, who had engaged as their secret agent a Jew money-lender, had started a bitter campaign against her, backed with the sum of a hundred thousand marks, placed by Hinckeldeym at the unscrupulous Hebrew's disposal with which to bribe the press. A little money can, alas! soon ruin a woman's good name, or, on the other hand, it can whitewash the blackest record.

This plot against an innocent, defenceless woman was as brutal as any conceived by the ingenuity of a corrupt Court of office-seekers and sycophants, for at heart the King had loved his wife—until they had poisoned his mind against her and besmirched her good name.

Of all this she was well aware, conscious of her own weakness as a woman. Yet she retained her woman's heart, for that was unalterable, and part of her being: but her looks, her language, her thoughts, even in those adverse circumstances, assumed the cast of the pure ideal; and to those who were in the secret of her humane and pitying nature, nothing could be more charming and consistent than the effect which she produced upon others.

As the hot, fevered days went by, she recognised that it became hourly more necessary for her to leave London, and conceal her identity somewhere in the country. She noticed at the Savoy, whenever she dined or lunched with Leucha, people were noting her beauty and inquiring who she was. At any moment she might be recognised by some one who had visited the Court at Treysa, or by those annoying portraits that were now appearing everywhere in the illustrated journals.

She decided to consult Guy Bourne, who, Leucha said, usually spent half his time in hiding. Therefore one evening, with "the Ladybird," she took a cab to a small semi-detached villa in Wolverton Gardens, off the Hammersmith Road, where she alighted and entered, in utter ignorance, unfortunately, that another hansom had followed her closely all the way from the Savoy, and that, pulling up in the Hammersmith Road, the fare, a tall, thin, middle-aged man, with a black overcoat concealing his evening dress, had alighted, walked quickly up the street, and noted the house wherein she and her maid had entered.

The stranger muttered to himself some words in German, and with a smile of self-satisfaction lit a cigar and strolled back to the Hammersmith Road to wait.

A fearful destiny had encompassed her.

XX

The Hermit of Hammersmith

Guy Bourne, in his shirt sleeves, was sitting back in a long cane lounge-chair in the little front parlour when the Princess and her companion entered. He had just finished his frugal supper.

He jumped up confusedly, threw the evening paper aside, and apologised that her Highness had discovered him without a coat.

"Please don't apologise, Mr. Bourne. This is rather an unusual hour for a visit, is it not? But pray forgive me," she said in English, with scarcely any trace of a German accent.

"Your Highness is always welcome—at any hour," he laughed, struggling into his coat and ordering his landlady to clear away the remnants of the meal. "Leucha was here yesterday, and she told me how you were faring. I am sorry that circumstances over which I, unfortunately, have no control have not permitted my calling at the Savoy. At present I can only go out after midnight for a breath of air, and time passes rather slowly, I can assure you. As Leucha has probably told you, certain persons are making rather eager inquiries about me just now."

"I understand perfectly," she laughed. "It was to obtain your advice as to the best way to efface myself that I came to see you this evening. Leucha tells me you are an expert in disappearing."

"Well, Princess," he smiled, offering her a chair, "you see it's part of my profession to show myself as little as possible, though self-imprisonment is always very irksome. This house is one among many in London which afford accommodation for such as myself. The landlady is a person who knows how to keep her mouth shut, and who asks no questions. She is, as most of them are, the widow of a person who was a social outcast like myself."

"And this is one of your harbours of refuge," her Highness exclaimed, looking around curiously upon the cheaply furnished but comfortable room. There was linoleum in lieu of carpet, and to the Londoner the cheap walnut overmantel and plush-covered drawing-room suite spoke mutely of the Tottenham Court Road and the "easy-payment" system.

The Princess was shrewd enough to notice the looks which passed between Leucha and the man to whom she was so much indebted.

She detected that a passion of love existed between them. Indeed, the girl had almost admitted as much to her, and had on several occasions begged to be allowed to visit him and ascertain whether he was in want of anything.

It was an interesting and a unique study, she found, the affection between a pair of the criminal class.

What would the world say had it known that she, a reigning Queen, was there upon a visit to a man wanted by the police for half a dozen of the most daring jewel robberies of the past half-century?

She saw a box of cheap cigarettes upon the table, and begged one, saying,—

"I hope, Mr. Bourne, you will not be shocked, but I dearly love a cigarette. You will join me, of course?"

"Most willingly, your Highness," he said, springing to his feet and holding the lighted match for her. She was so charmingly unconventional that people of lower station were always fascinated by her.

"You know," she exclaimed, laughing, "I used to shock them very much at Court because I smoked. And sometimes," she added mischievously, "I smoked at certain functions in order purposely to shock the prudes. Oh, I've had the most delightful fun very often, I assure you. My husband, when we were first married, used to enter into the spirit of the thing, and once dared me to smoke a cigarette in the Throne Room in the presence of the King and Queen. I did so—and imagine the result!"

"Ah!" he cried, "that reminds me. Pray pardon me for my breach of etiquette, but you have come upon me so very unexpectedly. I've seen in the *Mail* the account of his Majesty's death, and that you are now Queen. In future I must call you 'your Majesty.' You are a reigning sovereign, and I am a thief. A strange contrast, is it not?"

"Better call me your friend, Mr. Bourne," she said, in a calm, changed voice. "Here is no place for titles. Recollect that I am now only an ordinary citizen, one of the people—a mere woman whose only desire is peace."

Then continuing, she explained her daily fear lest she might be recognised at the Savoy, and asked his advice as to the best means of hiding herself.

"Well, your Majesty," said the past master of deception, after some thought, "you see you are a foreigner, and as such will be remarked in England everywhere. You speak French like a *Parisienne*. Why not pass as French under a French name? I should suggest that you go to some small, quiet South Coast town—say to Worthing. Many French people go there as they cross from Dieppe. There are several good hotels; or you might, if you wished to be more private, obtain apartments."

"Yes," she exclaimed excitedly; "apartments in an English house would be such great fun. I will go to this place Worthing. Is it nice?"

"Quiet—with good sea air."

"I was once at Hastings—when I was a child. Is it anything like that?"

"Smaller, more select, and quieter."

"Then I will go there to-morrow and call myself Madame Bernard," she said decisively. "Leucha will go with me in search of apartments."

Having gained her freedom, she now wanted to see what an English middle-class house was like. She had heard much of English home life from Allen and from the English notabilities who had come to Court, and she desired to see it for herself. Hotel life is the same all the world over, and it already bored her.

"Certainly. Your Majesty will be much quieter and far more comfortable in apartments, and passing as an ordinary member of the public," Leucha said. "I happen to know a very nice house where one can obtain furnished apartments. It faces the sea near the pier, and is kept by a Mrs. Blake, the widow of an Army surgeon. When I was in service with Lady Porthkerry we stayed there for a month."

"Then we will most certainly go there; and perhaps you, Mr. Bourne, will find it possible to take the sea air at Worthing instead of being cooped up here. You might come down by a night train—that is, if you know a place where you would be safe."

He shook his head dubiously.

"I know a place in Brighton—where I've stayed several times. It is not far from Worthing, certainly. But we will see afterwards. Does your Majesty intend to leave London to-morrow?"

"Yes; but please not 'your Majesty,'" she said, in mild reproach, and with a sweet smile. "Remember, I am in future plain Madame Bernard, of Bordeaux, shall we say? The landlady—as I think you call her in English—must not know who I am, or there will soon be paragraphs in the papers, and those seaside snap-shotters will be busy. I should quickly find myself upon picture postcards, as I've done, to my annoyance, on several previous occasions when I've wanted to be quiet and remain incognito."

And so it was arranged that she should establish herself at Mrs. Blake's, in Worthing, which she did about six o'clock on the following evening.

The rooms, she found, were rather frowzy, as are those of most seaside lodgings, the furniture early Victorian, and on the marble-topped whatnot was that ornament in which our grandmothers so delighted—a case of stuffed birds beneath a glass dome. The two windows of the first-floor sitting-room opened out upon a balcony before which was the promenade and the sea beyond—one of the best positions in Worthing, without a doubt.

Mrs. Blake recognised Leucha at once, terms were quickly fixed, and the maid—as is usual in such cases—received a small commission for bringing her mistress there.

When they were duly installed, Leucha, in confidence, told the inquisitive landlady that her mistress was one of the old French aristocracy, while at the same moment "Madame" was sitting out upon the balcony watching the sun disappear into the grey waters of the Channel.

In the promenade a few people were still passing up and down, the majority having gone in to dinner. But among them was one man, who, though unnoticed, lounged past and glanced upward—the tall, thin, grey-haired man who had on the previous night watched her enter the house in Hammersmith.

He wore a light grey suit, and presented the appearance of an idler from London, like most of the other promenaders, yet the quick, crafty look he darted in her direction was distinctly an evil one.

Yet in ignorance she sat there, in full view of him, enjoying the calm sundown, her eyes turned pensively away into the grey, distant haze of the coming night.

Her thoughts were away there, across the sea. She wondered how her husband fared, now that he was King. Did he ever think of her save with angry recollections; or did he ever experience that remorse that sooner or later must come to every man who wrongs a faithful woman?

That morning, before leaving the Savoy, she had received two letters, forwarded to her in secret from Brussels. One was from Treysa, and the other bore the postmark "Roma."

The letter from Treysa had been written by Steinbach three days after the King's death. It was on plain paper, and without a signature. But she knew his handwriting well. It ran:—

"Your Majesty will have heard the news, no doubt, through the newspapers. Two days ago our King George was, after luncheon, walking on the terrace with General Scheibe, when he was suddenly seized by paralysis. He cried, 'I am dying, Scheibe. Help me indoors!' and fell to the ground. He was carried into the palace, where he lingered until nine o'clock in the evening, and then, in spite of all the physicians could do, he expired. The Crown Prince was immediately proclaimed Sovereign, and at this moment I have just returned from the funeral, whereat the greatest pomp has been displayed. All the Sovereigns of Europe were represented, and your Majesty's absence from Court was much remarked and commented upon. The general opinion is that you will return—that your difference with the King will now be settled; and I am glad to tell you that those who were your Majesty's bitterest enemies a week ago are now modifying their views, possibly because they fear what may happen to them if you really do return. At this moment the Court is divided into two sets—those who hope that you will take your place as Queen, and those who are still exerting every effort to prevent it. The latter are still crying out that you left Treysa in company with Count Leitolf, and urging his Majesty to sue for a divorce—especially now that the Emperor of Austria has degraded you by withdrawing your Imperial privileges and your right to bear the Imperial arms of Austria, and by decree striking you off the roll of the Dames de la Croix Etoilee. From what I have gathered, a spy of Hinckeldeym's must have followed your Majesty to Vienna and seen you meet the Count. At present, however, although every effort is being made to find you, the secret agents have, it is said, been unsuccessful. I have heard that you are in Italy, to be near Leitolf; evidently a report spread by Hinckeldeym and his friends.

"The people are clamouring loudly for you. They demand that 'their Claire' shall be brought back to them as Queen. Great demonstrations have been made in the Dom Platz, and inflammatory speeches have been delivered against Hinckeldeym, who is denounced as your arch-enemy. The mob on two occasions assumed an attitude so threatening that it had to be dispelled by the police. The situation is serious for the Government, inasmuch as the Socialists have resolved to champion your cause, and declare that when the time is ripe they will expose the plots of your enemies, and cause Hinckeldeym's downfall.

"I am in a position to know that this is no mere idle talk. One of the spies has betrayed his employers; hence the whole Court is trembling.

What will the King do? we are all asking. On the one hand the people declare you are innocent and ill-judged, while on the other the Court still declares with dastardly motive that your friendship with Leitolf was more than platonic. And, unfortunately, his Majesty believes the latter.

"My own opinion is that your Majesty's best course is still to remain in concealment. A squadron of spies have been sent to the various capitals, and photographs are being purposely published in the illustrated press in order that you may be identified. I hope, however, that just at present you will not be discovered, for if so I fear that in order to stem the Socialistic wave even your friends must appear to be against you. Your Majesty knows too well the thousand and one intrigues which form the undercurrent of life at our Court, and my suggestion is based upon what I have been able to gather in various quarters. All tends to show that the King, now that he has taken the reins of government, is keenly alive to his responsibility towards the nation. His first speech, delivered to-day, has shown it. He appears to be a changed man, and I can only hope and pray that he has become changed towards yourself.

"If you are in Paris or in London, beware of secret agents, for both capitals swarm with them. Remain silent, patient and watchful; but, above all, be very careful not to allow your enemies any further food for gossip. If they start another scandal at this moment, it would be fatal to all your Majesty's interests; for I fear that even the people, faithful to your cause up to the present, would then turn against you. In conclusion, I beg to assure your Majesty of my loyalty, and that what ever there is to report in confidence I will do so instantly through this present channel. I would also humbly express a hope that both your Majesty and the Princess Ignatia are in perfect health."

The second letter—the one bearing the Rome postmark—was headed, "Imperial Embassy of Austria-Hungary, Palazzo Chigi," and was signed "Carl."

XXI

Love and "The Ladybird"

Re-entering the room she found herself alone, Leucha having gone downstairs into the garden to walk with Ignatia. Therefore she drew the letter from her pocket and re-read it.

"Dearest Heart," he wrote,—"To-night the journals in Rome are publishing the news of the King's death, and I write to you as your Majesty—my Queen. You are my dear heart no longer, but my Sovereign. Our enemies have again libelled us. I have heard it all. They say that we left Treysa in company, and that I am your lover; foul lies, because they fear your power. The *Tribuna* and the *Messagero* have declared that the King contemplates a divorce; yet surely you will defend yourself. You will not allow these cringing place-seekers to triumph, when you are entirely pure and innocent? Ah, if his Majesty could only be convinced of the truth—if he could only see that our friendship is platonic; that since the clay of your marriage no word of love has ever been spoken between us! You are my friend—still my little friend of those old days at dear old Wartenstein. I am exiled here to a Court that is brilliant though torn by internal intrigue, like your own. Yet my innermost thoughts are ever of you, and I wonder where you are and how you fare. The spies of Hinckeldeym have, I hope, not discovered you. Remember, it is to that man's interest that you should remain an outcast.

"Cannot you let me know, by secret means, your whereabouts? One word to the Embassy, and I shall understand. I am anxious for your sake. I want to see you back again at Treysa with the scandalous Court swept clean, and with honesty and uprightness ruling in place of bribery and base intrigue. Do not, I beg of you, forget your duty to your people and to the State. By the King's death the situation has entirely changed. You are Queen, and with a word may sweep your enemies from your path like flies. Return, assert your power, show them that you are not afraid, and show the King that your place is at his side. This is my urgent advice to you as your friend—your oldest friend.

"I am sad and even thoughtful as to your future. Somehow I cannot help thinking that wherever you are you must be in grave peril of new scandals and fresh plots, because your enemies are so utterly unscrupulous. Rome is as Rome is always—full of foreigners, and the Corso bright with movement. But the end of the season has come. The Court moves to Racconigi, and we go, I believe, to Camaldoli, or some other unearthly hole in the mountains, to escape the fever. I shall, however, expect a single line at the Embassy to say that my Sovereign has received my letter. I pray ever for your happiness. Be brave still, and may God protect you, dear heart.—Carl."

Tears sprang to her beautiful eyes as she read the letter of the man who was assuredly her greatest friend—the man whom the cruel world so erroneously declared to be her lover.

The red afterglow from over the sea streamed into the room as she sat with her eyes fixed away on the distant horizon, beyond which lay the wealthy, picturesque kingdom over which she was queen.

Leucha entered, and saw that she was *triste* and thoughtful, but, like a well-trained maid, said nothing. Little Ignatia was already asleep after the journey, and dinner would be served in half an hour.

"I hope Madame will like Worthing," the maid remarked presently, for want of something else to say. She had dropped the title of Majesty, and now addressed her mistress as plain "Madame."

"Delightful—as far as I have seen," was the reply. "More rural than Hastings, it appears. To-morrow I shall walk on the pier, for I've heard that it is the correct thing to do at an English watering-place. You go in the morning and after dinner, don't you?"

"Yes, Madame."

"Mr. Bourne did well to suggest this place. I don't think we shall ever be discovered here."

"I hope not," was Leucha's fervent reply. "Yet what would the world really say, I wonder, if it knew that you were in hiding here?"

"It would say something against me, no doubt—as it always does," she answered, in a hard voice; and then she recollected Steinbach's serious warning.

Dinner came at last, the usual big English joint and vegetables, laid in that same room. The housemaid, in well-starched cap, cuffs, and apron, was a typical seaside domestic, who had no great love for foreigners, because they were seldom lavish in the manner of tips. An English servant, no matter of what grade, reflects the same askance at the foreigner as her master exhibits. She regards all "forriners" as undesirables.

"Madame" endeavoured to engage the girl in conversation, but found her very loath to utter a word. Her name was Richards, she informed the guest, and she was a native of Thrapston, in Northamptonshire.

The bright, sunny days that followed Claire found most delightful. Leucha took little Ignatia down to the sea each morning, and in the afternoon, while the child slept, accompanied her mistress upon long walks, either along the sea-road or through the quiet Sussex lanes inland, now bright in the spring green. The so-called season at Worthing had not, of course, commenced; yet there were quite a number of people, including the "week-enders" from London, the people who came down from town "at reduced fares," as the railway company ingeniously puts it—an expression more genteel than "excursion." She hired a trap, and drove with Leucha to Steyning, Littlehampton, Shoreham, those pretty lanes about Amberley, and the quaint old town of Arundel, all of which highly interested her. She loved a country life, and was never so happy as when riding or driving, enjoying the complete freedom that now, for the first time in her life, was hers.

Weeks crept by. Spring lengthened into summer, and Madame Bernard still remained in Worthing, which every day became fuller of visitors, mostly people from London, who came down for a fortnight or three weeks to spend their summer holiday. And with Leucha she became more friendly, and grew very fond of her.

She had written to Leitolf the single line of acknowledgment, and sent it to the Austrian Embassy in Rome, enclosing it in the official envelope which he had sent her, in order to avoid suspicion. To Steinbach too she had written, urging him to keep her well informed regarding the undercurrent of events at Court.

In reply he had sent her other reports which showed most plainly that, even though the King might be contemplating an adjustment of their differences in order that she might take her place as Queen, her enemies were still actively at work in secret to complete her ruin. Up to the present, however, the spies of Hinckeldeym had entirely failed to trace her, and their cruel story that she was in Rome had on investigation turned out to be incorrect. Her enemies were thus discomfited.

In the London papers she read telegrams from Treysa—no doubt inspired by her enemies—which stated that the King had already applied to the Ministry of Justice for a divorce, and that the trial was to be heard *in camera* in the course of a few weeks.

Should she now reveal her whereabouts? Should she communicate with her husband and deny the scandalous charges before it became too late? By her husband's accession her position had been very materially altered. Her duty to the country of her adoption was to be at her husband's side, and assist him as ruler. Not that she regretted for one single instant leaving Treysa. She had not the slightest desire to re-enter that seething world of intrigue; it was only the call of duty which caused her to contemplate it. At heart, indeed, if the truth were told, she still retained a good deal of affection for the man who had treated her so brutally. When her mind wandered back to the early days of her married life and the sweetness of her former love, she recollected that he possessed many good traits of character, and felt convinced that only the bitterness of her enemies had aroused the demon jealousy within him and made him what he had now become.

If she were really able to clear herself of the stigma now upon her, there might, after all, be a reconciliation—if not for her own sake, then for the sake of the little Princess Ignatia.

These were the vague thoughts constantly in her mind during those warm days which passed so quietly and pleasantly before the summer sea.

Ignatia was often very inquisitive. She asked her mother why they were there, and begged that Allen might come back. From Leucha she was learning to speak English, but with that Cockney twang which was amusing, for the child, of course, imitated the maid's intonation and expression.

One calm evening, when Ignatia had gone to bed and they were sitting together in the twilight upon a seat before the softly-lapping waves up at the west end of the town, Leucha said,—

"To-day I heard from father. He is in Stockholm, and apparently in funds. He arrived in Sweden from Hamburg on the day of writing, and says he hopes in a few days to visit us here."

Claire guessed by what means Roddy Redmayne had replenished his funds, but made no remark save to express pleasure at his forthcoming visit. From Stockholm to Worthing was a rather far cry, but with Roddy distance was no object. He had crossed the Atlantic a dozen times, and was, indeed, ever on the move up and down Europe.

"Guy has also left London," "the Ladybird" said. "He is in Brighton, and would like to run over and call—if Madame will permit it."

"To call on you—eh, Leucha?" her royal mistress suggested, with a kindly smile. "Now tell me quite truthfully. You love him, do you not?"

The girl flushed deeply.

"I—I love him!" she faltered. "Whatever made you suspect that?"

"Well, you know, Leucha, when one loves one cannot conceal it, however careful one may be. There is an indescribable look which always betrays both man and woman. Therefore you may as well confess the truth to me."

She was silent for a few moments.

"I do confess it," she faltered at last, with downcast eyes. "We love each other very fondly; but, alas, ours is a dream that can never be realised! Marriage and happiness are not for such as we," she added, with a bitter sigh.

"Because you have not the means by which to live honestly?" Claire replied, in a voice of deep, heartfelt sympathy, for she had become much attached to the girl.

"That is exactly the difficulty, madame," was the lady's maid's reply. "Both Guy and myself hate this life of constant scheming and of perpetual fear of discovery and arrest. He is a thief by compulsion, and I an assistant because I—well, I suppose I was trained to it so early that espionage and investigation come to me almost as second nature."

"And yet you can work—and work extremely well," remarked her royal mistress, with a woman's tenderness of heart. "I have had many maids from time to time, in Vienna and at Treysa, but I tell you quite openly that you are the handiest and neatest of them all. It is a pity—a thousand pities—that you lead the life of an adventuress, for some day, sooner or later, you must fall into the hands of the police, and after that—ruin."

"I know," sighed the girl; "I know—only too well. Yet what can I do? Both Guy and I are forced to lead this life because we are without means. And again, I am very unworthy of him," she added, in a low, despondent tone. "Guy is, after all, a gentleman by birth; while I, 'the Ladybird' as they call me, am merely the daughter of a thief."

"And yet, Leucha, you are strangely unlike other women who are adventuresses. You love this man both honestly and well, and he is assuredly one worthy a woman's love, and would, under other circumstances, make you a most excellent husband."

"If we were not outlaws of society," she said. "But as matters are it is quite hopeless. When one becomes a criminal, one must, unfortunately, remain a criminal to the end. Guy would willingly cut himself away from my father and the others if it were at all possible. Yet it is not. How can a man live and keep up appearances when utterly without means?"

"Remain patient, Leucha," Claire said reassuringly. "One day you may be able to extricate yourselves—both of you. Who knows?"

But the girl with the dark eyes shook her head sadly, and spoke but little on their walk back to the house.

"Ah, Leucha," sighed the pale, thoughtful woman whom the world so misjudged, "we all of us have our sorrows, some more bitter than others. You are unhappy because you are an outlaw, while I am unhappy because I am a queen! Our stations are widely different; and yet, after all, our burden of sorrow is the same."

"I know all that you suffer, madame, though you are silent," exclaimed the girl, with quick sympathy. "I have never referred to it, because you might think my interference impertinent. Yet I assure you that I reflect upon your position daily, hourly, and wonder what we can do to help you."

"You have done all that can be done," was the calm, kind response. "Without you I should have been quite lost here in England. Rest assured that I shall never forget the kindnesses shown by all of you, even though you are what you are."

She longed to see the pair man and wife, and honest; yet how could she assist them?

Next evening, Guy Bourne, well-dressed in a grey flannel suit and straw hat, and presenting the appearance of a well-to-do City man on holiday, called upon her, and was shown up by the servant.

The welcome he received from both mistress and maid was a warm one, and as soon as the door was closed he explained,—

"I managed to get away from London, even though I saw a detective I knew on the platform at London Bridge. Very fortunately he didn't recognise me. I've found a safe hiding-place in Brighton, in a small public-house at the top of North Street, where lodgers of our peculiar class are taken in. Roddy is due to arrive at Hull to-day. With Harry and two others, he appears to have made a fine haul in Hamburg, and we are all in funds again, for which we should be truly thankful."

"To whom did the stuff belong?" Leucha inquired.

"To that German Baroness in whose service you were about eight months ago—Ackermann, wasn't the name? You recollect, you went over to Hamburg with her and took observation."

"Yes, I remember," answered "the Ladybird" mechanically; and her head dropped in shame.

Little Ignatia came forward, and in her sweet, childish way made friends with the visitor, and later, leaving Leucha to put the child to bed, "Madame Bernard" invited Guy to stroll with her along the promenade. She wished to speak with him alone.

The night was bright, balmy, and starlit, the coloured lights on the pier giving a pretty effect to the picture, and there were a good many promenaders.

At first she spoke to him about Roddy and about his own dull, cheerless life now that he was in such close hiding. Then, presently, when they gained the seat where she had sat with "the Ladybird" on the previous evening, she suddenly turned to him, saying,—

"Mr. Bourne, Leucha has told me the truth—that you love each other. Now I fully recognise the tragedy of it all, and the more so because I know it is the earnest desire of both of you to lead an honest, upright life. The world misjudges most of us. You are an outlaw and yet still a gentleman, while she, though born of criminal parents, yet has a heart of gold."

"Yes, that she has," he asserted quickly. "I love her very deeply. To you I do not deny it—indeed, why should I? I know that we both possess your Majesty's sympathy." And he looked into her splendid eyes in deep earnestness.

"You do. And more. I urge you not to be despondent, either of you. Endeavour always to cheer her up. One day a means will surely be opened for you both to break these hateful trammels that bind you to this unsafe life of fraud and deception, and unite in happiness as man and wife. Remember, I owe you both a deep debt of gratitude; and one day, I hope, I may be in a position to repay it, so that at least two loving hearts may be united." Though crushed herself, her great, generous heart caused her to seek to assist others.

"Ah, your Majesty!" he cried, his voice trembling with emotion as, springing up, he took her hand, raising it reverently to his lips. "How can I thank you sufficiently for those kind, generous words—for that promise?"

"Ah!" she sighed, "I myself, though my position may be different to your own, nevertheless know what it is to love, and, alas! know the acute bitterness of the want of love."

Then a silence fell between them. He had reseated himself, his manly heart too full for words. He knew well that this woman, whose unhappiness was even tenfold greater than his own, was his firm and noble friend. The world spoke ill of her, and yet she was so upright, so sweet, so true.

And while they sat there—he, a thief, still holding the soft white hand that he had kissed with such reverence—a pair of shrewdly evil eyes were watching them out of the darkness and observing everything.

At midnight, when he returned to Brighton, the secret watcher, a hard-faced, thin-nosed woman, slight, narrow-waisted, rather elegantly dressed in deep mourning, travelled by the same train, and watched him to his hiding-place; and having done so, she strolled leisurely down to the King's Road, where, upon the deserted promenade, she met a bent, wizened-faced, little old man, who was awaiting her.

With him she walked up and down until nearly one o'clock in the morning, engaged in earnest conversation, sometimes accompanied by quick gesticulation.

And they both laughed quietly together, the old man now and then shrugging his shoulders.

XXII

Shows Hinckeldeym's Tactics

Five weeks later.

A hot summer's night in Treysa. It was past midnight, yet before the gay, garish cafes people still lingered at the little tables, enjoying to the full the cool breeze after the heat and burden of the day, or strolled beneath the lime avenues in the Klosterstrasse, gossiping or smoking, all loth to retire.

In the great palace beyond the trees at the end of the vista the State dinner had ended, and the lonely King, glad to escape to the privacy of his own workroom in the farther wing of the palace, had cast himself into a long lounge-chair and selected a cigar. He was still in his military uniform, rendered the more striking by the many glittering orders across his breast—the Golden Fleece, the Black Eagle, the Saint Hubert, the Saint Andrew, and the rest. As he lit his cigar very slowly his face assumed a heavy, thoughtful look, entirely different from the mask of careless good-humour which he had worn at the brilliant function he had just left. The reception had not ended; it would continue for a couple of hours longer. But he was tired and bored to death of it all, and the responsibility as ruler already weighed very heavily upon him.

Though he made no mention of it to a single soul, he thought of his absent wife often—very often. Now and then a pang of remorse would cause him to knit his brows. Perhaps, after all, he had not treated her quite justly. And yet, he would reassure himself, she was surely not as innocent as she pretended. No, no; she was worthless. They were therefore better apart—far better.

Since his accession he had, on several occasions, been conscience-stricken. Once, in the empty nursery, he had noticed little Ignatia's toys, her dolls and perambulator, lying where the child had left them, and tears had sprung to his eyes. Allen, the kindly Englishwoman, too, had been to him and resigned her appointment, as she had no further duties to perform.

The Crown Princess's disappearance had at first been a nine-days' wonder in Treysa, but now her continued absence was regarded with but little surprise. The greatest scandal in the world dies down like grass in autumn. Those who had conspired against her congratulated themselves that they had triumphed, and were now busy starting fresh intrigues against the young Queen's partisans.

Since the hour that his sweet-faced wife had left the palace in secret, the King had received no word from her. He had learned from Vienna that she had been to Wartenstein, and that her father had cast her out; but after that she had disappeared—to Rome he had been told. As Crown Prince he had had his liberty, but now as King he lived apart, and was unapproachable. His was a lonely life. The duties of kingship had sobered him, and now he saw full well the lack of a clever consort as his wife was—a queen who could rule the Court.

Those about him believed him to be blind to their defects and their intrigues, because he was silent concerning them. Yet, if the truth were told, he was extremely wideawake, and saw with regret how, without the Queen's aid, he must fall beneath the influence of those who were seeking place and power, to the distinct detriment of the nation.

Serious thoughts such as these were consuming him as he sat watching the smoke rings ascend to the dark-panelled ceiling.

"Where is she, I wonder?" he asked himself aloud, his voice sighing through the room. "She has never reproached me—never. I wonder if all they have told me concerning her is really true." As he uttered these words of suspicion his jaws became firmly set, and a hardness showed at the corners of his mouth. "Ah, yes!" he added. "It is, alas! only too true—too true. Hinckeldeym would never dare to lie to me!"

And he sat with his serious eyes cast upon the floor, reflecting gloomily upon the past, as he now so very often reflected.

The room was luxurious in its appointments, for since his father's death he had had it redecorated and refurnished. The stern old monarch had liked a plain, severe, business-like room in which to attend to the details of State, but his son held modern ideas, and loved to surround himself with artistic things, hence the white-and-gold decorations, the electric-light fittings, the furniture and the pale green upholstery were all in the style of the *art nouveau*, and had the effect of exquisite taste.

A tiny clock ticked softly upon the big, littered writing-table, and from without, in the marble corridor, the slow, even tread of the sentry reached his ear.

Suddenly, while he was smoking and thinking, a low rap was heard; and giving permission to enter, he looked round, and saw Hinckeldeym, who, in Court dress, bowed and advanced, with his cocked hat tucked beneath his arm, saying,—

"I regret, sire, to crave audience at this hour, but it is upon a matter both imperative and confidential."

"Then shut the inner door," his Majesty said in a hard voice, and the flabby-faced old fellow closed the second door that was placed there as precaution against eavesdroppers.

"Well?" asked the King, turning to him in some surprise that he should be disturbed at that hour.

"After your Majesty left the Throne Room I was called out to receive an urgent dispatch that had just arrived by Imperial courier from Vienna. This dispatch," and he drew it from his pocket, "shows most plainly that his Majesty the Emperor is seriously annoyed at your Majesty's laxness and hesitation to apply for a divorce. Yesterday he called our Ambassador and remarked that although he had degraded the Princess, taken from her all her titles, her decorations, and her privileges, yet you, her husband, had done absolutely nothing. I crave your Majesty's pardon for being compelled to speak so plainly," added the wily old fellow, watching the disturbing effect his words had upon his Sovereign.

"That is all very well," he answered, in a mechanical voice. "The Emperor's surprise and annoyance are quite natural. I have been awaiting your reports, Hinckeldeym. Before my wife's disappearance you seemed to be particularly well-informed—through De Trauttenberg, I suppose—of all her movements and her intentions. Yet since she left you have been content to remain in utter ignorance."

"Not in entire ignorance, sire. Did I not report to you that she went to Vienna in the man's company?"

"And where is the man at the present moment?"

"At Camaldoli, a health resort in central Italy. The Ambassador and several of the staff are spending the summer up there."

"Well, what else do you know?" the King asked, fixing his eyes upon the crafty old scoundrel who was the greatest power in the Kingdom. "Can you tell me where my wife is—that's the question? I don't think much of your secret service which costs the country so much, if you cannot tell me that," he said frankly.

"Yes, your Majesty, I can tell you that, and very much more," the old fellow answered, quite unperturbed. "The truth is that I have known where she has been for a long time past, and a great deal has been discovered. Yet, for your Majesty's peace of mind, I have not mentioned so painful a subject. Had I not exerted every effort to follow the Princess I should surely have been wanting in my duties as Minister."

"Then where is she?" he asked quickly, rising from his chair.

"In England—at a small watering-place on the South Coast, called Worthing."

"Well—and what else?"

Heinrich Hinckeldeym made no reply for a few moments, as though hesitating to tell his royal master all that he knew. Then at last he said, with that wily insinuation by which he had already ruined the poor Princess's reputation and good name,—

"The rest will, I think, best be furnished to the counsel who appears on your Majesty's behalf to apply for a divorce."

"Ah!" he sighed sadly. "Is it so grave as that? Well, Hinckeldeym, you may tell me everything, only recollect I must have proof—proof. You understand?" he added hoarsely.

"Hitherto I have always endeavoured to give your Majesty proof, and on certain occasions you have complimented me upon my success in discovering the secrets of the pair," he answered.

"I know I have, but I must have more proof now. There must be no surmises—but hard, solid facts, you understand! In those days I was only Crown Prince. To-day I am King, and my wife is Queen—whatever may be her faults."

The old Minister was considerably taken aback by this sudden refusal on his royal master's part to accept every word of his as truth. Yet outwardly he exhibited no sign of annoyance or of disappointment. He was a perfect diplomatist.

"If your Majesty will deign to give them audience, I will, within half an hour, bring here the two secret service agents who have been to England, and they shall tell you with their own lips what they have discovered."

"Yes, do so," the King exclaimed anxiously. "Let them tell me the whole truth. They will be discreet, of course, and not divulge to the people that I have given them audience—eh?"

"They are two of the best agents your Majesty possesses. If I may be permitted, I will go at once and send for them."

And walking backwards, he bowed, and left the room. Three-quarters of an hour later he returned, bringing with him a middle-aged, thin-faced woman, rather tall and thin, dressed plainly in black, and a tall, grey-haired, and rather gentlemanly looking man, whom he introduced to their Sovereign, who was standing with his back to the writing-table.

The woman's name was Rose Reinherz and the man's Otto Stieger.

The King surveyed both of them critically. He had never seen any member of his secret service in the flesh before, and was interested in them and in their doings.

"The Minister Hinckeldeym tells me," he said, addressing Stieger, "that you are both members of our secret service, and that you have returned from England. I wish to hear your report from your own lips. Tell me exactly what you have discovered without any fear of giving me personal offence. I want to hear the whole truth, remember, however disagreeable it may be."

"Yes," added the evil-eyed old Minister. "Tell his Majesty all that you have discovered regarding the lady, who for the present purposes may remain nameless." The spy hesitated for a moment, confused at finding himself called so suddenly into the presence of his Sovereign, and without an opportunity of putting on another suit of clothes. Besides, he was at a loss how to begin.

"Did you go to Vienna?" asked the King.

"I was sent to Vienna the instant it became known that the Crown Princess—I mean the lady—had left the palace. I discovered that she had driven to her father's palace, but finding him absent had gone to Wartenstein. I followed her there, but she had left again before I arrived, and I entirely lost track of her. Probably she went to Paris, but of that I am not sure. I went to Rome, and for a fortnight kept observation upon the Count, but he wrote no letters to her, which made me suspect that she was hiding somewhere in Rome."

"You reported that she was actually in Rome. Hinckeldeym told me that."

The Minister's grey brows were knit, but only for a second.

"I did not report that she was actually there, sire. I only reported my suspicion."

"A suspicion which was turned into an actual fact before it reached my ears—eh?" he said in a hard voice. "Go on."

Hinckeldeym now regretted that he had so readily brought his spies face to face with the King.

"After losing touch with the lady for several weeks, it was discovered that she was staying under an assumed name at the Savoy Hotel, in London. I travelled from Rome to London post haste, and took a room at the hotel, finding that she had engaged a young Englishwoman named Redmayne as maid, and that she was in the habit of meeting in secret a certain Englishman named Bourne, who seemed to be leading a curiously secluded life. I reported this to the Minister Hinckeldeym, who at once sent me as assistant Rose Reinherz, now before your Majesty. Together we have left no stone unturned to fully investigate the situation, and—well, we have discovered many things."

"And what are they? Explain."

"We have ascertained that Count Leitolf still writes to the lady, sending her letters to the same address in Brussels as previously. A copy of one letter, which we intercepted, I placed in the Minister's hands. It is couched in terms that leave no doubt that this man loves her, and that she reciprocates his affection."

"You are quite certain that it is not a mere platonic friendship?" asked the King, fixing his eyes upon the spy very earnestly.

"As a man of the world, your Majesty, I do not think there is such a thing as platonic friendship between man and woman."

"That is left to poets and dreamers," remarked the wily Hinckeldeym, with a sneer.

"Besides," the spy continued, "we have carefully watched this man Bourne, and find that when she went to live at Worthing he followed her there. They meet every evening, and go long walks together."

"I have watched them many times, your Majesty," declared Rose Reinherz. "I have seen him kiss her hand."

"Then, to be frank, you insinuate that this man is her latest lover?" remarked the King with a dark look upon his face.

"Unfortunately, that is so," the woman replied. "He is with her almost always; and furthermore, after much inquiry and difficulty, we have at last succeeded in establishing who he really is."

"And who is he?"

"A thief in hiding from the police—one of a clever gang who have committed many robberies of jewels in various cities. This is his photograph—one supplied from London to our own Prefecture of Police in Treysa." And he handed the King an oblong card with two portraits of Guy Bourne, full face and profile, side by side.

His Majesty held it in his hand, and beneath the light gazed upon it for a long time, as though to photograph the features in his memory.

Hinckeldeym watched him covertly, and glanced at the spy approvingly.

"And you say that this man is at Worthing, and in hiding from the police? You allege that he is an intimate friend of my wife's?"

"Stieger says that he is her latest lover," remarked Hinckeldeym. "You have written a full and detailed report. Is not that so?" he asked.

The spy nodded in the affirmative, saying,—

"The fellow is in hiding, together with the leader of the association of thieves, a certain Redmayne, known as 'the Mute,' who is wanted by the Hamburg police for the theft of the Baroness Ackermann's jewels. The papers of late have been full of the daring theft."

"Oh! then the police are searching for both men?" exclaimed the King. "Is there any charge in Germany against this person—Bourne, you called him?"

"One for theft in Cologne, eighteen months ago, and another for jewel robbery at Eugendorf," was the spy's reply.

"Then, Hinckeldeym, make immediate application to the British Government for their arrest and extradition. Stieger will return at once to Worthing and point them out to the English police. It will be the quickest way of crushing out the—well, the infatuation, we will call it," he added grimly.

"And your Majesty will not apply for a divorce?" asked the Minister in that low, insinuating voice.

"I will reflect, Hinckeldeym," was the King's reply. "But in the meantime see that both these agents are rewarded for their astuteness and loyalty."

And, turning, he dismissed the trio impatiently, without further ceremony.

XXIII

Secret Instructions

"You did exceedingly well, Stieger. I am much pleased!" declared his Excellency the Minister, when, outside the palace, he caused them both to enter his carriage and was driving them to his own fine house on the opposite side of the capital. "His Majesty is taking a severe revenge," he laughed. "This Englishman Bourne will certainly regret having met the Queen. Besides, the fact of her having chosen a low-born criminal lover condemns her a thousandfold in the King's eyes. I, who know him well, know that nothing could cause him such anger as for her to cast her royalty into the mud, as she has done by her friendship with this gaolbird."

"I am pleased to have earned your Excellency's approbation," replied the man. "And I trust that his Majesty's pleasure will mean advancement for me—at your Excellency's discretion, of course."

"To-morrow I shall sign this decree, raising you to the post of functionary of the first class, with increased emoluments. And to you," he added, turning to the thin-nosed woman, "I shall grant a gratification of five thousand marks. Over an affair of this kind we cannot afford publicity. Therefore say nothing, either of you. Recollect that in this matter you are not only serving the King, but the whole Ministry and Court. The King must obtain a divorce, and we shall all be grateful to you for the collection of the necessary evidence. The latter, as I told you some time ago, need not be based on too firm a foundation, for even if she defends the action the mere fact of her alliance with this good-looking criminal will be sufficient to condemn her in the eyes of a jury of Treysa. Therefore return to England and collect the evidence carefully—facts that have foundation—you understand?"

The spy nodded. He understood his Excellency's scandalous suggestion. He was to manufacture evidence to be used against the Queen.

"You must show that she has lightly transferred her love from Leitolf to this rascal Bourne. The report you have already made is good, but it is not quite complete enough. It must contain such direct charges that her counsel will be unable to bring evidence to deny," declared the fat-faced man—the man who really ruled the Kingdom.

The old monarch had been a hard, level-headed if rather eccentric man, who had never allowed Hinckeldeym to fully reach the height of his ambition; yet now, on the accession of his son, inexperienced in government and of a somewhat weak and vacillating disposition, the crafty President of the Council had quickly risen to be a power as great, if not greater than, the King himself.

He was utterly unscrupulous, as shown by his conversation with Stieger. He was Claire's bitterest enemy, yet so tactful was he that she had once believed him to be her friend, and had actually consulted him as to her impossible position at Court. Like many other men, he had commenced life as a small advocate in an obscure provincial town, but by dint of ingenious scheming and dishonest double-dealing he had wormed himself into the confidence of the old King, who regarded him as a necessity for the government of the country. His policy was self-advancement at any cost. He betrayed both enemies and friends with equal nonchalance, if they were unfortunate enough to stand in his way. Heinrich Hinckeldeym had never married, as he considered a wife an unnecessary burden, both socially and financially, and as far as was known, he was without a single relative.

At his own splendid mansion, in a severely furnished room, he sat with his two spies, giving them further instructions as to how they were to act in England.

"You will return to-morrow by way of Cologne and Ostend," he said, "and I will at once have the formal requisition for their arrest and extradition made to the British Foreign Office. If this man Bourne is convicted, the prejudice against the Queen will be greater, and she will lose her partisans among the people, who certainly will not uphold her when this latest development becomes known." And his Excellency's fat, evil face relaxed into a grim smile.

Presently he dismissed them, urging them to carry out the mission entrusted to them without scruple, and in the most secret manner possible. Then, when they were gone, he crossed the room to the telephone and asked the Ministers Stuhlmann, Meyer, and Hoepfner—who all lived close by—whether they could come at once, as he desired to consult them. All three responded to the President's call, and in a quarter of an hour they assembled.

Hinckeldeym, having locked the door and drawn the heavy *portiere*, at once gave his friends a resume of what had taken place that evening, and of the manner in which he had rearoused the King's anger and jealousy.

"Excellent!" declared Stuhlmann, who held the portfolio of Foreign Affairs. "Then I shall at once give Crispendorf orders to receive Stieger and to apply to the British Foreign Office for the arrest of the pair. What are their names? I did not quite catch them."

Hinckeldeym crossed to his writing-table and scribbled a memorandum of the names Bourne and Redmayne, and the offences for which they were wanted.

"They will be tried in Berlin, I suppose?" Stuhlmann remarked.

"My dear friend, it does not matter where they are tried, so long as they are convicted. All we desire to establish is the one fact which will strike the public as outrageous—the Queen has a lover who is a criminal. Having done that, we need no longer fear her return here to Treysa."

"But is not the Leitolf affair quite sufficient?" asked Meyer, a somewhat younger man than the others, who, by favour of Hinckeldeym, now held the office of Minister of Justice.

"The King suspects it is a mere platonic friendship."

"And it really may be after all," remarked Meyer. "In my opinion—expressed privately to you here—the Queen has not acted as a guilty woman would act. If the scandal were true she would have been more impatient. Besides, the English nurse, Allen, came to me before she left Treysa, and vowed to me that the reports were utterly without foundation. They were lovers, as children—that is all."

Hinckeldeym turned upon him furiously.

"We have nothing to do with your private misgivings. Your duty as Minister is to act with us," he said in a hard, angry voice. "What does it matter if the English nurse is paid by the Queen to whitewash her mistress? You, my dear Meyer, must be the very last person to express disbelief in facts already known. Think of what would happen if this woman returned to Treysa! You and I—and all of us—would be swept out of office and into obscurity. Can we afford to risk that? If you can, I tell you most plainly that I can't. I intend that the King shall obtain a divorce, and that the woman shall never be permitted to cross our frontier again. The day she does, recollect, will mark our downfall."

Meyer, thus reproved by the man to whom he owed his present office, pursed his lips and gave his shoulders a slight shrug. He saw that Hinckeldeym had made up his mind, even though he himself had all along doubted whether the Queen was not an innocent victim of her enemies. Allen had sought audience of him, and had fearlessly denounced, in no measured terms, the foul lies circulated by the Countess de Trauttenberg. The Englishwoman had declared that her mistress was the victim of a plot, and that although she was well aware of her friendliness with Count Leitolf, yet it was nothing more than friendship. She had admitted watching them very closely in order to ascertain whether what was whispered was really true. But it was not. The Queen was an ill-treated and misjudged woman, she declared, concluding with a vow that the just judgment of God would, sooner or later, fall upon her enemies. What the Englishwoman had told him had impressed him. And now Hinckeldeym's demeanour made it plain that what Allen had said had very good foundation.

He, Ludwig Meyer, was Minister of Justice, yet he was compelled to conspire with the others to do to a woman the worst injustice that man's ambition could possibly conceive. His companion Hoepfner, Minister of Finance, was also one of Hinckeldeym's creatures, and dared not dissent from his decision.

"You forget, my dear Meyer," said the old President, turning back to him. "You forget all that the Countess Hupertz discovered, and all that she told us."

"I recollect everything most distinctly. But I also recollect that she gave us no proof."

"Ah! You, too, believe in platonic friendship!" sneered the old man. "Only fools believe in that."

"No," interposed Stuhlmann quickly. "Do not let us quarrel over this. Our policy is a straightforward and decisive one. The King is to apply for a divorce, and our friend Meyer will see that it is granted. The thing is quite simple."

"But if she is innocent?" asked the Minister of Justice.

"There is no question of her innocence," snapped Hinckeldeym. "It is her guilt that concerns you—you understand!"

Then, after some further consultation, during which time Meyer remained silent, the three men rose and, shaking hands with the President, departed.

When they had gone Hinckeldeym paced angrily up and down the room. He was furious that Meyer should express the slightest doubt or compunction. His hands were clenched, his round, prominent eyes wore a fierce, determined expression, and his gross features were drawn and ashen grey.

"We shall see, woman, who will win—you or I!" he muttered to himself. "You told me that when you were Queen you would sweep clean the Augean stable—you would change all the Ministers of State, Chamberlains—every one, from the Chancellor of the Orders down to the Grand Master of the Ceremonies. You said that they should all go—and first of all the *dames du palais*. Well, we shall see!" he laughed to himself. "If your husband is such a fool as to relent and regard your friendship with Leitolf with leniency, then we must bring forward this newest lover of yours—this man who is to be arrested in your company and condemned as a criminal. The people, after that, will no longer call you 'their Claire' and clamour for your return, and in addition, your fool of a husband will be bound to accept the divorce which Meyer will give him. And then, woman," he growled to himself, "you will perhaps regret having threatened Heinrich Hinckeldeym!"

XXIV

Romance and Reality

Roddy Redmayne, having returned safely from abroad, was living in quiet seclusion with Guy in apartments in a small, pleasantly situated cottage beyond West Worthing, on the dusty road to Goring. Immediately on his arrival from Hull he had gone to Brighton, but after a few days had taken apartments in the ancient little place, with its old-world garden filled with roses.

Both he and Guy, under assumed names, of course, represented themselves as clerks down from London, spending their summer holidays, and certainly their flannel suits, white shoes, and Panama hats gave them that appearance. Kinder was in hiding in a house up in Newcastle-on-Tyne, having crossed to that port from Antwerp. The Baroness's jewels, which were a particularly fine lot, had been disposed of to certain agents in Leyden, and therefore Roddy and his friends were in funds, though they gave no sign of wealth to their landlady, the thrifty wife of a cab proprietor.

It was a very pleasant little cottage, standing quite alone, and as the two men were the only lodgers they were quite free to do as they liked. The greater part of the day they smoked and read under the trees in the big, old-fashioned garden, and at evening would walk together into Worthing, and generally met Claire upon the pier.

"Madame," as they called her, went with Leucha several times and lunched with them at the little place, while once or twice they had had the honour of dining at her table, when they had found her a most charming hostess. Both men tried to do all they could to render her what little services lay in their power, and each day they sent her from the florist's large bunches of tea-roses, her favourite flowers. Little Ignatia was not forgotten, for they sent her dolls and toys.

Claire's life was now at last calm and peaceful, with her three strange friends. Leucha was most attentive to Ignatia, and took her each morning for a run with bare feet upon the sands, while the two men who seldom, if ever, went out before dusk, generally met her and walked with her after dinner beside the sea.

Often, when alone, she wondered how her husband fared at Treysa, and how Carl was enduring the broiling heat of the long, thirsty Italian summer. Where was that traitress, the Trauttenberg, and what, she wondered, had become of those two faithful servants, Allen and Henriette? Her past unhappiness at Treysa sometimes arose before her like some hideous but half-remembered dream. In those days she lived among enemies, but now she was with friends, even though they might be outlawed from society. With all her timid flexibility and soft acquiescence Claire was not weak; for the negative alone is weak, and the mere presence of goodness and affection implies in itself a species of power, power with repose—that soul of grace.

Many a pleasant stroll after sundown she took with the courtly old adventurer, who looked quite a gay old dog in his flannels and rakish Panama pulled down over his eyes; or with Guy, who dressed a trifle more quietly. The last-named, however, preferred, of course, the society of Leucha, and frequently walked behind with her. Claire treated Roddy's daughter more as an equal than as a dependant—indeed, treated her as her lady-in-waiting, to fetch and carry for her, to tie her veil, to button her gloves, and to perform the thousand and one little services which the trained lady-in-waiting does so deftly and without ceremony.

Though at first very strange to the world, Claire was now beginning to realise its ways, and to enjoy and appreciate more and more the freedom which she had at last gained. She delighted in those evening walks beneath the stars, when they would rest upon a seat, listening to the soft music of the sea, and watching the flashing light of the Owers and the bright beacon on Selsea Bill.

Yes, life in the obscurity of Worthing was indeed far preferable to the glare and glitter of the Court at Treysa. The people in the town—shopkeepers and others—soon began to know Madame Bernard by sight, and so many were her kindly actions that the common people on the promenade—cabmen, baggage-porters, bath-chair men, and the like—touched their hats to her in respect, little dreaming that the beautiful, sweet-faced foreigner with the pretty child was actually queen of a German kingdom.

As the summer days went by, and the two men met her each evening at the entrance to the pier, she could not close her eyes to the fact that the affection between Guy and Leucha had increased until it now amounted to a veritable passion. They loved each other both truly and well, yet what could be done? There was, alas! the ghastly barrier of want between them—a barrier which, in this cruel, hard world of ours, divides so many true and loving hearts.

And as those peaceful summer days went by, the two strangers, a man and a woman, who lived at separate hotels, and only met on rare occasions, were ever watchful, noting and reporting the Queen's every action, and keeping close observation upon the two men who were living at that rose-embowered cottage in calm ignorance of the dastardly betrayal that was being so ingeniously planned.

One evening, just before she sat down to dinner, the maidservant handed her a letter with a Belgian stamp, and opening it, she saw that enclosed was a communication from the faithful Steinbach.

She tore open the envelope with breathless eagerness, and read as follows:—

"Your Majesty.—In greatest haste I send you warning to acquaint you with another fresh conspiracy, the exact nature of which I am at present unaware. Confidential papers have, however, to-day passed through my hands in the Ministry—a report for transmission to Crispendorf, in London. This report alleges that you are unduly friendly with a certain Englishman named Guy Bourne, said to be living in the town of Worthing, in the county of Sussex. This is all I can at present discover, but it will, I trust, be sufficient to apprise you that your enemies have discovered your whereabouts, and are still seeking to crush you. The instant I can gather more I will report further. Your Majesty's most humble and obedient servant.—S."

She bit her lip. Then they had discovered her, and, moreover, were trying now to couple her name with Bourne's! It was cruel, unjust, inhuman. In such a mind as hers the sense of a cruel injury, inflicted by one she had loved and trusted, without awakening any violent anger or any desire of vengeance, sank deep—almost incurably and lastingly deep.

Leucha, who entered the room at that moment, noticed her grave expression as she held the letter in her hand, but was silent.

The tender and virtuous woman reread those fateful lines, and reflected deeply. Steinbach was faithful to her, and had given her timely warning. Yes, she had on many occasions walked alone with Guy along the promenade, and he had, unseen by any one, kissed her hand in homage of her royal station. She fully recognised that, unscrupulous liars as her enemies were, they might start another scandal against her as cruel as that concerning Carl Leitolf.

She had little appetite for dinner but afterwards, when she went out with Leucha into the warm summer's night, and, as usual, they met the two men idling near the pier, she took Guy aside and walked with him at some distance behind Roddy and his daughter.

At first their conversation was as usual, upon the doings of the day. She gave him permission to smoke, and he lit his cigar, the light of the match illuminating his face.

It was a delightful August night, almost windless, and with a crescent moon and calm sea, while from the pier there came across the waters the strains of one of the latest waltzes. She was dressed all in white, and Guy, glancing at her now and then, thought he had never seen her looking more graceful and beautiful. Nevertheless her Imperial blood betrayed itself always in her bearing, even on those occasions when she had disguised herself in her maid's gowns.

Presently, when father and daughter were some distance ahead, she turned to him and, looking into his countenance, said very seriously,—

"Much as I regret it, Mr. Bourne, our very pleasant evenings here must end. This is our last walk together."

"What! Madame!" he exclaimed. "Are you leaving?" and he halted in surprise.

"I hardly know yet," she replied, just a trifle confused, for she hesitated to tell the cruel truth to this man who had once risked his life for hers. "It is not, however, because I am leaving, but our parting is imperative, because—well—for the sake of both of us."

"I don't quite follow your Majesty," he said, looking inquiringly at her. They were quite alone, at a spot where there were no promenaders.

"No," she sighed. "I expect not. I must be more plain, although it pains me to be so. The fact is that my enemies at Court have learnt that we are friends, and are now endeavouring to couple our names—you and I. Is it not scandalous—when you love Leucha?"

"What!" he cried, starting back amazed. "They are actually endeavouring to again besmirch your good name! Ah! I see! They say that I am your latest lover—eh? Tell me the truth," he urged fiercely. "These liars say that you are in love with me! They don't know who I am," he laughed bitterly. "I, a thief—and you, a sovereign!"

"They are enemies, and will utter any lies to create scandal concerning me," she said, with quiet resignation. "For that reason we must not be seen together. To you, Mr. Bourne, I owe my life—a debt that I fear I shall never be able to sufficiently repay. Mr. Redmayne and yourself have been very kind and generous to me, a friendless woman, and yet I am forced by circumstances to withdraw my friendship because of this latest plot conceived by the people who have so ingeniously plotted my ruin. As you know, they declared that Count Leitolf was my lover, but I swear before God that he was only my friend—my dear, devoted friend, just as I believe that you yourself are. And yet," she sighed, "it is so very easy to cast scandal against a woman, be she a seamstress or of the blood royal."

"I am certainly your devoted friend," the man declared in a clear, earnest tone. "You are misjudged and ill-treated, therefore it is my duty as a man, who, I hope, still retains some of the chivalry of a gentleman, to stand your champion."

"In this, you, alas! cannot—you would only compromise me," she declared, shaking her head sadly.

"We must part. You and Mr. Redmayne are safe here. Therefore I shall to-morrow leave Worthing."

"But this is dastardly!" he cried in fierce resentment. "Are you to live always in this glass house, for your enemies to hound you from place to place, because a man dares to admire your beauty? What is your future to be?"

She fixed her calm gaze upon him in the pale moonlight.

"Who can tell?" she sighed sadly. "For the present we must think only of the present. My enemies have discovered me, therefore it is imperative that we should part. Yet before doing so I want to thank you very much for all the services you and Mr. Redmayne have rendered me. Rest assured that they will never be forgotten—never."

Roddy and Leucha had seated themselves upon a seat facing the beach, and they were now slowly approaching them.

"I hardly know how to take leave of you," Guy said, speaking slowly and very earnestly. "You, on your part, have been so good and generous to Leucha and myself. If these scandalmongers only knew that she loved me and that I reciprocated her affection, they surely would not seek to propagate this shameful report concerning us."

"It would make no difference to them," she declared in a low, hoarse voice of grief. "For their purposes—in order that I shall be condemned as worthless, and prevented from returning to Treysa—they must continue to invent their vile fictions against my honour as a woman."

"The fiends!" he cried fiercely. "But you shall be even with them yet! They fear you—and they shall, one day, have just cause for their fears.

We will assist you—Roddy and I. We will together prove your honesty and innocence before the whole world."

They gained the seat whereon Leucha and her father were sitting, and Claire sat down to rest before the softly sighing sea, while her companion stood, she having forgotten to give him permission to be seated. She was so unconventional that she often overlooked such points, and, to her intimate friends, would suddenly laugh and apologise for her forgetfulness.

While all four were chatting and laughing together—for Roddy had related a droll incident he had witnessed that day out at Goring—there came along the sea-path two figures of men, visitors like themselves, judging from their white linen trousers and straw hats. Their approach was quite unnoticed until of a sudden they both halted before the group, and one of them, a brown-bearded man, stepping up to the younger man, said, in a stern, determined voice,—

"I identify you as Guy Bourne. I am Inspector Sinclair of the Criminal Investigation Department, and I hold a warrant for your arrest for jewel robbery!" Claire gave vent to a low cry of despair, while Leucha sprang up and clung to the man she loved. But at that same instant three other men appeared out of the deep shadows, while one of them, addressing Roddy, who in an instant had jumped to his feet, said,—

"I'm Detective-sergeant Plummer. I identify you as Roddy Redmayne, *alias* Scott-Martin, *alias* Ward. I arrest you on a charge of jewel robbery committed within the German Empire. Whatever statement you may make will be used in evidence against you on your trial." Both men were so utterly staggered that neither spoke a word. Their arrest had been so quickly and quietly effected that they had no opportunity to offer resistance, and even if they had they would have been outnumbered.

Roddy uttered a fierce imprecation beneath his breath, but Guy, turning sadly to Claire, merely shrugged his shoulders, and remarked bitterly,—

"It is Fate, I suppose!"

And the two men were compelled to walk back with a detective on either side of them, while Leucha, in a passion of tears, crushed and heart-broken, followed with her grave-faced mistress—a sad, mournful procession.

Claire spoke to them both—kind, encouraging words, urging them to take courage—whereupon one of the detectives said,—

“I really think it would be better if you left us, madam.” But she refused, and walked on behind them, watched from a distance by the German agent Stieger and Rose Reinherz, and, alas! in ignorance of the vile, despicable plot of Hinckeldeym—the plot that was to ruin her for ever in the eyes of her people.

XXV

Some Ugly Truths

Poor Leucha was beside herself with grief, for she, alas! knew too well the many serious charges upon which her father and her lover were wanted. Both would receive long terms of penal servitude. Against them stood a very ugly list of previous convictions, and for jewel robbery, judges were never lenient.

Claire was in deadly fear that Roddy's daughter might also be arrested for the part she had played in the various affairs, but it appeared that the information received by the police did not extend to "the Ladybird."

The blow was complete. It had fallen and crushed them all.

That night Leucha lay awake, reflecting upon all that might be brought against the pair—the Forbes affair, when the fine pearls of Mrs. Stockton-Forbes, the wife of the American railroad king, were stolen from the house in Park Lane; the matter of the Countess of Henham's diamonds; the theft of Lady Maitland's emeralds, and a dozen other clever jewel robberies that had from time to time startled readers of the newspapers.

Claire, on her part, also lay wondering—wondering how best to act in order to extricate the man who had so gallantly risked his life to save hers, and the easygoing old thief who had showed her such great kindness and consideration. Could she extricate them? No; she saw it was quite impossible. The English police and judges could not be bribed, as she had heard they could be in some countries. The outlook was hopeless—utterly and absolutely hopeless. Somebody had betrayed them. Both men had declared so, after their arrest. They had either been recognised and watched, or else some enemy had pointed them out to the police. In either case it was the same. A long term of imprisonment awaited both of them.

Though they were thieves, and as such culpable, yet she felt that she had now lost her only friends.

Next morning, rising early, she sent Leucha to the police station to inquire when they would be brought before the magistrate. To her surprise, however, "the Ladybird" brought back the reply that they had been taken up to London by the six o'clock train that morning, in order to be charged in the Extradition Court at Bow Street—the Court reserved for prisoners whose extradition was demanded by foreign Governments.

Post-haste, leaving little Ignatia in charge of the landlady and the parlour-maid, Madame Bernard and Leucha took the express to London, and were present in the grim, sombre police court when the chief magistrate, a pleasant-faced, white-headed old gentleman, took his seat, and the two prisoners were placed in the dock.

Guy's dark eyes met Claire's, and he started, turning his face away with shame at his position. She was a royal sovereign, and he, after all, only a thief. He had been unworthy her regard. Roddy saw her also, but made no sign. He feared lest his daughter might be recognised as the ingenious woman who had so cleverly acted as their spy and accomplice, and was annoyed that she should have risked coming there.

The men were formally charged—Redmayne with being concerned with two other men, not in custody, in stealing a quantity of jewellery, the property of the Baroness Ackermann, at Uhlenhorst, outside Hamburg.

The charge against Guy Bourne was "that he did, on June 16th, 1903, steal certain jewellery belonging to one Joseph Hirsch of Eugendorf."

In dry, hard tones Mr. Gore-Palmer, barrister, who appeared on behalf of the German Embassy, opened the case.

"Your Worship," counsel said, "I do not propose to go into great length with the present case to-day. I appear on behalf of the German Imperial Embassy in London to apply for the extradition of these men, Redmayne and Bourne, for extensive thefts of jewels within the German Empire. The police will furnish evidence to you that they are members of a well-known, daring, and highly ingenious international gang, who operate mainly at the large railway stations on the Continent, and have, it is believed, various accomplices, who take places as domestic servants in the houses of persons known to be in possession of valuable jewellery. For the last two years active search has been made for them; but they have always succeeded in eluding the vigilance of the police until last night, when they were apprehended at Worthing, and brought to this Court. The first case, that against Redmayne, is that one of the gang, a woman unknown, entered the service of the Baroness Ackermann in London, and after a few weeks accompanied her to Hamburg, where, on discovering where this lady kept her jewels, she made an excuse that her mother was dying, and returned to England. Eight months afterwards, however, the prisoner Redmayne, *alias* Ward, *alias* Scott-Martin, made a daring entry into the house while the family were at dinner, opened the safe, and escaped with the whole of its precious contents, some of which were afterwards disposed of in Leyden and in Amsterdam. The charge against Bourne is that, on the date named, he was at the Cologne railway station, awaiting the express from Berlin, and on its arrival snatched the dressing-case from the Countess de Wallwitz's footman and made off with it. The servant saw the man, and at the police office afterwards identified a photograph which had been supplied to the German police from Scotland Yard as that of a dangerous criminal. Against both men are a number of charges for robbery in various parts of France and Germany, one against Bourne being the daring theft, three years ago, of a very valuable ruby pendant from the shop of a jeweller named Hirsch, in the town of Eugendorf, in the Kingdom of Marburg. This latter offence, as your Worship will see, has been added to the charge against Bourne, and the Imperial German Government rely upon your Worship granting the extradition sought for under the Acts of 1870 and 1873, and the Treaty of 1876." Mention of the town of Eugendorf caused Claire to start quickly. He had actually been guilty of theft in her own Kingdom! For that reason, then, he had escaped from Treysa the instant he was well enough to leave the hospital.

"I have here," continued counsel, "a quantity of evidence taken on commission before British Consuls in Germany, which I will put in, and I propose also to call a servant of the Baroness Ackermann and the jeweller Hirsch, both of whom are now in the precincts of the Court. I may add that the Imperial German Government have, through their Ambassador, made diplomatic representations to the Secretary of State for Foreign Affairs, as they attach the greatest importance to this case. The men, if my instructions are correct, will be found to be the leaders of a very dangerous and daring gang, who operate mostly in Germany, and seek refuge here, in their own country. I therefore hope that your Worship, after reading the depositions and hearing the evidence, will make the order for them to be handed over to the German authorities to be dealt with."

"I must have direct evidence," remarked the magistrate. "Evidence on commission is not sufficient. They are both British subjects, remember."

"I have direct evidence of identification against each prisoner," counsel replied. "I take it that your Worship will be obliged to adjourn the case for seven days, as usual; and if further evidence is required from Germany, it will be forthcoming."

"Very well," said the magistrate, taking the mass of documents handed to him, and proceeding to hear the formal evidence of arrest, as given by the inspector and sergeant from New Scotland Yard.

Afterwards the interpreter of the Court was sworn, and following him a tall, clean-shaven, yellow-haired German entered the witness-box, and gave his name as Max Wolff, in the employ of the Baroness Ackermann, of Uhlenhorst, near Hamburg. The instant "the Ladybird" saw him she made an excuse to Claire, and rising, escaped from the Court. They had been in service together, and he might recognise her!

The man's evidence, being translated into English, showed that suspicion fell upon an English maid the Baroness had engaged in London, and who, a few days after arriving in Hamburg, suddenly returned. Indeed, she had one day been seen examining the lock of the safe; and it was believed that she had taken an impression of the key, for when the robbery was committed, some months later, the safe was evidently opened by means of a duplicate key.

"And do you identify either of the prisoners?" inquired the magistrate.

"I identify the elder one. I came face to face with him coming down the principal staircase with a bag in his hand. I was about to give the alarm; but he drew a revolver, and threatened to blow out my brains if I uttered a word."

The accused man's face relaxed into a sickly smile.

"And you were silent?"

"For the moment, yes. Next second he was out into the road, and took to the open country. I am quite certain he is the man; I would know him among ten thousand."

"And you have heard nothing of this English lady's maid since?" asked the magistrate.

"No; she disappeared after, as we suppose, taking the impression of the key."

The next witness was a short, stout, dark-faced man with a shiny bald head, evidently a Jew. He was Joseph Hirsch, jeweller, of the Sternstrasse, Eugendorf, and he described how, on a certain evening, the prisoner Bourne—whom he identified—had entered his shop. He took him to be a wealthy Englishman travelling for pleasure, and showed him some of his best goods, including a ruby pendant worth about fifty thousand marks. The prisoner examined it well, but saying that the light was not good, and that he preferred to return next morning and examine it in the daylight, he put it down and went out. A quarter of an hour later, however, he had discovered, to his utter dismay, that the pendant had been cleverly palmed, and in its place in the case was left a cheap ornament, almost a replica, but of brass and pieces of red glass. He at once took train to Treysa and informed the chief of police, who showed him a photograph of the prisoner—a copy of one circulated by Scotland Yard.

"And do you see in Court the man who stole the pendant?" asked the magistrate.

"Yes; he is there," the Jew replied in German—"the younger of the two."

"You have not recovered your property?"

"No, sir."

The court was not crowded. The London public take little or no interest in the Extradition Court. The magistrate glanced across at the well-dressed lady in dark grey who sat alone upon one of the benches, and wondered who she might be. Afterwards one of the detectives informed him privately that she had been with the men at Worthing when they were arrested.

"I do not know, your Worship, if you require any further evidence," exclaimed Mr. Gore-Palmer, again rising. "Perhaps you will glance at the evidence taken on commission before the British Consul-General at Treysa, the British Consul in Hamburg, and the British Vice-Consul at Cologne. I venture to think that in face of the evidence of identification you have just heard, you will be convinced that the German Government have a just right to apply for the extradition of these two persons."

He then resumed his seat, while the white-headed old gentleman on the bench carefully went through folio after folio of the signed and stamped documents, each with its certified English translation and green Consular stamps.

Presently, when about half-way through the documents, he removed his gold pince-nez, and looking across at counsel, asked,—

"Mr. Gore-Palmer, I am not quite clear upon one point. For whom do you appear to prosecute—for the Imperial German Government, or for the Ministry of Foreign Affairs of the Kingdom of Marburg?"

"I appear for both, your Worship, but I am instructed by the latter."

"By the Minister Stuhlmann himself, on behalf of the Government—not by Herr Hirsch?"

"Yes, your Worship, by the Minister himself, who is determined to crush out the continually increasing crimes committed by foreign criminals who enter the Kingdom in the guise of tourists, as in the case of the present prisoners."

Claire, when counsel's explanation fell upon her ears, sat upright, pale and rigid.

She recollected Steinbach's warning, and in an instant the vile, dastardly plot of Hinckeldeym and his creatures became revealed to her.

They would condemn this man to whom she owed her life as a low-bred thief, and at the same time declare that he was her latest lover!

For her it was the end of all things—the very end!

XXVI

Place and Power

The grey-faced London magistrate had remanded the prisoners in custody for seven days, and the papers that evening gave a brief account of the proceedings under the heading: "Smart Capture of Alleged Jewel Thieves."

During the return journey to Worthing Claire remained almost silent at Leucha's side. The girl, whose gallant lover had thus been snatched from her so cruelly, was beside herself in utter dejection and brokenness of heart. Surely they were a downcast pair, seated in the corners of an empty first-class carriage on the way back to the seaside town which possessed no further charm for them.

To Claire the plot was now revealed as clear as day. She had, however, never dreamed that Hinckeldeym and Stuhlmann would descend to such depths of villainy as this. Their spies had been at work, without a doubt. She had been watched, and the watchers, whoever they were, had evidently established the identity of the two men to whom she owed so very much. And then Hinckeldeym, with that brutal unscrupulousness that distinguished him, had conceived the hellish plot to create a fresh scandal regarding the jewel thief Guy Bourne and herself.

The man who had risked his life for hers had now lost his liberty solely on her account. It was cruel, unjust, inhuman! Night and day she had prayed to her Maker for peace and for protection from the thousand pitfalls that beset her path in that great complex world of which she was almost as ignorant as little Ignatia herself. Yet it seemed as though, on the contrary, she was slowly drifting on and on to a ruin that was irreparable and complete.

She felt herself doubting, but instantly her strong faith reasserted itself. Yes, God would hear her; she was sure He would. She was a miserable sinner, like all other women, even though she were queen of an earthly kingdom. He would forgive her; He would also forgive those two men who stood charged with the crime of theft. God was just, and in Him she still placed her implicit trust. In silence, as the train rushed southward, she again appealed to Him for His comfort and His guidance.

Her bounden duty was to try and save the men who had been her friends, even at risk to herself. Their friendliness with her had been their own betrayal. Had they disappeared from Paris with her jewels they would still have been at liberty.

Yet what could she do? how could she act?

Twenty years' penal servitude was the sentence which Leucha declared would be given her father if tried in England, while upon Bourne the sentence would not be less than fifteen years, having in view his list of previous convictions. In Germany, with the present-day prejudice against the English, they would probably be given even heavier sentences, for, according to Mr. Gore-Palmer, an attempt was to be made to make an example of them.

Ah! if the world only knew how kind, how generous those two criminals had been to her, a friendless, unhappy woman, who knew no more of the world than a child in her teens, would it really judge them harshly, she wondered. Or would they receive from the public that deep-felt compassion which she herself had shown them?

Many good qualities are, alas! nowadays dead in the human heart; but happily chivalry towards a lonely woman is still, even in this twentieth century, one of the traits of the Englishman's character, be he gentleman or costermonger.

Alone in her room that night, she knelt beside the bed where little Ignatia was sleeping so peacefully, and besought the Almighty to protect her and her child from this last and foulest plot of her enemies, and to comfort those who had been her friends. Long and earnestly she remained in prayer, her hands clasped, her face uplifted, her white lips moving in humble, fervent appeal to God.

Then when she rose up she pushed back the mass of fair hair from her brow, and paced the room for a long time, pondering deeply, but discerning no way out of the difficulties and perils that now beset her. The two accused men would be condemned, while upon her would be heaped the greatest shame that could be cast upon a woman.

Suddenly she halted at the window, and leaning forward, looked out upon the flashing light far away across the dark, lonely sea. Beyond that far-off horizon, mysterious in the obscurity of night, lay the Continent, with her own Kingdom within. Though freedom was so delightful, without Court etiquette and without Court shams, yet her duty to her people was, she recollected, to be beside her husband; her duty to her child was to live that life to which she, as an Imperial Archduchess, had been born, no matter how irksome it might be to her.

Should she risk all and return to Treysa? The very suggestion caused her to hold her breath. Her face was pale and pensive in her silent, lofty, uncomplaining despair.

Would her husband receive her? Or would he, at the instigation of old Hinckeldeym and his creatures, hound her out of the Kingdom as what the liars at Court had falsely declared her to be?

Again she implored the direction of the Almighty, sinking humbly upon her knees before the crucifix she had placed at the head of her bed, remaining there for fully a quarter of an hour.

Then when she rose again there was a calm, determined look on her pale, hard-set face.

Yes; her patience and womanhood could endure no longer. She would take Leucha and go fearlessly to Treysa, to face her false friends and ruthless enemies. They would start to-morrow. Not a moment was to be lost. And instead of retiring to bed, she spent the greater part of the night in packing her trunks in readiness for the journey which was to decide her fate.

THE SUMMER'S EVENING WAS BREATHLESS and stifling in Treysa. Attired in Henriette's coat and skirt, and wearing her thick lace veil, Claire alighted from the dusty *wagon-lit* that had brought her from Cologne, and stood upon the great, well-remembered platform unrecognised.

The *douaniers* at the frontier had overhauled her baggage; the railway officials had clipped her tickets; the *wagon-lit* conductor had treated her with the same quiet courtesy that he had shown to her fellow-passengers, and she had passed right into the splendid capital without a single person recognising that the Queen—"their Claire"—had returned among them.

Leucha descended with Ignatia, who at once became excited at hearing her native tongue again; and as they stood awaiting their hand-baggage an agent of police passed them, but even he did not recognise in the neat-waisted figure the brilliant and beautiful soft-eyed woman who was his sovereign.

At first she held her breath, trembling lest she might be recognised, and premature information of her return be conveyed to Hinckeldeym or to the Prefect of Police, who, no doubt, had his orders to refuse her admittance. Yet finding her disguise so absolutely complete, she took courage, and passed out of the station to hail a closed cab.

They were all three utterly tired out after thirty-six hours of rail, crossing by way of Dover and Ostend.

When Leucha and Ignatia had entered the cab she said to the man sharply, in German,—

"Drive to the royal palace."

The man, who took her for one of the servants, settled himself upon his box and drove up the straight tree-lined avenue to the great entrance gates of the royal park, which were, as usual, closed.

As they approached them, however, her Majesty raised her veil, and waited; while Leucha, with little Ignatia upon her knee, sat wondering. She, "the Ladybird," the accomplice of the cleverest gang of thieves in Europe, was actually entering a royal palace as intimate friend of its Queen!

The cab halted, the sentries drew up at attention, and the gorgeous porter came forward and put in his head inquisitively.

Next instant he recognised who it was, and started back; then, raising his cocked hat and bowing low, gave orders to the cabman to drive on. Afterwards, utterly amazed, he went to the telephone to apprise the porter up at the palace that her Majesty the Queen had actually returned.

When they drew up at the great marble steps before the palace entrance, the gaudily-dressed porter stood bare-headed with three other men-servants and the two agents of police who were always on duty there.

All bowed low, saluting their Queen in respectful silence as she descended, and Leucha followed her with the little Princess toddling at her side. It was a ceremonious arrival, but not a single word was uttered until Claire passed into the hall, and was about to ascend the grand staircase on her way to the royal private apartments; for she supposed, and quite rightly, that her husband had, on his accession, moved across to the fine suite occupied by his late father.

Bowing slightly to acknowledge the obeisance of the servants, she was about to ascend the broad stairs, when the porter came forward, and said apologetically,—

"Will your Majesty pardon me? I have orders from the Minister Hinckeldeym to say that he is waiting in the blue anteroom, and wishes to see you instantly upon your arrival."

"Then he knows of my return?" she exclaimed surprised.

"Your Majesty was expected by him since yesterday." She saw that his spies had telegraphed news of her departure from London.

"And the King is in the palace?"

"Yes, your Majesty; he is in his private cabinet," responded the man, bowing.

"Then I will go to him. I will see Hinckeldeym afterwards."

"But, your Majesty, I have strict orders not to allow your Majesty to pass until you have seen his Excellency. See, here he comes!"

And as she turned she saw approaching up the long marble hall a fat man, her arch-enemy, attired in funereal, black.

"Your Majesty!" he said, bowing, while an evil smile played upon his lips. "So you have returned to us at Treysa! Before seeing the King I wish to speak to you in private."

Deadly and inexorable malice was in his countenance. She turned upon him with a quick fire in her eyes, answering with that hauteur that is inherent in the Hapsbourg blood,—

"Whatever you have to say can surely be said here. You can have nothing concerning me to conceal!" she added meaningly.

"I have something to say that cannot be said before the palace servants," he exclaimed quickly. "I forbid you to go to the King before I have had an opportunity of explaining certain matters."

"Oh! you forbid—*you*?" she cried, turning upon him in resentment at his laconic insolence. "And pray, who are you?—a mere paid puppet of the State, a political adventurer who discerns further advancement by being my enemy! And you *forbid*?"

"Your Majesty—I—"

"Yes; when addressing me do not forget that I am your Queen," she said firmly, "and that I know very well how to deal with those who have endeavoured to encompass my ruin. Now go to your fellow-adventurers, Stuhlmann, Hoepfner, and the rest, and give them my message." Every word of hers seemed to blister where it fell. Then turning to Leucha, she said in English,—

"Remain here with Ignatia. I will return to you presently."

And while the fat-faced officer of State who had so ingeniously plotted her downfall stood abashed in silence, and confused at her defiance, she swept past him, mounted the stairs haughtily, and turning into the corridor, made her way to the royal apartments.

Outside the door of the King's private cabinet—that room wherein

Hinckeldeym had introduced his spies—she held her breath. She was helpless at once, and desperate. Her hand trembled upon the door knob, and the sentry, recognising her, started, and stood at attention.

With sudden resolve she turned the handle, and next second stood erect in the presence of her husband.

XXVII

A Woman's Words

The King sprang up from his writing-table as though electrified.

"You!" he gasped, turning pale and glaring at her—"you, Claire! Why are you here?" he demanded angrily.

"To speak with you, Ferdinand. That scheming reptile Hinckeldeym forbade me to see you; but I have defied him—and have come to you."

"Forbade you! why?" he asked, in a deep voice, facing her, and at once noticing that she was disguised as Henriette.

"Because he fears that I may expose his ingenious intrigue to you. I have discovered everything, and I have come to you, my husband, to face you, and to answer any charges that this man may bring against me. I only ask for justice," she added, in a low, earnest voice. "I appeal to you for that, for the sake of our little Ignatia; for the sake of my own good name, not as Queen, but as a woman!"

"Then Hinckeldeym was aware that you were returning?"

"His spies, no doubt, telegraphed information that I had left London. He was awaiting me in the blue anteroom when I arrived, ten minutes ago."

"He told me nothing," her husband remarked gruffly, knitting his brows in marked displeasure.

"Because he fears the revelation of his dastardly plot to separate us, and to hurl me down to the lowest depths of infamy and shame."

Her husband was silent; his eyes were fixed upon hers. Only yesterday he had called Meyer, the Minister of Justice, and given orders for an application to the Court for a divorce. Hinckeldeym, by continually pointing out the Imperial displeasure in Vienna, had forced him to take this step. He had refrained as long as he could, but at last had been forced to yield.

As far as government was concerned, Hinckeldeym was, he considered, an excellent Minister; yet since that night when the man had introduced his spies, he had had his shrewd suspicions aroused that all he had told him concerning Claire was not the exact truth. Perhaps, after all, he had harshly misjudged her. Such, indeed, was the serious thought that had a thousand times of late been uppermost in his mind—ever since, indeed, he had given audience to the Minister Meyer on the previous morning.

Claire went on, shining forth all her sweet, womanly self. Her intellectual powers, her elevated sense of religion, her high honourable principles, her best feelings as a woman, all were displayed. She maintained at first a calm self-command, as one sure of carrying her point in the end; and yet there was, nevertheless, a painful, heart-thrilling uncertainty. In her appeal, however, was an irresistible and solemn pathos, which, falling upon her husband's heart, caused him to wonder, and to stand open-mouthed before her.

"You allege, then, that all this outrageous scandal that has been the talk of Europe has been merely invented by Hinckeldeym and his friends?" asked the King, folding his arms firmly and fixing his eyes upon his wife very seriously.

"I only ask you, Ferdinand, to hear the truth, and as Sovereign to render justice where justice is due," was her calm response, her pale face turned to his. "I was too proud in my own honesty as your wife to appeal to you: indeed, I saw that it was hopeless, so utterly had you fallen beneath the influence of my enemies. So I preferred to leave the Court, and to live incognito as an ordinary person."

"But you left Treysa with Leitolf, the man who was your lover! You can't deny that, eh?" he snapped.

"I deny it, totally and emphatically," was her response, facing him unflinchingly. "Carl Leitolf loved me when I was a child, but years before my marriage with you I had ceased to entertain any affection for him. He, however, remained my friend—and he is still my friend."

"Then you don't deny that to-day he is really your friend?" he said, with veiled sarcasm.

"Why should I? Surely there is nothing disgraceful that a man should show friendliness and sympathy towards a woman who yearns for her husband's love, and is lonely and unhappy, as I have been? Again, I did not leave Treysa with him. He joined my train quite by accident, and we travelled to Vienna together. He left me at the station, and I have not seen him since."

"When you were in Vienna, a few days before, you actually visited him at his hotel?"

"Certainly; I went to see him just as I should call upon any other friend. I recognised the plot against us, and arranged with him that he should leave the Court and go to Rome."

"I don't approve of such friends," he snapped again quickly.

"A husband should always choose his wife's male friends. I am entirely in your hands, Ferdinand."

"But surely you know that a thousand and one scandalous stories have been whispered about you—not only in the palace, but actually among the people. The papers, even, have hinted at your disgraceful and outrageous behaviour."

"And I have nothing whatever to be ashamed of. You, my husband, I face boldly to-night, and declare to you that I have never, for one single moment, forgotten my duty either to you or to our child," she said, in a very low, firm voice, hot tears at that moment welling in her beautiful eyes. "I am here to declare my innocence—to demand of you justice, Ferdinand!"

His lips were pressed together. He was watching her intently, noticing how very earnestly and how very boldly she refuted those statements which, in his entire ignorance of the conspiracy, he had believed to be scandalous truths. Was it really possible that she, his wife, whom all Europe had admired for her grace, her sweetness, and her extraordinary beauty, was actually a victim of a deeply-laid plot of Hinckeldeym's? To him it seemed utterly impossible. She was endeavouring, perhaps, to shield herself by making these counter allegations. A man, he reflected, seldom gets even with a woman's ingenuity.

"Hinckeldeym has recently revealed to me something else, Claire," he said, speaking very slowly, his eyes still fixed upon hers—"the existence of another lover, an interesting person who, it appears, is a criminal!"

"Listen, Ferdinand, and I will tell you the truth—the whole truth," she said very earnestly. "You will remember the narrow escape I had that day when my cob shied at a motor car and ran away, and a stranger—an Englishman—stopped the animal, and was so terribly injured that he had to be conveyed to the hospital, and remained there some weeks in a very precarious state. And he afterwards disappeared, without waiting for me to thank him personally?"

"Yes; I remember hearing something about him."

"It is that man—the criminal," she declared; and then, in quick, breathless sentences, she explained how her jewels had been stolen in Paris, and how, when the thieves knew of her identity, the bag had been restored to her intact. He listened to every word in silence, wondering. The series of romantic incidents held him surprised. They were really gallant and gentlemanly thieves, if—if nothing else, he declared.

"To this Mr. Bourne I owe my life," she said; "and to him I also owe the return of my jewels. Is it, therefore, any wonder when these two men, Bourne and Redmayne, have showed me such consideration, that, lonely as I am, I should regard them as friends? I have Redmayne's daughter with me here, as maid. She is below, with Ignatia. It is this Mr. Bourne, who is engaged to be married to Leucha Redmayne, that Hinckeldeym seeks to denounce as my lover!"

"He says that both men are guilty of theft within the Empire; indeed, Bourne is, it is said, guilty of jewel robbery in Eugendorf."

"They have both been arrested at Hinckeldeym's instigation, and are now in London, remanded before being extradited here."

"Oh! he has not lost very much time, it seems."

"No. His intention is that Mr. Bourne shall stand his trial here, in Treysa, and at the same time the prisoner is to be denounced by inspired articles in the press as my lover—that I, Queen of Marburg, have allied myself with a common criminal! Cannot you see his dastardly intention? He means that this, his last blow, his master stroke, shall crush me, and break my power for ever," she cried desperately. "You, Ferdinand, will give me justice—I know you will! I am still your wife!" she implored. "You will not allow their foul lies and insinuations to influence you further; will you?" she asked. "In order to debase me in your eyes and in the eyes of all Europe, Hinckeldeym has caused the arrest of this man to whom I owe my life—the man who saved me, not because I was Crown Princess, but because I was merely a woman in peril. Think what betrayal and arrest means to these men. It means long terms of imprisonment to both. And why? Merely in order to attack me—because I am their friend. They may be guilty of theft—indeed they admit they are; nevertheless I ask you to give them your clemency, and to save them. You can have them brought here for trial; and there are ways, technicalities of the law, or something, by which their release can be secured. A King may act as he chooses in his own Kingdom."

Every word she spoke was so worthy of herself, so full of sentiment and beauty, poetry and passion. Too naturally frank for disguise, too modest to confess her depth of love while the issue remained in suspense, it was a conflict between love and fear and dignity.

"I think you ask me rather too much, Claire," he said, in a somewhat quieter tone. "You ask me to believe all that you tell me, without giving me any proof whatsoever."

"And how can I give you proof when Mr. Bourne and his friend are in custody in London? Let them be extradited to Treysa, and then you may have them brought before you privately and questioned."

For some moments he did not speak. What she had just alleged had placed upon the matter an entirely different aspect. Indeed, within himself he was compelled to admit that the suspicions he had lately entertained regarding Hinckeldeym had now been considerably increased by her surprising statements. Was she speaking the truth?

Whenever he allowed his mind to wander back he recollected that it had been the crafty old President who had first aroused those fierce jealous thoughts within his heart. It was he who had made those allegations against Leitolf; he who, from the very first weeks of his marriage, had treated Claire with marked antipathy, although to her face he had shown such cordiality and deep obeisance that she had actually believed him to be her friend. Yes, he now recognised that this old man, in whom his father had reposed such perfect confidence, had been the fount of all those reports that had scandalised Europe. If his calm, sweet-faced wife had, after all, been a really good and faithful woman, then he had acted as an outrageous brute to her. His own cruelty pricked his conscience. It was for her to forgive, not for her to seek forgiveness.

She saw his hesitation, and believed it due to a reluctance to accept her allegations as the real truth.

"If you doubt me, Ferdinand, call Hinckeldeym at this instant. Let me face this man before you, and let me categorically deny all the false charges which he and his sycophants have from time to time laid against me. Here, at Court, I am feared, because they know that I am aware of all my secret enemies. Make a clearance of them all and commence afresh," she urged, a sweet light in her wonderful eyes. "You have clever men about you who would make honest and excellent Ministers; but while you are surrounded by such conspirators as these, neither you nor the throne itself is safe. I know," she went on breathlessly, "that you have been seized by a terrible jealousy—a cruel, consuming jealousy, purposely aroused against me in order to bring about the result which was but the natural outcome—my exile from Treysa and our estrangement. It is true that you did not treat me kindly—that you struck me—that you insulted me—that you have disfigured me by your blows; but recollect, I beg, that I have never once complained. I never once revealed the secret of my dire unhappiness; only to one man, the man who has been my friend ever since my childhood—Carl Leitolf. And if you had been in my place, Ferdinand, I ask whether you would not have sought comfort in relating your unhappiness to a friend. I ask you that question," she added, in a low, intense, trembling voice. "For all your unkindness and neglect I have long ago really forgiven you. I have prayed earnestly to God that He would open your eyes and show me in my true light—a faithful wife. I leave it to Him to be my judge, and to deal out to my enemies the justice they deserve."

"Claire!" he cried, suddenly taking her slim white hand in his and looking fiercely into her beautiful eyes, "is this the real truth that you have just told me?"

"It is!" she answered firmly; "before God, I swear that it is! I am a poor sinner in His sight, but as your wife I have nothing with which to reproach myself—nothing. If you doubt me, then call Leitolf from Rome; call Bourne. Both men, instead of being my lovers, are your friends—and mine. I can look both you and them in the face without flinching, and am ready to do so whenever it is your will."

All was consummated in that one final touch of truth and nature. The consciousness of her own worth and integrity which had sustained her through all her trials of heart, and that pride of station for which she had contended through long years—which had become more dear by opposition and by the perseverance with which she had asserted it—remained the last strong feeling upon her mind even at that moment, the most fateful crisis of her existence.

Her earnest, fearless frankness impressed him. Was it really possible that his wife—this calm-faced woman who had been condemned by him everywhere, and against whom he had already commenced proceedings for a divorce—was really, after all, quite innocent?

He remembered Hinckeldeym's foul allegations, the damning evidence of his spies, the copies of certain letters. Was all this a tissue of fraud, falsehood, and forgery?

In a few rapid words she went on to relate how, in that moment of resentment at such scandalous gossip being propagated concerning her, she had threatened that when she became Queen she would change the whole entourage, and in a brief, pointed argument she showed him the strong motive with which the evil-eyed President of the Council had formed the dastardly conspiracy against her.

"Claire," he asked, still holding her soft hand with the wedding ring upon it, "after all that has passed—after all my harsh, inhuman cruelty to you—can you really love me still? Do you really entertain one single spark of love for me?"

"Love you!" she cried, throwing herself into his arms in a passion of tears; "love you, Ferdinand!" she sobbed. "Why, you are my husband; whom else have I to love, besides our child?"

"Then I will break up this damnable conspiracy against you," he said determinedly. "I—the King—will seek out and punish all who have plotted against my happiness and yours. They shall be shown no mercy; they shall all be swept into obscurity and ruin. They thought," he added, in a hard, hoarse voice, "to retain their positions at Court by keeping us apart, because they knew that you had discovered their despicable duplicity. Leave them to me; Ferdinand of Marburg knows well how to redress a wrong, especially one which concerns his wife's honour," and he ran his hand over his wife's soft hair as he bent and kissed her lips.

So overcome with emotion was she that at the moment she could not speak. God had at last answered those fervent appeals that she had made ever since the first year of their marriage.

"I have wronged you, Claire—deeply, very deeply wronged you," he went on, in a husky, apologetic voice, his arm tenderly about her waist, as he again pressed his lips to hers in reconciliation. "But it was the fault of others. They lied to me; they exaggerated facts and manufactured evidence, and I foolishly believed them. Yet now that you have lifted the scales from my eyes, the whole of their devilishly clever intrigue stands plainly revealed. It utterly staggers me. I can only ask you to forgive. Let us from to-night commence a new life—that sweet, calm life of trust and love which when we married we both believed was to be ours for ever, but which, alas! by the interference and malignity of our enemies, was turned from affection into hatred and unhappiness."

"I am ready, Ferdinand," she answered, a sweet smile lighting up her beautiful features. "We will bury the past; for you are King and I am Queen, and surely none shall now come between us. My happiness tonight, knowing that you are, after all, good and generous, and that you really love me truly, no mere words of mine can reveal. Yet even now I have still a serious thought, a sharp pang of conscience for those who are doomed to suffer because they acted as my friends when I was outcast and friendless."

"You mean the men Bourne and Redmayne," the King said. "Yes, they are in a very perilous position. We must press for their extradition here, and then their release will be easy. To-morrow you must find some means by which to reassure them."

"And Hinckeldeym?"

"Hinckeldeym shall this very night answer to his Sovereign for the foul lies he has spoken," replied the King, in a hard, meaning tone. "But, dearest, think no more of that liar. He will never cross your path again; I shall take good care of that. And now," he said, imprinting a long, lingering caress upon her white, open brow—"and now let us call up our little Ignatia and see how the child has grown. An hour ago I was the saddest man in all the kingdom, Claire; now," he laughed, as he kissed her again, "I admit to you I am the very happiest!"

Their lips met again in a passionate, fervent caress.

On her part she gazed up into his kind, loving eyes with a rapturous look which was more expressive than words—a look which told him plainly how deeply she still loved him, notwithstanding all the bitterness and injustice of the black, broken past.

XXVIII

Conclusion

The greatest flutter of excitement was caused throughout Germany—and throughout the whole of Europe, for the matter of that—when it became known through the press that the Queen of Marburg had returned.

Reuter's correspondent at Treysa was the first to give the astounding news to the world, and the world at first shrugged its shoulders and grinned.

When, however, a few days later, it became known that the Minister Heinrich Hinckeldeym had been summarily dismissed from office, his decorations withdrawn, and he was under arrest for serious peculation from the Royal Treasury, people began to wonder. Their doubts were, however, quickly set at rest when the Ministers Stuhlmann and Hoepfner were also dismissed and disgraced, and a semi-official statement was published in the Government *Gazette* to the effect that the King had discovered that the charges against his wife were, from beginning to end, a tissue of false calumnies "invented by certain persons who sought to profit by her Majesty's absence from Court."

And so, by degrees, the reconciliation between the King and Queen gradually leaked out to the English public through the columns of their newspapers.

But little did they guess that the extradition case pressed so very hard at Bow Street last August against the two jewel thieves, Redmayne, *alias* Ward, and Guy Bourne, had any connection with the great scandal at the Court of Marburg.

The men were extradited, Redmayne to be tried in Berlin and Bourne at Treysa; but of their sentences history, as recorded in the daily newspapers, is silent. The truth is that neither of them was sentenced, but by the private request of his Majesty, a legal technicality was discovered, which placed them at liberty.

Both men afterwards had private audience of the King, and personally received the royal thanks for the kindness they had shown towards the Queen and to little Ignatia. In order to mark his appreciation, his Majesty caused a lucrative appointment in the Ministry of Foreign Affairs, where a knowledge of English was necessary, to be given to Roddy Redmayne, while Guy Bourne, through the King's recommendation, was appointed to the staff of an important German bank in New York; and it has been arranged that next month Leucha—who leaves her Majesty and Ignatia with much regret—goes to America to marry him. To her place, as Ignatia's nurse, the faithful Allen has now returned, while the false de Trauttenberg, who, instantly upon Hinckeldeym's downfall, went to live in Paris, has been succeeded by the Countess de Langendorf, one of Claire's intimate friends of her days at the Vienna Court, prior to her marriage.

What actually transpired between Hinckeldeym and his Sovereign on that fateful night will probably never be known. The people of Treysa are aware, however, that a few hours after "their Claire's" return the President of the Council was commanded to the royal presence, and left it ruined and disgraced. On the following day he was arrested in his own mansion by three gendarmes and taken to the common police office, where he afterwards attempted suicide, but was prevented.

The serious charges of peculation against him were, in due course, proved up to the hilt, and at the present moment he is undergoing a well-merited sentence of five years' imprisonment in the common gaol at Eugendorf.

Count Carl Leitolf was recalled from Rome to Treysa a few days later, and had audience in the King's private cabinet. The outcome was, however, entirely different, for the King, upon the diplomat's return to Rome, signed a decree bestowing upon him *di moto proprio* the Order of Saint Stephen, one of the highest of the Marburg Orders, as a signal mark of esteem.

Thus was the public opinion of Europe turned in favour of the poor, misjudged woman who, although a reigning sovereign, had, by force of adverse circumstances, actually resigned her crown, and, accepting favours of the criminal class as her friends, had found them faithful and devoted.

Of the Ministers of the Kingdom of Marburg only Meyer retains his portfolio at the present moment, while Steinbach has been promoted to a very responsible and lucrative appointment. The others are all in obscurity. Ministers, chamberlains, *dames du palais* and *dames de la cour*, all have been swept away by a single stroke of the pen, and others, less prone to intrigue, appointed.

Henriette—the faithful Henriette—part of whose wardrobe Claire had appropriated on escaping from Treysa, is back again as her Majesty's head maid; and though the popular idea is that little real, genuine love exists between royalties, yet the King and Queen are probably the very happiest pair among the millions over whom they rule to-day.

Her Majesty, the womanly woman whose sweet, even temperament and constant solicitude for the poor and distressed is so well known throughout the Continent, is loudly acclaimed by all classes each time she leaves the palace and smiles upon them from her carriage.

The people, who have universally denounced Hinckeldeym and his unscrupulous methods, still worship her and call her "their Claire." But, by mutual consent, mention is no longer made of that dark, dastardly conspiracy which came so very near wrecking the lives of both King and Queen—that dastardly affair which the journalists termed "The Great Court Scandal."

THE END

A Note About the Author

William Le Queux (1864–1927) was an Anglo-French journalist, novelist, and radio broadcaster. Born in London to a French father and English mother, Le Queux studied art in Paris and embarked on a walking tour of Europe before finding work as a reporter for various French newspapers. Towards the end of the 1880s, he returned to London where he edited *Gossip* and *Piccadilly* before being hired as a reporter for *The Globe* in 1891. After several unhappy years, he left journalism to pursue his creative interests. Le Queux made a name for himself as a leading writer of popular fiction with such espionage thrillers as *The Great War in England in 1897* (1894) and *The Invasion of 1910* (1906). In addition to his writing, Le Queux was a notable pioneer of early aviation and radio communication, interests he maintained while publishing around 150 novels over his decades long career.

A Note from the Publisher

Spanning many genres, from non-fiction essays to literature classics to children's books and lyric poetry, Mint Edition books showcase the master works of our time in a modern new package. The text is freshly typeset, is clean and easy to read, and features a new note about the author in each volume. Many books also include exclusive new introductory material. Every book boasts a striking new cover, which makes it as appropriate for collecting as it is for gift giving. Mint Edition books are only printed when a reader orders them, so natural resources are not wasted. We're proud that our books are never manufactured in excess and exist only in the exact quantity they need to be read and enjoyed.

Printed in the USA
CPSIA information can be obtained
at www.ICGtesting.com
JSHW022338140824
68134JS00019B/1564

9 781513 280882